# FILFY O'DURR

## By

## Michael Gould

Published in 2009 by YouWriteOn.com

Previously Published in 2008 as "Filfy O'Durr Lives!"

# ACKNOWLEDGMENTS

To Jeannette for her loyalty and inspiration

To Edmund Clements, Adrienne Morgan, Helen Anderson, Christopher Finch, Sue Law, Samira Harris, Chandra Masoliver, and Julia Noakes for all their gracious and loving support.

To Umilla Sinha  for her searing critiques and constant encouragement.

To Liam and Eve Gould, who laughed at the very first Filfy O'Durr story.

And to all those who see the love of God in a dog.

Cover Illustration by Samira Harris
(samira@samiraharris.com)

# CONTENTS

# CHAPTER ONE
## December

## FILFY'S BEAT

It was Christmas Eve, and it was very cold. Filfy O'Durr padded out of the remains of the front gate with the thick leather lead trailing behind him. Mr. O'Durr had promised him a walk before bedtime, but had then collapsed on the blow-up settee after too much Buster's lager, and gone to sleep.

Filfy was not too disappointed. Although he enjoyed the company of his master, he could walk a lot faster without him, and freely investigate many more fascinating smells without being violently jerked by the throat. And tonight was a night for walking faster. It was crisp and clear, his breath was like steam, and the cold threatened to get into the old dog's bones. But then Filfy stopped.

Next door someone was getting into a car. He caught a whiff of the yogurt and fear that was Mr. Noble, and the sickly sweet perfume that was his wife. He stood for a moment, and let out a perfunctory bark. Jennifer Noble said "Oh look, there's Filfy!" Charles Noble, who was adjusting his driving mirror and locking the doors of his dove-grey Rover 200 from inside, froze for a moment.

"Thanks for telling me, dear," he replied stiffly as he felt the old tension rise within him. He engaged first gear, and jerking out of the short driveway into Hillside Close, he gave the dog a blast on his horn. A few yards up the street, he had to stop when his wife reminded him about his seat belt.

Filfy began to trot as he turned the corner into Pinchley Crescent. There was no-one else on the street. Coloured fairy

1

lights twinkled discreetly in some of the windows of the mature semi-detached houses  Filfy's night vision wasn't as good as it used to be, but the full moon was bright, reflecting bleakly from the tiled rooftops, and projecting sharp shadows on the dog's path.  His sense of smell was totally unimpaired however, and as he lifted his head and sniffed, the faintest of cooking smells, spicy and inviting, warmed and suffused the chill air.  He lengthened his stride into the long mile-eating gait of his ancestors.

Ice was starting to form on the windscreens of the cars parked in Greenways and Hillside Avenue, and some of the house lights were starting to go out as Filfy reached The Green. He immediately put his nose down and started to tack across the grass, moving this way and that and abruptly changing direction like an electric pinball.  No other dogs were out so late.  Most of them were safely tucked up in beds and baskets across Pinchley whilst their owners wearily wrapped little gifts and put them in stockings and pillowcases and giant plastic sacks purchased at Fesco as their children feigned sleep.  But although there were no dogs, their scents, despite the cold, were everywhere.  Oh, joy! Just as well George O'Durr wasn't there shouting at him.  Filfy went straight from the odiferous leg of a park bench through the prickly municipal rosebed into a small shrubbery where he squeezed between aggressive boughs which sprang back on him as he passed by.  Wow! That was a particularly jazzy scent.  Filfy lifted his leg against a blackthorn trunk.

A London train was in the station as Filfy crossed the footbridge, and smelled for a moment the warm miasma that rose from the two deserted carriages below.  Spilled beer, electricity, perspiration, and abandoned newspapers.  Then, following his old familiar route, he crossed the garden at the front of the station into Cheeseman Circus.  He took the bridge over the North Circular, and with rising excitement padded up Broadway into The Precinct for his first nourishment of the night.  If his master had been walking him, as he had promised, Filfy knew he would have been taken straight to either the Red Lion or the Gay Trooper, where a few begrudged and dusty crisps or pork scratchings would have been his lot.

But now, on his own, he had the run of the town, and Filfy O'Durr knew his priorities well. He trotted up to the garishly lit Ed's Supergrill and put his nose to the window. Good; Osman, with his brilliant white hat and heavy black stubble was on duty, and had seen him. The only other customer, an elderly lady with very red hands, was in the corner eating a portion of chips out of some expanded polystyrene. In her haste she was dropping them all over the floor. Filfy padded round to the back of the shop, where he waited in the yard for a few moments in perfect trust that he would be fed. The rear door was unmarked except for the spray painted "PAKIS." The dog watched it open, just as he knew it would, and he heard Osman's intense whisper.
"Filfy!"
As the old dog gave a subdued welcoming growl, the man tossed a handful of cold lamb shish-kebab in his general direction, and swiftly closed the door. Very good it was too, despite its landing in a pool of diesel oil.

There was somebody going through the rubbish at the back of Hoots Chemists next door as Filfy trotted round the corner to check out Fagg's Café. The café was in darkness and no-one responded to the black nose pressed against the window. Bert Fagg, who would always find something for Filfy, was absent but there were some scraps left in a bin in the back yard. Filfy polished off some congealed Jumbo Breakfasts before continuing his patrol through the deserted precinct. "Big and Classy" were closed, of course, but the dog stopped for a moment before the window, in which a very chunky mannequin dressed as Father Christmas was sitting on a sleigh. An electric motor was causing her to move her head from side to side and wave rather unnaturally. Filfy stood impressed. The model looked awfully like Mrs. O'Durr in one of her better moods. Well, a bit like her. It had a healthier complexion and displayed a greater variation between waist and hip than did his beloved mistress. A notice on the window screamed "HALF PRICE SALE!"

Filfy didn't linger in front of "Big and Classy" which hadn't been open long, and still said "Pinchley Modes" on the fascia. He trotted up the Precinct, passing "L'Homme" with its lingering floral scents, and accelerated as he passed a dark figure vomiting outside "Suez Nights", and shouting between convulsions "Shit, oh sodding shit!" The Pinchley Sauna was still open for business. More floral scents, this time sweeter and of a more exotic nature lingered on the night air, and from the shadows Filfy watched a dark-suited man emerge, anxiously checking his wallet and walking unsteadily in the direction of the station. Not much hope there.

Now then! This was more like it! The rich and pungent aroma of Indian spices suddenly filled the old dog's universe as he came to the front of the Naff Tikka. Oh! The joy of it! He sat contentedly down on the tiled walkway and looked up adoringly at the window, which contained a brightly coloured picture of the Taj Mahal in a dusty gold frame, a Christmas garland, and a menu on imitation parchment headed "For Your Delactation Our Chef Reckomends". The Blu Tack used to stick the parchment to the rear of the window space had perished at one corner, causing the menu to start to roll itself up, so only starters and a few main courses were visible. But to Filfy O'Durr, the Naff Tikka had no imperfections. He had developed a taste for Indian fare after Mrs. O'Durr had started bringing home tins of "Brahmaputra Vindaloo Doggie Chunks" from Fesco, and in exploring the bins at the back of the restaurant, Filfy had discovered a whole new world of flavour. For a few moments, he sat and let the lamb, diesel, and jumbo breakfast settle inside him as he breathed deeply of the scents of the sub-continent.
The door opened. A young couple wearing red and white furry hats came out to the strains of "Jingle Bells" played on a sitar, and a blast of warm spice and jasmine-infused air. They walked tightly in step, arms around each other, in the direction of the car park, as Filfy disappeared round the back.

4

Most of the unwanted delights from the restaurant had been placed securely in a wheelie bin with a heavy lid, but Filfy found a conglomeration of Pillau Rice, Onion Bhajis, and Korma Sauce on a plate, with an accompanying seasonal serviette. He was not to know it had been left out for Father Christmas and his reindeer. Nor was he to know that for the last three Christmases, Bert Bonallack of the tattered overcoat and whiskers, and his longsuffering dog Jack had made this their Christmas Eve dinner. It didn't take Filfy long to clear the plate, and if he felt a little overfilled afterwards, he certainly experienced no remorse about Santa, Bert or Jack being so deprived.

"1975 SKODA IN BYPASS CRASH!" "64 YEAR OLD HEAD LASHES OUT!" "FUNERAL DIRECTOR IN MERCY DASH!" "TRAFFIC WARDEN ABUSED!"
Filfy O'Durr was licking his lips as he stood in front of the window of the "Pinchley Gazette". He liked Mr. Cheeseman, who had once given him a ham roll. Well, actually Mr. Cheeseman had put down a ham roll on a bench in Pinchley Park after leaving his office for a bit of lunchtime fresh air and Filfy had thoroughly enjoyed it. Well; everything was for him, wasn't it?

"TEENAGE IMMIGRANT BEATEN UP!" "PANTOMIME CLOSED BY COUNCIL!" "TRAFFIC WARDEN ABUSED ME!" "CELEBRITY FAILS TO SHOW AT BATTS PIES ANNIVERSARY!" "55 YEAR OLD MAYOR HOSPITALISED!" "FREE TICKETS FOR ST. WILFRED'S – THE MUSICAL!" "VICAR CAUGHT WITH AMPHETAMINES!" The headlines in the window were supplemented by shiny black and white photos of dignitaries, school nativity plays, disgusted residents, and car crashes, themselves decorated with golden bells and glitter. The old dog craned his neck. Mr Cheeseman was clearly not in residence. The upstairs office, so frequently illuminated well into the night hours, was in darkness. Filfy turned away.
Usually at this point, Filfy would retrace his steps as far as

Hoots and cross the road to the George and Dragon yard, and then explore Old Pinchley with its cobbled alleys and quiet backyards. But tonight, he remembered Witless Road, with its B&B's and municipal tip, and hurrying past Hunwick's Army Surplus, Pinchley Sports, and Sparks and Mincer, he trotted down Short Street and through the subway. Emerging on the nameless road between the Griplock Garden Centre and Kitchen Sink, he padded past the abandoned cars and bright orange streetlights, and stood at the gate of the garden centre, looking in through the steel bars at the collection of unsold twinkling dwarves and reindeer within.

"Oy! You! Get the hell out of here!"

Filfy froze in the wandering beam of the flashlight. It moved closer, and Filfy gulped. The man was wearing a dark uniform with a peaked cap. Suddenly the dog felt very cold; he hated uniforms. Turning with his belly pressed to the ground he crept abjectly into the interstices of a shrubbery. In summer the gay colours of the flowering shrubs lit up the threshold of the Griplock Garden Centre and made a nice relief from the speeding traffic on the Downtown Expressway. But at this time of year the deciduous shrubs were bare, and the flashlight beam followed Filfy unerringly. He was caught amongst the skeletal plants like a bomber in a searchlight beam.

"Okay, you bastard. I got you now. Fugging bastard! You're the bastard who shat on our fugging Christmas display, aren't you? Bastard!"

He could hear the man jangling his keys as he opened the gate, and in panic, Filfy sprinted blindly from the shrubbery into the street, and into the path of a gleaming Rover 200 that was proceeding serenely down the Downtown Expressway at 20 m.p.h. Charles Noble had only just left the car park of the Pinchley Excelsior Hotel after an abridged visit to the Prood's Educational Books office party, and was struggling to clear the windscreen as he drove when he saw the dark canine shadow trailing a leash career across his bows. Mr. Noble moved his highly polished size twelve from the accelerator to the brake. His long white fingers tightened on the steering wheel as the car skidded softly on the black ice and, in slow motion, mounted a small traffic island. A soft crunching sound disturbed the still air.

"Oh my God!" Charles Noble looked in his wing mirror. "Wait here, dear."

There was no other traffic. He rose from his seat, stepped gingerly on to the slippery tarmac, and walked carefully to the front of the car, dreading what he would find. Someone at the party had plied him with a small glass of cheap wine. He could be over the limit, and the sooner he got off the main road and safely home to Hillside Close the better. But he had to see for himself. He had hit the illuminated traffic bollard and it was leaning at a drunken angle with its light extinguished. And there was a dent in the offside wing.

"Oh, no!"

Jennifer, who had insisted on accompanying her husband after a lone shopping expedition to Sparks and Mincer's and who had not enjoyed the party because everyone else had been talking about educational books, cooed from the well-filled passenger seat where she was sitting with a self-basting turkey on her lap:

"Everything all right, dear?" Mrs. Noble hadn't drunk Champagne for a long time, and felt quite tiddly and at peace with the world, even though the wine had in fact been an inexpensive Spanish substitute that Mr. Noble had insisted on. He was after all the Accountant, and his frugality was well known.

"No. It's not all right." Mr. Noble started the engine. "Did you see the dog? Confounded creature. That's my no claims bonus down the drain, damn it."

"Oh dear. Is he all right?"

"What? The dog? Are you more interested in the dog? What about my no claims? No, the dog's all right. No sign of him. But the wing's dented to hell."

"Oh, thank heavens. I don't know what I would have said to you-know-who if you'd hit him. And watch your language please, Charles."

"Hit who, darling?" A peculiar edge had come into Mr. Noble's voice.

"Filfy, of course."

Charles Noble revved up and crashed the gears badly as he put

7

the car into first. The vehicle jumped as the engine stalled violently, and the Painsbury's frozen turkey shot into the footwell. Mrs. Noble said "Careful, dear." Her husband's knuckles had gone white and his lips had disappeared. "Filfy O'Durr!!" He restarted the car and checked his mirror, as he always did. And then he checked it again. A flashing blue light filled his rear window.

As Mr. Noble was blowing into a bag, Filfy O'Durr was far away. He had doubled across the wasteground between the impressive Vault Disney (Europe) building and the even more impressive Pinchley Mosque, and crossed Bendon New Road into Pinchley cemetery. The gravestones stood out like bones, stark and white in the moonlight as Filfy sat on the comfortable grey tomb of Sir Redvers Cheeseman and his family. Filfy wasn't to know that below him also lay the bones of Sir Redvers's two favourite hunting dogs. Horatio and Wellesley might not have been too impressed with the scruffy hound who now bestrode their resting place.
It was at the top of the cemetery, far away from the main road, and it was the perfect place for Filfy to recover. He always came here. The lichen-covered stone seemed to harbour its own warmth on a cold night like this, and the dog spread himself out across the top of the tomb which, with its slightly bowed configuration, lent itself to the contours of Filfy's prostrate body. It was very peaceful here.
Filfy went to sleep on a full stomach, only to be wakened by a nightmare in which a man in a dark uniform was hitting him with a rough stick. The old dog whimpered and trembled in his sleep, and awoke as he fell off the tomb on to the frosty ground. Filfy lifted his head and sniffed the hard air. It was time to return to Hillside Close Filfy shook himself and checked himself over. Then, passing by the markers of centuries, of old men, and housewives, of nurses and immigrants and soldiers and schoolboys and babies, he left the cemetery and set course for home.

# CHAPTER TWO
## December


## CHRISTMAS NIGHT


Hillside Close was deserted, and it was raining. Lights winked and shone from the windows of some of the semi-detached houses, and you could tell who was entertaining visitors by the extra cars parked on the kerbside, and filling driveways. The Grinders were entertaining both sets of parents for the first time. A Range Rover and a Porsche Mustard 4x4 spilled over from their short drive on to the pavement, and a squashed and sodden hillock of empty Sparks and Mincers wine boxes squelched by their garage door. Randy Breed and his partner, Jenda Steamwell, were away entertaining senior citizens with a 'Turkey 'n' Western Weekend' at the Southport Sunset Hotel, so their house was in darkness. Tonight no scarlet and silver Chevvie pickup bestrode the puddles on the concrete front apron. The Nobles driveway sported Mr. Noble's dove-grey Rover 200 Passe, freshly washed and polished, and parked so close to the road that no-one else could enter. His son's Fiat Newt SRI was pulled up on the kerb outside.

The rain hissed softly on the shimmering surfaces of a large motor cycle, parked like an unexploded bomb in the driveway next door. Number 27 was the one house in the close where the excitement of Christmas shone out for all to see. The huge illuminated polar bear, slightly askew over the garage door, flashed intermittently, and the light was reflected in the seasonal tones of red and silver from the sea of squashed sardine cans that passed for a front lawn. As the raindrops became heavier and larger, so the tune they played on the squashed cans became louder. Ping! Ting! Ponk! Plop! The giant polar bear sizzled loudly and went out.

The curtains in the front room were open, and a large Christmas tree covered in flashing fairy lights seemed to fill the window from floor to ceiling. Vertically speaking, it did indeed occupy every centimetre of this area, because George O'Durr had purchased such a big tree that when he'd got it home, it had been at least a foot too tall for the room. So he had had to borrow a saw from Mr. Noble next door (he didn't like asking Noble for favours, but it was Christmas) to cut the top off. He had miscalculated the amount to be pruned and had ended up wedging the oversize tree, tubless, between floor and ceiling. He had also ruined Mr. Noble's new Wilkinson Scimitar Executive hacksaw.

Mrs. O'Durr and their daughter, Channelle, had decorated the tree together in a rare afternoon of bonding, and it now looked quite beautiful, sporting flashing multicoloured lights and some antique decorations that had belonged to Mrs. O'Durr's grandmother. As a result of her husband's miscalculations, the tree wasn't quite vertical. It proved to be immovable, too.

Channelle and her new boyfriend, Leroy Kitt, had just finished the washing up from lunchtime, and were squeezing each other warmly on the blow-up settee, whilst George O'Durr snored in his armchair, and his mother gave herself a strict lecture as she tried to remember how to play Patience at the table. Mr. Huq, from the Anglo-Pakistani Friendship League, was feeling embarrassed at the display of lust from the young people, and the intermittent sounds of breaking wind from the armchair. He was reading a book with a plain brown paper dust jacket. He bit his lip as he tried to concentrate on his book, but the old lady kept asking "You're from Pakistan, aren't you?" He also tried to ignore the television, where the Reverend Jim Manley was starring in another episode of St. Wilfred's. Mr. Huq looked up, and wondered what was keeping Mrs. O'Durr, as Jim Manley unmasked an elderly flasher in the vestry.

Upstairs, Dolly O'Durr was feeling bereft. This was

the first Christmas without her mother, Violet. Mum. Mum of the big heart, and the endless energy. Mum, who always invited people with less than herself to their home at Christmas, and however short of money, had always found enough to give her family a feast of love and laughter at the festival. Mrs. O'Durr slumped on the edge of the bed holding a photo. Things didn't feel the same somehow. She had been looking forward to the holiday. But she knew it would never be the same again.

Her mother would have known what to say when the visitor had declined her roast pork with crackling. She would have passed off the awkward moment with a quip, instead of allowing her husband to turn it into an international incident. And Mum would have poured oil on troubled waters when Filfy had greeted Mr. Huq with total abandon and head-butted him in the testicles. She would have laughed at Alice O'Durr's infuriating confusion, and even her chain smoking. She would have just smiled that gentle smile of hers, and said "It's Christmas." Dolly spoke softly to the picture and the tears welled up. Filfy was confused. He felt certain she was speaking to him, and yet she was clearly distressed. Filfy sidled over, and sitting on her foot, pressed the warm bulk of his body against her leg.

Mr. Huq was also feeling confused. He had heard that Christmas was the major Christian festival in England, and that everyone celebrated wildly; indeed that the festivities often took on a truly Babylonian quality. But this family seemed strangely divorced one from the other, and seemed to spend most of the time watching awful programmes on the television. He wasn't to know that Mr. and Mrs. O'Durr had argued loud and long over inviting a lonely stranger into their midst at the holiday, and that Mrs. O'Durr had prevailed.

"Call yourself a Christian, George? You should be ashamed of yourself. Mum would turn in her grave she would. Come on George. Let's give someone a day they'll never forget."

"Are you from Pakistan?"
Mr. Huq looked up from his book, wishing he had stayed in

his quiet comfortable room in Tufnell Park, where he could have studied for his forthcoming examinations. But then he had looked at the noticeboard at the Anglo-Pakistani Friendship League.

"Yes, Alice."

Grandma O'Durr turned to Leroy, and after controlling with difficulty a sudden coughing spasm asked "Are you from Pakistan?"

"No, grandma. I'm from Streatham."

"How am I supposed to know that? They never told me. They never tell me nothing."

Alice crushed her cigarette butt in the brimming 'Pinchley Health and Fitness Centre' ashtray with a sense of finality. Mr. O'Durr stirred in his chair.

"Shut up, mum, will you?"

"So you are awake. Where are you from?"

Channelle and Leroy burst out laughing, and on the television, the Reverend Jim Manley announced to a shocked congregation that he wouldn't be giving Christmas presents this year.

"I love Christmas. Get me another drink, Lee."

Channelle O'Durr caressed Leroy's cheek. Leroy didn't move.

"Mean bastard! He's not giving any Christmas presents this year!"

"Are you from Pakistan?"

"He must be giving the money to charity. What about that drink? I'll have a Between the Sheets… If you've got the energy, that is."

"Oh, I got the energy, gorgeous. I got plenty of that. Coming upstairs then, princess?"

"Ooh, you …. In your dreams!"

"Are you from Pakistan?"

Mr. Huq looked up expectantly as Dolly O'Durr entered the room, accompanied by Filfy, who was walking very close to his mistress, keeping his body in contact with her thigh and almost tripping her up. But she didn't seem to mind.

"You look bloody awful. You don't look like Christmas. You look more like Hallowe'en!"

George O'Durr didn't look much like Christmas, either. His torn yellow paper hat clashed with his red white and blue singlet, and he appeared to need a shave.

"It's like the bloody United Nations in here."

"That's no bad thing at Christmas, George," his wife replied wearily.

"I'd say it's more like a smokehouse! Someone open a window!"

Mr. Huq put his book down on the table and sprang athletically from his cane chair.

"No sooner said than done, dear lady." Mr. Huq had been breathing very shallowly to protect himself from the poisonous fumes for the last two hours.

"Oh. The windows seem to be locked."

"George! What did you do with the key? For the double glazing."

"I dunno. I never seen no key."

"Yes you did. You insisted on having it. Remember? You said Don't give no key to no woman, or you'll never see it again. Remember? When that Mr. Whatsisname finished the job. After I'd got after him. If we'd left it to you, we'd have been waiting till Christmas next year!"

"Oy! Mum! Watch out!"

The table cloth was on fire. In trying to light a cigarette, Alice O'Durr had contrived to light the cloth. George O'Durr lurched out of his armchair, grabbed the nearest thing to extinguish the fire, which happened to be Mr. Huq's book, and whacked it down hard on the flames that licked around the table edge. The cards from the permanently uncompleted game of Patience took off in all directions. Whack! Whack! Mrs. O'Durr senior put up her hands to protect herself from the whirlwind, as her son, like an avenging angel, first subdued and then crushed the flames.

"If you've finished?"

Mr. Huq put out his hand for the book.

"Mr. O'Durr?"

George O'Durr wiped the sweat from his brow with his forearm and handed the book to the guest without looking at him.

"Thank-you sir."

If Mr. O'Durr had looked at Mr. Huq in that moment, he might have seen in the dark eyes a very deep and dark emotion. "Just look what you and your mum have done to my tablecloth!"

Dolly O'Durr's voice was shrill. She sounded almost hysterical. It had been her mother's. It was the one Mum always brought out at Christmas. Now it was browned all along one edge like a piece of toast heated under a faulty grill, and there was a tattered circular hole which her mother-in-law was trying to hide with a trembling hand. An acrid, bitter smell hung in the air.

"No use trying to hide the hole, Alice. We've all seen it. And if Mum could see it, she'd turn in her grave."

Dolly O'Durr rounded on her husband.

"And if she could see you, George O'Durr, she's turn again and all! She knew what Christmas was all about. She'd open her house to anyone who needed shelter or a good square meal. But look at you! Just look at you! Never did anything for anybody. You're selfish, you are, George O'Durr. Just plain bleeding selfish!"

Dolly moved towards the table, trembling, and Filfy could feel the vibration of her thigh as he walked closely at her side. But as she turned back to her husband, she almost fell over the dog.

"Filfy! Right! Now get out of the house! And you George. Go on! Take him out for a walk before I do something I'll regret!"

It was a rare thing for Dolly O'Durr to be so upset, and everyone in the room, except Mr. Huq, knew it.

"Come on, Filf."

George O'Durr took the lead from the back of the door.

"We know when we're not wanted."

By the time George O'Durr had accompanied Filfy to the bottom of the close, while the dog had christened a Porsche, a Range Rover, three gateposts, a saucer of milk left out for Santa, and a squashed hedgehog, he had decided he needed a drink. His wife's reproving words were still ringing in his ears, and he was not happy.  So he yanked on the thick leash, and the pair returned whence they had come, stopping only outside number twenty-six where Filfy was allowed off the lead to do a sizeable poo in the middle of Mr. Noble's lawn.

"Evening, George.  Nice hat."
George O'Durr snatched the party hat from his head, screwed it up and tossed it in the direction of the roaring fire.
"Large Scotch, Nige.  And some pork scratchings for Filf."
"Blotcher's, Chavs, or Porkies?"
"You taking the piss?"
"What sort do you want?"
"Oh, just give me some pork scratchings will you, and the drink what I asked for."
George O'Durr grabbed the glass of whisky and tossed back the burning liquid in one. He tore open the packet of scratchings and emptied it on the parquet floor.  Filfy wolfed down the contents, and then frantically licked the grimy floor until a light patch appeared, reminiscent of those that appeared on his master's trousers when Mrs. O'Durr had spilled neat bleach on them.
"And another."
George O'Durr banged the empty glass down on the bar, and looked around him.  The only other occupant of the saloon bar at the Gay Trooper was a little old lady, who seemed to be asleep. She was very close to the fire.  Her face was pale and shrunken, and her grey hair protruded untidily from under a grey felt hat. On the table before her was a half-drunk glass of beer with a screwed-up party hat stuck in the top.
"Right rave-up in here tonight, Nige.  Who's the old bird then? Might as well give me another, while you've got a quiet moment."
The barman placed another large whisky before his old customer, who was starting to warm up, and feel a bit more like Christmas.
"Dunno, George.  Never seen her before.  Says she don't have nowhere to go."
George O'Durr looked across the bar.  His gaze took in the

bony red hands, the scuffed flat shoes, and he felt something move inside him. His wife's words came back to him for the second time that night.

"Never did nothing for nobody!"

Then a very odd thing happened. It was as if Filfy had read his thoughts. The dog suddenly rose from his snooze, padded across to the old lady, and started pulling hard at her coat.

"Oy! Filf! Filf!"

The dog continued to haul at the sleeping woman's coat, and then George O'Durr saw the smoke. Her coat was on fire! He jumped off his bar stool, stumbled across the room and threw the contents of his whisky glass at the smouldering flames. This was not a sensible idea. The flames shot up as Nigel scooted across the bar and hurled the contents of an ice bucket over the old woman, who was now coming out of a deep sleep. Seeing the barman with his reindeer antlers whacking at her thighs, the large scruffy hound pulling at her coat, and the plump little man in the Union Jack singlet with his head in his hands intoning "Dolly, Oh Dolly" she thought she had gone to hell. Or maybe Heaven. She didn't know which.

But later in the evening, after she had been taken by the strangely charitable George O'Durr to his home, and given some Christmas dinner, some cheap Ginger Wine, had a party hat slapped on her head, and asked seventeen times if she was from Pakistan, she decided it was neither. It was just a nice day. A very nice Christmas day.

George O'Durr didn't notice the warm glances given him by his wife that Christmas night. He was too busy working out his selections for the Boxing Day race meeting at Boncaster. But he did sit up when his wife said:

"You can move your stuff out of the boxroom, George O'Durr. You're with me tonight."

# CHAPTER THREE
## February


## VALENTINES DAY


Charles Noble bent down and pulled the chair out. Jennifer Noble looked around to see if others had noticed her husband's chivalry. But they hadn't. Everyone else at the new restaurant in Bendon High Street seemed distracted.

The Bistro de Paris had been opened to fanfares from the local press just before Christmas, and had swiftly become known for its legendary service. Neither the chic sign in the window "Ici on parle Francais" nor the notice under the plastic Regency lady and gentleman on the toilet door "Please be patient. Everything is cooked freshly on the premises" could compensate for the inordinate delays in getting anything to eat.

The Nobles, like the rest of the company, were greeted with welcoming "complementary" red roses that stood in a Tupperware jug by the door with a sign "Please Take One." They helped each other pin roses on Mrs. Noble's gauzy stole and her husband's new grey suit, and sat down. It was as if they didn't exist. Veronica Hargreaves and a young waitress who kept disappearing into the kitchen for long periods and emerging with prominent love bites and a blank expression, didn't seem to notice them. At the end of the evening the roses would be added to the bill. Mr. Noble tried to lighten the atmosphere.
"You're looking very lovely this evening, dear. If I may say so."
His wife primped her new perm and flushed.
"Yes, you may, Charles. Can you catch her eye?"

Veronica Hargreaves was known in Pinchley for her well-established Dance Studio, but her graceful ballroom smoothery was missing this evening. Charles Noble gave a little cough next time she approached, but it went unregistered as the proprietress set course for the kitchen clutching a plate of returned salmon. The table wobbled as she stumped past. Mr. Noble raised his hand rather vaguely, and said "I say." But this raised as little reaction as the cough.

At last Veronica Hargreaves approached the Nobles' table. The attempted smile looked painful.
"Bon soir. This table's reserved."
Mr. Noble swallowed, and his Adam's apple went up and down like the dumb waiter in the corner. He clutched the corner of the tablecloth.
"We have a reservation. Noble. Mr and Mrs. Noble."
Veronica Hargreaves fished in the breast pocket of her dinner jacket, and her fading red rose fell on the floor. She squinted at a handwritten list.
"You're in the corner over there by the Eiffel Tower. You should have waited to be seated."
Mrs. Noble stuck her chin and her chest out. It was an awesome combination.
"No, my dear", she said with awful clarity. "This is our table. And we're staying here. Now, the menu if you please."
Veronica Hargreaves was feeling the pressure; she wasn't used to having a full restaurant. She handed the Nobles a rather grand looking menu. The cover was imitation leather and said "Bistro de Paris" on it in small gold letters, and "Cheeseman's Wine Warehouses" in ostentatious capitals. Mr. Noble was not to be outdone.
"And we'd like two small glasses of Muscadet, please. As soon as possible."

Back in Hillside Close, Mr. and Mrs. O'Durr had just finished a home-cooked Valentine's Dinner of Painsburys Double Chicken Kievs, Aunt Agatha's Instant Yorkshire Puddings, Chips and Mushy Peas. They were having a romantic post prandial interlude, with lots of Baileys, on the blow-up settee when Filfy, feeling even more left out than usual, started whining at the door. He was still wearing his thick lead after having been prepared for a walk earlier in the evening. Dolly O'Durr disentangled herself from her husband's arms, and rising unsteadily, accompanied Filfy to the front door. She flung it open.

"There you go, Filf. Happy Valentines!"

With that, she slammed the door, and turning on her heel, tripped over her feet and fell on the dusty hall floor.

Filfy never knew what made him turn up the Bendon Road that night. His usual route through Pinchley was forgotten as he padded up the deserted country route out of town. It may have had something to do with the fresh air he needed after Mrs. O'Durr had burned the Chicken Kievs and filled the house with smoke. But whatever it was, the old dog knew he needed a trip to somewhere new and exciting. And although Bendon wasn't strictly exciting, it would offer some new and life-enhancing smells. Of course Filfy didn't know it was Valentine's night. He had just experienced an uncharacteristic closeness between his mistress and Mr. O'Durr, which had made him feel quite uneasy. And he wasn't to know that Veronica Hargreaves who had once given him a Doggy Chew was running a restaurant in Bendon with her new boyfriend, Jacques Fournier.

Filfy closed on the "Bistro de Paris" like a guided missile. He was standing outside the front door sniffing at the carbon and garlic scented air, when Jacques Fournier came tiptoeing out with a flaming pan of "Chicken Kiev Parisienne" and dumped it in the gutter. When he and Veronica Hargreaves had planned the restaurant during languorous afternoons in his louche apartment on the Left Bank, he had omitted to tell her that his only catering qualification was a 'D' in "Cuisine Generale" at the now defunct "Ecole Culinaire" in the 14th Arondissement.

Filfy's keen sense of smell informed him that the Chicken Kievs were not worth a sniff, no more indeed than those of Mrs. O'Durr.    In fact, the smell was precisely the same.    Which was scarcely surprising as they had all come from the Special Offer counter at Painsburys.

"Delicious!" Mrs. Noble chewed the tender mouthful. "Don't wait for me, dear", said her husband, looking longingly in the direction of the kitchen and then at his Timex watch. He didn't see the shaggy face pressed against the lace-curtained window, nor the twitching nostrils that registered every subtle change in the olfactory register. Mr. Noble was suffering stomach cramps, which he always did when he didn't eat regularly. He raised his hand, and said "I say", but Veronica Hargreaves disappeared into the kitchen, as she drained a half drunk glass of red wine from a table she had just cleared.

The other customers all seemed to be leaving as Mr. Noble's "Steak à l'Arc de Triomphe" was triumphantly brought from the kitchen, and as Filfy O'Durr and his quivering nostrils sidled into the restaurant.
Mrs. Noble said "About time too" as her gaze moved to the flashing light on top of the Eiffel Tower in the corner.
As the cold plate thumped on to the stained cloth and Charles Noble looked up into the hard, mesmeric eyes of Veronica Hargreaves for the first time, and asked for a "nice glass of red wine, please",  the "Steak a l'Arc de Triomphe" was lifted gently from his plate in Filfy's whiskery jaws and disappeared out of the front door.

Mrs. Noble had been focusing so hard on the flashing light on top of the Eiffel Tower that she simply hadn't noticed the crime that had taken place under her husband's nose.  She looked at the dried up vegetables and the smear of sauce and saliva on the plate opposite and then at Mr. Noble's sagging jaw.
"You wolfed that down!  Oh, do keep your mouth closed when you're eating, Charles."
And then "Are you all right dear?"

# CHAPTER FOUR
## March


## THE BONE


Mrs. O'Durr had just arrived home in a taxi with the shopping. She was in a very bad mood. She had failed to tip Mr. Caries of Polite Taxis after he had humped her plastic bags of cheap food from Fesco's all the way up her front path. Mrs. O'Durr had been attempting to light a Cheerio Number One High Tar in the force eight gale that blew down Hillside Close as the nicotine withdrawal symptoms hit her once again. A few minutes previously Mr. Caries had bared his khaki-coloured teeth in the rear-view mirror as his passenger had tried to light up surreptitiously in the back seat in his smart 'non-smoking' cab, and had stopped the vehicle, drumming his pale fingers ostentatiously in irritation, until the offending object was extinguished.

He wouldn't have worn such a wolfish grin all the way back if he had realised his fare had extinguished her cigarette on his imitation leather upholstery, leaving a smoking roundel, not unlike a Lee Enfield .303 bullet hole.

Upon leaving Mrs. O'Durr's kitchen with his exact fare, and nothing more, Mr. Caries of Polite Taxis saluted as he had been trained to do, and shouted "Get lost, you old pisshead!"

Then he slammed the front door so hard that it almost shattered the glass. But the only real damage done was to a faded glamour-pic of the late Princess Diana, that fell to the dusty parquet floor, and smashed.

In the utility room Filfy O'Durr was barking at the top of his voice. His mistress had refused to take him shopping, and he wasn't at all happy. So, knowing that she would by now be flopping on to the new red, yellow and green inflatable armchair recently delivered from Spittlewoods, and pouring herself a generous Pernod on the rocks, Filfy took executive canine action.

First, he started to bark as loudly as he could (which wasn't very loud on account of the emphysema that seemed to run in his family). When this failed to elicit a response, he tried his very authentic 'Hound of the Baskervilles' impression. Filfy's voice went very deep indeed, and the gaps between the barks became extended. It was like a great bass bell tolling. Mrs. O'Durr banged on the wall with her discarded shoe and shouted "Shut up! Shut up, Filf!"

So Filfy started to gnaw the scarred plywood of the utility room door, knowing that this always did the trick. And it did. Mrs. O'Durr, hearing her nest being destroyed once again, exploded into the room, but was, as usual, completely disarmed by the welcome inflicted upon her by the old dog. After leaping up to wash his mistress's face with stringy dogspittle, Filfy, now quite delirious with delight, rushed into the kitchen and started to sniff around the bags that Mr. Caries had left strewn on the floor. He located the two bags containing his special 'Brahmaputra Vindaloo Doggie Chunks', and peed on the floor in ecstasy. And, joy of joys, he found a bone!

Yes; a real bone! On her way home from Fesco's, Mrs. O'Durr had popped in to see Mr. Heffernan at Herdsman's, the old fashioned butcher's shop in Gore Square, for some of their High Fat Minced Beef Parts, which they sold at a very low price. She liked Mr. Heffernan, who treated her as one of the boys as he stood gesticulating in his straw hat and bloodied apron and told Mrs. O'Durr jokes about honeymoons, undergarments, and sexual disasters of all kinds. Mr. Heffernan found Mrs. O'Durr very liberating. She was quite unlike Mrs. Heffernan . His wife was vegetarian for a start, and very squeamish when it came to either animal or human body parts. But Mrs. O'Durr cracked up at his jokes, and didn't seem to have any irritating inhibitions at all. He knew she was married; she never made a secret of that burden. But that made their assignations over the offal even more exciting, somehow.

Mr. Heffernan always felt his life a little colder after Mrs.

O'Durr's departure, and looked after her longingly as she strode out to the taxi, swinging her hips in the most tantalising way possible. As for the lady, well, she found Mr. Heffernan's blueberry complexion most alluring. Such a refreshing change from her husband's which was more banana-like. She had almost blushed today as she had left the shop with six pounds of minced beef fat and sinew, together with a really chunky bone from the leg of a cow. The rogue had called after her: "I knew you'd like a chunky one! Come back soon, darling! You can see my chitterlings any time!"

So this was Filfy's lucky day! He grabbed the huge bone, tugging it this way and that, and soaking up in his doggie soul the wonderful smell of the shambles. Mrs. O'Durr bent down to make an attempt to play with the elderly hound, but Filfy growled horribly and, waggling his hindquarters, backed into the space between the broken-down washing machine and the intermittently operable tumbledryer. There he challenged all the world to come and take his new possession.
There were few things that Filfy would kill for, he knew, but he was certain that this bone was one of them.

For the rest of the day, whilst Mrs. O'Durr lounged on her inflatable armchair, fascinated by television quizzes with strangely hollow chairmen in suits, and excited contestants who didn't know the capital of France, the level in the bottle of Pernod went inexorably down, and Mr. O'Durr remained at the betting shop with a strong inexplicable feeling that his luck would change. In fact it had to bloody change.

Filfy just loved his bone. He felt his great jaw muscles flexing. Time after time. And, time after time, he thought to himself "I'm a real dog. This is what real dogs do!!"
He thought this because his father, the late, feared, and sorely missed Whizzbang Finnegan had told him this was what real dogs did. And his father was never wrong.
Whizzbang had told him you never knew when you would need your jaw muscles and teeth to be in perfect order, and

23

that a crazed brontosaurus, for example, could appear from the direction of Hillside Avenue at any moment. Filfy had first thought it a silly idea, rather like humans putting on clean pants or knickers each day in case they got knocked over by a bus. But when Whizzbang had told him he could become a hero and save the family from certain death and even get his name in the papers, Filfy warmed to the idea.

Of course, a crazed brontosaurus had not yet crossed Filfy's path; the biggest intruder had been Murphy, the Irish wolfhound, from Fuggs Hill, who had eaten Filfy's dinner before allowing Filfy to escort him to the gate. And if, one day, a self-respecting brontosaurus did come down the close looking for food, it would probably not be attracted by a heap of rancid high-fat minced beef bits, or, come to that, a tin of Brahmaputra Vindaloo Doggie Chunks. It would probably go to number six, where the Grinders bought exotic dishes like Veal a la Creme and Salmon Mousse from Sparks and Mincers.

Of course, whilst Filfy had that bone, he was constitutionally incapable of concentrating on anything else at all, and as he gnawed and gnawed at the thing that had once been alive and part of a living world, he began to lose all interest in everything else. He refused to come out and play, even briefly, with the orange chiming ball Mr. O'Durr had bought him the previous year in a fit of drunken generosity. He refused to come out of his den and play with the bedraggled Brer Rabbit with the missing ears and the mouse-like squeak that had charmed him for so long. And, unbelievably, he even started to refuse to go out for walkies with either his master or his mistress. He just sat and gnawed. And gnawed. It was as if his very life depended upon that bone.

Filfy became constipated, which was very unlike him. He wasn't getting his usual roughage, nor his usual exercise. He was in love with the bone. He was obsessed by it. He just couldn't stop gnawing, nor thinking of that awful brontosaurus and what he was going to do to it when it arrived in Hillside Close. Filfy had never seen a brontosaurus, but Whizzbang had made very sure that Filfy was in fear of it. He started at every movement, and at every sound. He lost weight.

And when Mr. and Mrs. O'Durr sat down to watch "The Creature from Hell", starring Ronald Reagan and a very voluble dinosaur, Filfy set up such a cacophony of barking and howling in the utility room that they had to switch to Channel 91 and "The Great War" for a little peace. Filfy was not well. He was becoming a very sick mongrel indeed.

Mr. and Mrs. O'Durr did everything they could to persuade Filfy to eat again. They unpacked tins of dog food in the utility room, they fried him a fillet steak, and even brought him a bag of biscuits. But none of these elicited the slightest response. Mr. O'Durr became so upset that he actually opened a tin of Brahmaputra Vindaloo Doggie Chunks in front of Filfy, and crouching awkwardly on the utility room floor, spooned the highly flavoured contents into his own mouth whilst making ecstatic noises of evident enjoyment as he did so. Filfy just kept gnawing, and effected not to notice when his master threw up outside on the hall carpet as soon as he had hurriedly left the room.

Out of Filfy's hearing, (and he had very good hearing) the O'Durrs decided that the vet must be called, despite the cost, and they made a contract with each other to cut down their smoking by half for the next month to pay for the call-out. Filfy could certainly not be moved from the utility room; he was far too ill. The O'Durrs had never attempted to cut down on their smoking before, and their contract was a measure of the deep concern they felt for their beloved friend. Somewhere, also, they both recognised that the continuance of their marital arrangement, which at least provided some mutual comfort, depended in some mysterious way on the continuance of Filfy.

That night, after calling the unmanned surgery and being told to try again in the morning, Mr. O'Durr decided to revisit the Punter's Joy Betting Shop in Fleece Lane to see if he could recoup at least a part of his day's losses, and even see if a friendly greyhound might make it unnecessary for him to cut down his nicotine intake. He hadn't even started, but he was already feeling withdrawal symptoms by the time he got to the window and placed his last tenner on Lightning Strike to win the last race of the evening. The animal, that looked more like a dachshund than a greyhound, had an undisclosed history of agoraphobia, and only slunk out of its trap as the race was finishing. Mr. O'Durr crept home with a skinful, and his tail between his legs.

Herr Wittgenstein, Pet Psychologist from Baden-Württemberg, who was on a lecture tour of England, answered the phone at the Pinchley Pets Clinic in Scoop Lane. He might have expected the first call of the day to be less challenging.
"Mrs. Oder, you say"?"
"Yes. I just told you. He's not at all well. I think he's dying. You got to do something!"
"Zees sounds like a very interesting case."
The psychologist, stroking his greying goatee beard with one hand, and scratching his shrunken bottom with another, turned the pages of his appointments diary.
"Ah! I have a window!" he exclaimed.
"So have I!" screamed the distraught woman on the end of the line. "I got half a dozen windows, but that's not going to help Filfy. I want a vet!!!"
"Sh. Sh. Calm down now please," purred Herr. Wittgenstein, writing 'Filthy Oder' carefully in his diary, accompanied by the note 'Freudian?'
"My dear Mrs. Oder. Try to calm your poor self, please. Hysterical outbursts like zees are not in the best interests of your hound. Animals are very sensitive creatures, you know."
There was a hysterical silence at the other end of the line. Encouraged, Herr. Wittgenstein continued.
"It sounds very much like Distraction Syndrome to me".
"Destruction Shinbone?" screeched Mrs. O'Durr. The scientist took a deep controlled breath, but not before he had allowed a sharply hissed "Gott in Himmel!" to escape his lips.
"Nein. Distraction Syndrome."

"What; you mean like Hitler?"

"Oh, no!"  "Nein, nein, no, no" cooed the psychologist, trying desperately to visualise the peaceful green hills of his homeland, as Mr. O'Durr grabbed the receiver from his distracted spouse.

"You sound like a very lovely lady, if I may say so, Mrs. Oder. Please call me Adolf.  I am cancelling my conference call with the direktor of Bayerische Hund.  I know you need me at your place.  I hear your passion so I'm coming around to service you now.  Number twenty-seven, you said?"

Mr. O'Durr, who had just changed his Union Jack vest, was so shocked that all he could say was "Yes" before the phone went dead.  This was their last hope, and if Filfy could be saved by his wife giving her body to a Nazi, then that was the way it was.


Herr. Wittgenstein had widespread experience of calming both neurotic and obsessional dogs and their owners, so it was with some confidence that he took his own cherished German Shepherd, Tonto, along to Hillside Close that day. Tonto was highly trained in canine Gestalt Therapy and was an excellent listener, and in relation to humans, he was altogether a model of his kind.

He conducted himself perfectly, as a guest should, as the O'Durrs described in whispers Filfy's extraordinary behaviour. Of course, Filfy could hear every word from his lair in the utility room, but he was finding it hard to concentrate.  He was feeling exhausted, and he felt sure he had a fever.  His nose was dry and his eyes were swimming, and if truth be told, he was only just hanging on to consciousness, when he heard a word he had never expected to pass the lips of a human being. Mr. O'Durr was behaving quite out of character in trying to relate to a foreigner in a friendly manner.  In trying awkwardly, and it must be said, rather fawningly, to establish a relationship with the splendid German Shepherd and the German who had come for his wife, he said in all innocence "When we looked out of the front window, Tonto saw us."

Mr. O'Durr assumed the best smile he could manage without his teeth in, whilst Tonto totally ignored the odiferous man and looked adoringly up at his master.

But in the utility room, a very different dog was all of a tremble. "BRONTOSAURUS!!!!!!!!" His master had seen a Brontosaurus through the tattered yellow lace curtains in the front room. Gradually Filfy O'Durr's jaw muscles relaxed for the first time that week, and the heavy dead bone hit the chipped tiles with a KLONK! Filfy felt the hairs prickle on the back of his neck.

Dad was right! So that was what that dry old bone was for! To prepare him for this very moment! To protect his toothless master and mistress from the dreaded creature that even now was cowing them into silence. Filfy started to growl. It was an awful sound that was dragged from deep within him by a primeval and irresistible force. His heart was pumping so fast he thought he was going to have a heart attack. But in that pumping, he could feel the resolve that characterised all the bastard mongrels sired by Whizzbang Finnegan.

Filfy O'Durr felt the blood of his ancestors course through his arteries, and he felt his muscle and sinew come alive for the first time in five long years of recycling Brahmaputra Vindaloo Doggie Chunks all over the trim gardens of Hillside Close, and scratching himself. But this was the Canine Life Force that now filled his heart and his veins. This was a power not yet experienced in the raw by Herr. Wittgenstein and his colleagues, but it was one they would shortly come to include with regularity in their esoteric vocabulary.

Filfy O'Durr heard them coming, as he drained the demi-john of reverse osmosis water. Herr Wittgenstein and the brontosaurus didn't stand a chance. As the perfectly behaved and balanced Tonto entered the utility room to befriend his poor sick brother, and ask him some very revealing questions about his past, Filfy O'Durr used every ounce of strength left in him to pick up the heavy beef bone in his jaws and smash it down on the head of the poised brontosaurus.

Tonto was k.o.'d before he knew what hit him. "Brontosaurus, huh?" grated Filfy. "Looks just like a German Shepherd to me."

With a lightning strike, he turned his attention to the creature's master and his swiftly retreating bottom.

Adolf Wittgenstein, pet psychologist, doesn't make house calls any more, and Tonto lies at his feet as his master sits on a rubber cushion in Baden-Württemberg dictating his memoirs. He is also editing his book entitled "Dealing with Difficult Dogs" in which he is continually trying to rewrite the chapter headed "Bones".

His publisher can't wait to receive the manuscript after receiving a wonderful picture of a rabid mongrel baring its teeth and showing the whites of its eyes. It looks remarkably like Filfy O'Durr.

# CHAPTER FIVE
## March

## THE DOGGIE CHUNKS PROMOTION

"Effing useless!" said the voice, and the phone was slammed down.

Mrs. Noble said "Well!" to herself, wiped her hands on her apron, and returned to the kitchen table where a healthy vegetable flan was taking shape. Jennifer Noble's mother had been an enthusiastic feminist, and had refused to cook anything for her father, who had gone on, out of necessity, to be an eminent chef. Jennifer now felt a sense of great fulfilment when she created something tasty, especially when it looked so beautiful.

The bright colours of the peppers, and the peas and tomatoes looked so appetising, and as she poured in the egg mixture, the little pieces of vegetable, in their bright profusion, took on the character of a great mosaic. She stood contemplating the colours and the spirit of the dish, much as some would stand before a Monet or a Turner, and her eyes prickled at the beauty of it. Charles Noble was usually very appreciative of her healthy cooking style and she hoped he'd like it. There was something hugely rewarding about feeding her thin husband well.

Sonya Steen was on the radio, chairing the popular phone-in programme, "A Question of Abuse." As Jennifer Noble bent to put the flan in the oven, a caller who had been abused as a child was asking if castration might be a viable option for men who couldn't control their impulses. The chairperson, who had been in an abusive marriage, agreed strongly, but Melody Long, who had run a home for abused teenagers, and who was a committed Christian, made a case for forgiveness. Sonya Steen asked her if she was serious. Then a man, who was not identified, broke into the studio, and started to verbally abuse Sonya Steen and her team before Jennifer Noble and the entire radio audience were cut off from the programme and played soothing music for a full five minutes, before the next programme, "Footballing Airheads."

"Like a bloody old woman!" said another voice before the phone was slammed down.
"Well; I don't know" said Jennifer, returning to her armchair, and turning up the sound once more on "St. Wilfred's". The Reverend Jim Manley was visiting a woman parishioner imprisoned for killing her abusive husband with a cricket bat.
"Get me out of here, Rev", she implored, grabbing Jim's collar through the bars with a grip of iron. The hands went around Jim's manly neck and squeezed, and the closing shot was a close up of his face as he gritted "In the name of Heaven, I can't breathe, Magda!"

"Like a sodding blind man!" Click!
Jennifer said "Oh, dear" wearily and switched the phone off before sitting down once more with a cup of foxglove tea and a chocolate brownie. A group of very beautiful pensioners was smiling and singing a jingle.
"We love MacShambles Stairlifts, cos they're so good for you."
The closing shot was of a senior Adonis being born up a grand staircase as he read "Secrets of Ascension", the celebrated new-age bestseller by Dwane Atlantis.

A newsreader with a foreign accent explained that England was now officially overpopulated, and a man standing in Parliament Square explained that road, pavement, carboot, Parliament, hospital, and doctor's waiting-room rage were set to rocket in the forthcoming year, before he was attacked by a group of miniskirted teenagers. The Deputy Prime Minister had launched an unprecedented attack on the Ramsbottom Multicultural Gay Pride Festival, and the Prime Minister had launched an unprecedented attack on the England football manager who had been caught with unadjusted dress in the gardens of the Belgravia Refuge for Footballers' Wives. The chimes in the hall sounded, and Mrs. Noble switched off the set just as the familiar signature tune of "Tunbridge Wells Vice" filled the room.

"Yes, I've had a somewhat upsetting day, dear".
Mr. Noble sipped tea from the bone china cup that had belonged to his mother.
"The world's gone mad. I've had people shouting at me from their cars, and hooting their horns at me all the way home."
When he had parked his Rover Passé in the drive, he had made a point of removing the little sign in his rear window that said "How's My Driving? Call 0208 5256513 ." He had only put it in that morning.
"Oh, my" said his wife. "I suppose it must be something you're doing, dear. I've had phone calls."
"Phone calls? What phone calls?"

Next door, the thin, muffled electronic tones of "I Want Satisfaction" issued from Mrs. O'Durr's mobile which was in the fridge. Mrs. O'Durr started throwing cushions from the chairs and the inflatable settee in the front room as she searched for the instrument whilst Filfy opened the fridge and retrieved it. "Good boy, Filf!" she said as Filfy proudly presented her with the device. Filfy received a few muscular strokes, a couple of unintended sloshes of Pernod on the rocks from his mistress's glass, and a strong sense of once more having a life purpose. Mr. Mac Swear, the manager at Fesco's was on the phone, querying the quantity of Brahmaputra Vindaloo Doggie Chunks on Mrs. O'Durr's order.

Mr. MacSwear hated Mrs. O'Durr, and he had only agreed to make the call when his secretary had refused to do so, after having had to seek counselling after her last exchange with the customer. There wasn't much that Blodwen would refuse her boss, in fact surprisingly little considering his boorish ways and smelly breath, but when it came to dealing with Mrs. O'Durr, she put her dainty foot down. As for Mr. MacSwear, he would have to tread carefully, as the last time he'd spoken to her, Mrs. O'Durr had complained to his

Regional Manager about his foul language and he'd received a warning.

"What do you want?"

Mrs. O'Durr collapsed on the blow-up settee, spilling more Pernod on her elasticated trainer pants, and turning down the sound on "Tunbridge Wells Vice."

"It's about the Doggie Chunks, madam."

Mr MacSwear never called anyone madam, and he flinched as he mouthed the word. Nobody ever called Mrs. O'Durr madam, and she softened as she heard it.

"Well, what about it? Don't tell me you've run out again! If you've run out again, I'll be reporting you. Mr. Bulger won't forget me in a hurry, you dickhead."

Mr. MacSwear took a deep breath, just as Ernst Kesselring, the new security guard, propelled a teenager with green hair into his office.

"Get out!"

Mr. Kesselring and the teenager did a smart about turn as Mrs. O'Durr shouted into the phone.

"Don't you use that tone to me!" Mr. MacSwear took another deep breath. It was so deep that he saw spots before his eyes.

"Sorry madam. Someone came in. I wasn't shouting at you, madam."

The manager's insides twisted into a knot of extraordinary complexity, one not yet included in either the "Boy Scouts Handbook" or "The Sailor's Companion."

"You ordered 36 tins of Vindaloo Doggie Chunks, but the manufacturers have asked us to send you two for the price of one. It's a goodwill gesture."

"Hang on" said Mrs. O'Durr. "Why are you phoning me? If it's a two for one offer, course I want the extra. What do you think I am, a muppet?!"

Mr. MacSwear kept his thoughts about what his customer was to himself.

"No; this is a special for you. And your dog. You're our best customers. For Brahmaputra."

Mr. MacSwear's words were sticking painfully to the back of his throat.

"They want to say 'Thank-you'."

Mrs. O'Durr was puzzled, but she said "I should think so. If you're asking me if I can take an extra 36 cans for free, course I can."

Mr. MacSwear took another deep breath. His mouth was very dry.

"In that case, madam, I'll have them sent round tonight. With the rest of your order."

"I should bloody well hope so."

Mrs. O'Durr switched the phone off, and turned up the sound on her remote. A man from Tunbridge Wells wearing a pair of lace panties and a blindfold was screaming for mercy.

The Doggie Chunks promotion had gone very well. Raj and Veejay Chaudhury were celebrating with Mr. MacSwear and his wife, Fiona, at the Naff Tikka. Mr.MacSwear was on his fourth pint of Buster's Lager. Fiona had had one sip of oxidised dry white wine. The Chaudhurys were on "Brahmaputra" fizzy water.

"Nice wallpaper" said Mr. MacSwear, who was in an Indian Restaurant for the first time.

"It's been a jolly good show," Veejay announced as he bit into a leathery poppadom. His brother removed a dollop of hot lime pickle that Mr. MacSwear had just spat out on his pinstripe suit, and agreed.

"Yes; jolly good show, everyone. I want to propose a toast."

Raj Chaudhury raised his glass. "To Brahmaputra Doggie Chunks."

Everyone raised their glass. Mr. MacSwear's was empty.

Cullum MacSwear was gone for an awfully long time. Long enough indeed for his wife to rise from the table and excuse herself as her hosts scalded their hands on superheated jasmine flannels from the microwave.

"Are you okay, Mac?" Mrs. MacSwear stood, a mite embarrassed, by the door to the gents. She raised her voice.

"Are you all right, Mac?"

"Yes, fine thanks" answered a young man with a shaved head and a problem with his zip.

A sound like a hippo belching in a bucket came from behind

the closed door, and Mrs. MacSwear took a step back before deciding to use the ladies room.  The ladies room was empty but for a girl in jeans injecting something into her arm and a strong smell of disinfectant mixed with something indefinable.

It was almost time to go, and the foursome was sucking earnestly on rock hard sweets, when Raj Chaudhury turned to thank the subdued Fesco manager for all his support. "No problem, laddie" said Mr. MacSwear as the sweet popped out of his mouth and cracked a "Naff Tikka" crested sideplate. Raj Chaudhury raised his glass once more.
"I want to propose a toast."
Mr. MacSwear raised his empty brandy balloon.
"Here's to Filfy.  Filfy O'Durr."
"Filfy O'Durr" everyone chorused.  The waiter looked up apprehensively.

The Pinchley branch of Fesco sold more Brahmaputra Doggie Chunks than any other.  But their success went farther. Sales of the Vindaloo blend, which was the Chaudhurys most profitable line, were especially high in Mr. MacSwear's store, and indeed represented a higher percentage of the whole than at any other outlet.  As one might expect, the Korma was the most popular, accounting for some fifty per cent of the total, and downed in large quantities by the dogs of more delicate sensibilities and digestion.  It was particularly popular with Poodles, Pekingese, and Whippets.  The Madras and Balti blends went down well with the hardier eaters like Labradors, Spaniels, and South African Ridgebacks, but it was Bulldogs, Staffordshire Bull Terriers, and Jack Russells who went for the Vindaloo.  And, of course, the coarser bred animals, the mongrels.  And of all the mongrels in Pinchley, Filfy O'Durr took the biscuit.

Henry Smythe, of Touchy and Touchy had been called in by the Chaudhurys to reinvigorate the Brahmaputra brand and bring its image firmly into the 21st Century.
"I'm a people person."
Henry Smythe was sitting at the Chaudhurys' teak boardroom

table in Bloxton-under-Lyne, flanked by Veejay and Raj Chaudhury and surrounded by other board members.

"And my mission, our mission, is to personalise your excellent brand in such a way that punters relate to it in a very personal way."

Mr. Smythe stood up, and picked up a tin of Brahmaputra Doggie Chunks from an illuminated display set in the wall.

"Take this tin. Nice label. Legible. Colourful. Legal. But what is there to truly differentiate it from say "Rover" or "Rex" or "Canine Dreams?""

Nobody seemed to know. The board sat, awaiting Henry Smythe's answer. They trusted him; he had come up with right answers before.

"Gentlemen. We need a role model."

There was silence. Everyone looked at everyone else, wondering who it was going to be. Henry Smythe took his time as he opened his leather briefcase and withdrew a studio portrait of a black mongrel.

"Gentlemen, I'd like you to meet Filfy. Filfy O'Durr."

"Filfy is a remarkable animal. As you know, I met him recently."

Henry Smythe's enthusiastic tone cooled markedly.

"With his owner, Mr. O'Durr." It cooled again. "And his wife."

The portrait of Filfy O'Durr was passed around the table. Filfy had been shampooed and brushed for the occasion and was looking much younger than his years as he seemed to look up at what might have been a distant star with an ecstatic smile on his face and a distinct twinkle in his eye. Filfy always loved to be photographed and made a fuss of, and the day of the photographs had been a good day. The make-up artists had feted Filfy and the studio manager had taken a shine to him and kept him supplied with biscuits and bones all day. Filfy wasn't quite so sure of the photographer, who kept giving him orders in a squeaky voice, and had a funny walk. Filfy had thought to himself "Wouldn't fancy going walkies with him!"

Henry Smythe moved to the overhead projector as Raj

Chaudhury dimmed the lights.

"Now, gentlemen, we come to the campaign."

He switched on the projector, and loaded a CD into an expensive portable player.

"At Touchy and Touchy, we concluded first that the name Filfy O'Durr is not suitable."

Sounds of assent went round the boardroom table.

"And today, we have prepared for you two different characters, both based upon the same dog. Here, I'll show you what I mean."

Henry Smythe pressed a button, and a sketch of Filfy O'Durr in a classic gun-dog pose with a forepaw raised, somewhere on a grousemoor appeared on the screen. Next to him was a distinguished, tweedy looking man aiming a shotgun into the air. Henry Smythe pressed another button, and the strains of "Land of Hope and Glory" filled the room. There was a discreet round of applause from those around the table.

"Gentlemen; meet Pelham Vane-Fortescue of Chagford Vale."

After a short silence, a junior member of the board spoke. "Is that the man or the dog?"

The next transparency was of a very different Filfy. The dog in this case was nosing in a dustbin in a darkened street with tall buildings and a derelict air. It could have been Brooklyn, or Pinchley East Side.

"Gentlemen, meet Fred Kred."

Henry Smythe pressed a button and the poignant tones of "The Streets of London" filled the room.

"How can you say that you're lonely, and say for you that the sun don't shine?"

There was no applause from the board; just an embarrassed silence. Raj Chaudhury spoke on behalf of everyone. "Mr. Smythe; that, I think, is not the image we want for Brahamaputra Chunks."

"I quite understand you, Raj" said Henry Smythe, adjusting his silk tie. He had been ready for the objection and had prepared his answer.

"But I must point out that there are a lot more Fred Kreds

about than there are Pelham Vane-Fortescues er..."
Veejay interrupted "of Chagford Vale."  The words rolled off his tongue like honey.
 "That's right" said Henry Smythe.  "And of course, there are a lot more owners of dogs like Fred than there are owners of – er..."
"Pelham Vane-Fortescue of Chagford Vale" said Veejay.
"Thank-you, Veejay" replied the marketeer, looking at the screen.
"Doesn't look like he has an owner to me" said a young Chaudhury with a toothbrush moustache.
"He looks like a stray.  Plenty of those in Mumbai.  But this is Pinchley Park!"
Henry Smythe's manner suddenly became confidential.
"Ah, yes.  He looks like a stray but he's not.  Fred's got cred. Street Cred.  He knows what he wants, and he gets it.  He's a- er- sort of role model for your customers."
"I don't think our customers want to be pilfering from dustbins" said Raj Chaudhury, with finality.  "We'll go with Pelham Vane-Fortescue."
"Of Chagford Vale" added Veejay.
Raj continued "That is the image we want to foster for our products."
Everyone in the room except Henry Smythe murmured their assent as Fred Kred disappeared from the screen for ever.

Algernon Rockinghorse-Fopp looked concerned as he pressed keys on his calculator.
"Well?" asked Raj Chaudhury.  "Will you do it for ten grand or not?  We're wasting time here if you can't."
Algernon's generous margins were being squeezed, but he needed the work.  Times had been tough since his attempted makeover of the Finsbury Park mosque, and he fidgeted in the leather chair, twiddling with his turquoise neckerchief.
"A scheme on this scale would normally be more than twenty. It's not just the house.  It's the people."
Algernon spoke this last word with a tone of incredulity.
"They're just, well, wrong."
Raj Chaudhury was losing patience, and he was due on Bloxton

Heath golf course with his uncle in ten minutes.

"That's exactly why I'm employing you. We want the O'Durrs and their house to be transformed. That's what you do, isn't it?"

The client rose from his large, leather-topped desk.

"Eleven. Eleven grand. That's my last word."

Filfy O'Durr thought he was dreaming, when the large, gold plated bowl, brimming with Brahmaputra Vindaloo Doggie Chunks was placed before him. He usually ate from a small encrusted plastic dish, in much smaller quantities. But he thought it must be a nightmare when his master and mistress started to talk posh, and call him "Pelham", as they sipped gin and tonics from crystal glasses, and went mad if a single hair found its way on to their designer clothing.

The living room was quite unrecognisable. The red and yellow blow-up settee had gone, and a huge L-shaped black leather battery stood in its place, before a television screen that took up half one wall. The windows had been cleaned for the first time in living memory, and bright, white lace curtains from Sloane Square covered the window. The carpet was deep and thick, and strange minimalist glass-framed pictures had replaced the daub of Ballybunnion by a drunken Uncle Seamus that had sat in a dusty, chipped old frame since the family had moved in. But the worst thing of all was that Filfy wasn't even allowed in there.

Filfy had been presented with a hand-crafted kennel with a golden plaque above the door saying "Pelham Vane-Fortescue of Chagford Vale," together with a vindaloo flavoured bone and a golden water bowl, branded "Brahmaputra". He had received a magnificent thick green leather collar with great golden studs, and a woollen waistcoat in Royal Stuart tartan for colder days. He was going to need it. Filfy was no longer allowed in the house.

"Action!" The director snapped his fingers, and George O'Durr awoke in his uncomfortable new silk pyjamas. The old singlet that he usually wore to bed had been disposed of.

"Oh, darling," he said in a strangely plummy voice. "It's half eight already, and I'm due on the jolly old golf course at nine. I'll just go and feed Filf, I mean Pel...."

"Cut!!"

Mrs. O'Durr sat up in bed in a nightie that looked like the queen's coronation gown, and a wig that seemed to have a life of its own. Her accent was unrecognisable.

"Oh, Piers. Don't you think it's time you fed the bleedin' 'ound?"

"Cut!!"

"Oh, Piers. I really must get up out of this four-poster and shower. I have Mrs. Chol-mond-ley – Fitzroy coming round for coffee. And she's a right pain in the bum - oh!"

"CUT!"

Later shots included Mrs. O'Durr waving her husband off to golf in the Mercedes that had replaced his smoking Datsun Gooseberry, and, of course, Pelham Vane-Fortescue of Chagford Vale at last receiving his breakfast in the golden bowl bearing his name. Filfy had, by now, completely lost his appetite, and was in a very neurotic state. As Dolly O'Durr bent regally to scrape the Brahmaputra Vindaloo Doggie Chunks into the bowl, wafting Emile de Grafton Street perfume into his face, Filfy brought up his breakfast.

"CUT!" I said "CUT!!!"

By the time that Mrs. O'Durr had managed to smash all the crystal wine glasses after drinking far more free Mumbai Gin than was good for her, and Mr. O'Durr had written off the Mercedes in a confrontation with Ms. Elspeth Parker's Nissan Miniscule outside the RSPCA, the Chaudhurys realised that the end had come for Pelham Vane-Fortescue of Chagford Vale, and indeed, his entire entourage. Although the commercial was never completed, the family honoured their contract with Algernon Rockinghorse-Fopp, who was able to pay off some of his debts, and go on to make his name with a makeover of the MacShambles Drive-Thru at Hampton Court.

George and Dolly O'Durr received a good price for

their new leather settee, spending the proceeds on Pernod, Buster's Lager, and Cheerio Number One Tipped, but they kept the television set, and gave the old one to Channelle for her birthday, together with the lace curtains from Sloane Square. Although Mr. O'Durr persevered with his silk pyjamas for a night or two, they ended up in Filfy's basket in the utility room, after his old singlet had been reclaimed from the tip.

Mr. and Mrs. MacSwear never visited the Naff Tikka again, but Mr. MacSwear continued to stock Brahmaputra Vindaloo Doggie Chunks, doubling up on the facings in his store as a "thank-you" for his first and last "Indian."

And Filfy O'Durr? Filfy never again entered his handcrafted kennel, which was left to rot in the back garden, and he went back, thankfully, to his plastic doggie bowl with its friendly encrustations. Filfy just continued to be happy and grateful for his modest lot, and never gave a thought to what might have been.

# CHAPTER SIX
## April


## THE HOLIDAY


"It looks a very nice hotel, dear."
Jennifer Noble put down the brochure on the glass-topped coffee table, and took a bite out of a large cream doughnut.
"Are you sure we can afford it?"
"Of course we can afford it. Don't forget I'm Chief Accountant now. We can't just stay anywhere, you know. I have a.. er.. position to maintain. Please don't forget that."
Charles Noble gave his wife a withering look as a dollop of cream fell on to her lap. She lifted up her crimplene skirt and licked it off.
"Mm. Nice." she said.
Mrs. Noble picked up the brochure from the Grosvenor Travel Agency once more, and looked at the colourful pictures. The Palacio Grande Hotel looked wonderful. It was a very new hotel with its own private beach, the only hotel, apparently, to have been built in the sleepy little fishing village of Silencio de Mar. Her husband nibbled testily at a sesame seed biscuit, and took a very deep breath.
"I'm ready for a holiday, dear. It's been a hard year. What with the promotion and taking over Shorthaul for All."
"Did they get you something off?"
"Well er yes. How did you know that?"
"Oh, you know me dear. I know a lot more than you think."
"Yes. That's the trouble. Um - they gave us 50% off the flight and 20% off the hotel. Probably we've saved 40% off the holiday. Well, 35% if you count in the taxes and landing charges and the excess fuel. Probably 33% in all. Not to be sneezed at."
"The hairdressing salon looks very nice, dear."
Jennifer Noble read from the brochure

"Senor Philippe will put you at your ease with a glass of Sangria before giving your hair the treatment. Which look do you want? The Sophia Loren? The Dolly Parton? The Amy Winehouse? The Queen Elizabeth? Just tell Philippe exactly what you want, and watch him go to work on your follicles with effortless precision and the passion that only a true Spaniard can offer."

"I'd like to go there, dear!"

Mr. Noble gave a little sigh. "No, I don't think so, dear. That's not for you. Why don't you go to Peggy's in The Precinct? They were perfectly adequate last time."

He looked up at his wife's startling coiffure and wondered what he had just said.

"Yes. It'll be good to get away. Work's been getting me down lately. And as for that dog! It's like living in hell with him next door. Oh! The joy of it! Thank heavens! Three weeks without that filthy animal. And without his subhuman owners!"

"Charles! You mustn't talk like that. They are our neighbours after all. And just think how lucky we are. They're not well off. They can't afford a nice break like we can. Just look at that awful car!"

At that very moment there was an ear splitting grating sound from next door and a cloud of blue smoke floated across the Nobles' front lawn. Charles Noble leapt athletically from his chair, still clutching a miniscule piece of sesame snap, and strode to the window, where he ostentatiously slammed shut the casement. Then he stood looking with a look of pure hatred at the rusty Datsun Gooseberry that bucked noisily out into the street. Suddenly there was the sound of barking, and Filfy O'Durr appeared seemingly following a scent on to the Nobles' front lawn. He stopped suddenly, and adopted the unmistakeable evacuation asana right in the centre of the perfectly manicured lawn.

"Oh no you don't!"

Mr. Noble flung open the window once more and shouted.

"Oh no you don't!" Filfy seemed quite unworried by the move and continued to concentrate on his work. Mr. Noble put his foot on the window sill and levered his long body up into the frame.

"Oh no you don't!"

"Charles!" Jennifer Noble was becoming concerned for her husband's safety. But it was too late. Charles Noble had launched himself through the window, propelled by the rocket fuel of pure loathing. Unfortunately his foot slipped on the window ledge, and he fell heavily into a hydrangea bush just below the window, spraining his wrist and sustaining a number of minor bloody abrasions on the dry, carefully pruned branches of the plant.

"Oh, Charles. Do be careful!" Jennifer Noble took another bite of her cream doughnut, as outside a playful Filfy O'Durr came over to investigate the prostrate form in the desecrated bush.

"I could have blood poisoning, you know."

Mr. Noble was sitting in his favourite Parker Knoll chair with his feet up on a flowery foot stool, sipping a mug of beef tea which his wife had made for him.

"Oh, I don't think so, dear."

There was a very slight edge to Jennifer Noble's reassuring tone.

"Tetanus. Lockjaw." Mr. Noble warmed to his theme. "There was a case in the paper just last week."

He flexed his jaw and made exaggerated lateral movements with it. Then he opened his jaws as widely as he could.

"Seems to be all right. It's not locked up. Yet. But just to be on the safe side, I think I'd better get you to take me down to the outpatients."

Mr. Noble was well known at the outpatients department at Pinchley General.

"Oh really dear. Is that really necessary?"

Jennifer Noble had planned to watch the omnibus edition of "St. Wilfreds" that afternoon, in which, apparently, the Reverend Jim Manley was to be seduced by a Brazilian Go-Go dancer.

"Yes dear. I fear so. Yes. I'd say it's absolutely necessary. We're off next week. And you still want Philippe to do your hair, don't you?"

Whilst Charles Noble sat in the outpatients department next to a young man with a tattooed head and a nasty gash in his cheek, George O'Durr was leaping out of the blow-up armchair in his front room.

"Hey! Doll! We won! We won!"

Dolly O'Durr was on the double bed upstairs listening to Mozart's Clarinet Concerto on her i-pod. She was feeling quite transported by the music, and didn't hear her husband at all. Then suddenly he was there, jumping up and down in his singlet in front of her and waving that day's copy of the Bum newspaper.

"Hey! Wake up, Doll! Wake up!"

His wife opened an eye, and tried to come back into the room.

"We won the holiday. In Spain. Next month! We're going to Spain!!"

Dolly O'Durr sat bolt upright.

"Wot? We won? We won something? What did we win?"

"We won the competition. To er…" Mr. O'Durr looked again at the paper.

"To Spain. To er.. Silencio de Mar." George O'Durr pronounced the name as if it were a very quiet female racehorse.

"Look, it's all here. And there's your name..Mrs. D. O'Durr, Pinchley Park. It's next month. I'd better get some gear."

Dolly O'Durr snatched the newspaper and read aloud, with a tone of wonder in her voice.

"The winner of our two week holiday at the Grand Hotel in Silencio de Mar is Mrs. D. O'Durr of Pinchley Park.."

She slumped back on the bed.

"Oh God, George! We won something! Maybe our luck is changing."

Mr. O'Durr snatched back the newspaper, and read once more.

"The Grand Hotel is the biggest and most modern hotel in Silencio, with two hundred bedrooms, all with luxurious en-suite facilities and balconies, two swimming pools, a fitness club, bollocks to that, and three international standard restaurants."

Suddenly, the bedroom door was pushed open, and Filfy

45

arrived with the post. He put it carefully down on the coverlet, and waited for his mistress to pat his head as she always did. But Mrs. O'Durr was so excited that she forgot to do so, as she riffled through the letters, and came across a large envelope bearing the crest "Royal Iberian Holidays." She tore open the envelope, and read from the letter.

'Dear Mrs. Odour,
Congratulations! We are delighted to inform you that the Bum newspaper has today been in contact with our PRIZES department to advise that you have won a two week holiday, with companion, at the Grand Hotel in Silencio de Mar. You will enjoy a twentieth floor luxury suite with all facilities and a balcony with sea views. Our Representative, Mr. Gary Bolsover, as seen on "Big Bugger" will be delighted to greet you at the hotel and attend to your every need. In the meantime, sit back and be assured that your holiday will be a truly memorable one. You will be travelling in Economy Class on Gung-Ho Airways, and leaving at 3am on Saturday 16th April from Gatwick, with our very own Captain Brent Bolsover at the controls.
Your tickets will follow within ten working days.

Yours very sincerely,
Keith Bolsover
Chairman, Royal Iberian Holidays'

Dolly O'Durr looked down at the shaggy head that was pressed against the coverlet, and she looked into the sombre dark eyes that sought her own. A fearful look came over her face.
"What we going to do about Filf?" she asked.

The proprietor of The Happy Cattery had expelled Filfy into an adjoining field on his last visit to the kennels, after the dog had destroyed his cage, and Mr. Job would not be entertaining the O'Durrs again. And Channelle O'Durr had refused ever to accommodate Filfy again after the attack on her last boyfriend but one. Stefan Grodzinski's favourite cowboy motor cycle boots had never looked the same after Filfy had given them a good overnight chewing.  And after that, Channelle's relationship with their owner had never looked the same either.

"Get him a passport.  A pet passport."

Sean Lift seemed to know so much about everything.

"What?  A passport for a bleeding dog?"  George O'Durr's incredulity could not be mistaken.

"I could probably get you one cheap."

"No thanks, mate.  The last passport you got me cheap got me in stook."

"Stook?"  Sean Lift raised his bushy eyebrows as he tidied the new rail of Arsenal Football Shirts of which he had just taken delivery.  He had paid the lorry driver in £50 notes.

"Yeah.  We got the fuzz on our backs.  Dolly didn't like that one bit."

"All right.  Just trying to help.  You need a new EU Pet Passport.  Obtainable from DEFRA.  You'll have to have him microchipped.  And give them a photo."

"A photo?!  What?  You mean a photo of a bleeding dog?"

"And you'll need a Rabies vaccination…"

"Who, me?"

"And tick and tapeworm clearance."

"Bloody hell!"

"And then of course, you'll need the container."  "Container?"  George O'Durr wasn't feeling well.  "Container for what, for crying out loud?"

"The container for Filfy.  Your dog, mate.  Wake up, sunshine."

George O'Durr ran his hand through his thinning hair.  "Cor.  This is going to cost ain't it?"

"It'll cost you a bomb.  But then it's your bleeding dog."

"It's not my bleeding dog.  It's Dolly's bleeding dog.  It was her that got him.  For company she said.  And she won't go nowhere without him nowadays  What's wrong with my company?  That's what I'd like to know."

George O'Durr  belched orchestrally.

"And don't forget the air fare" said Sean Lift helpfully.  "That'll set you back an arm and a leg."

Mr. Noble was sitting in a gangway seat, listening to Spanish Flamenco music, as the great aircraft whistled quietly through the night, when he felt a tug on his sleeve. He opened his eyes to see his neighbour's eyes bulging into his.

"I've got to go to the toilet. Sorry I've got a weak bladder."

Mr. Noble gave her a withering look, disengaged his earphones, lifted his uncollected tray vaguely in the air, unbuckled his seat belt with one hand, dropped his miniscule blanket and reading glasses on the floor, together with his Spanish Phrase Book, and red white and blue neck cushion, and attempted to rise by clinging to the back of the seat in front whilst still balancing the tray in his free hand.

The seat in front gave way with a clunk, and its elderly occupant, who had been mugged in the passenger lounge prior to take-off, awoke in fear. Another withering look was directed, this time towards Mr. Noble, by the disagreeable looking stewardess who now relieved him of the tray she had forgotten to collect after the 4am breakfast, and patted the grey head in front with a beringed and muscular hand which was of an unnatural orange colour. She pressed a button, and the elderly passenger grunted as she was projected violently back into the upright position.

The young woman with the bulging eyes disappeared whilst Charles Noble went for a stroll down the gangway. Everyone seemed to be asleep, or trying to be, caught in horribly uncomfortable looking poses. There were trainers sticking up over the backs of seats, there were necks craned at crazy angles into flimsy pillows, there were tousled heads on jean-clad laps, and occasionally there was a body that sat bolt-upright as if it had been struck by lightning.. When Charles Noble came abreast of his wife, from whom he had been separated when the stewardess had examined their tickets, he found her in animated conversation with a much younger man, some sort of foreign dago, he thought  This didn't please him at all. He leaned across his wife's newfound friend even as the man was speaking

"Don't you think you'd better get some sleep, dear?  We've got a long day tomorrow."

Mrs. Noble looked up for a moment. "No. I'm fine dear. Thank-you."

Mr Noble hung on to the back of the man's seat. (The stranger had gallantly given Mrs. Noble his window seat) and stretched his long right leg across the aisle, dislodging a sleeping head from an armrest.

"Oooh! That's better. I think you really should consider what's best for you dear. Remember what happened in Bridlington. You really mustn't overdo it."

Jennifer Noble didn't often get the chance to talk to fascinating strangers.

"Would you please stop fussing dear and go back to your seat? I'm perfectly all right, thank-you."

Her companion looked up for the first time. He had black eyes that were hard and shiny, and Mr. Noble couldn't help noticing the bull-like shoulders and the mat of hairs that poked like dark creatures through the scarlet singlet. The man twisted in his seat and gently, but very firmly, removed Mr. Noble's hand from the seatback, and said "Hasta la vista, senor!"

Then he turned once more to his companion.

Mr. Noble returned to his own seat after a circumnavigation of the cabin, during which he indulged in some rather exaggerated callisthenics designed to get his circulation and his muscles going again. He awoke several more strangers by dint of lunges and kicks on his way around the aircraft. When he arrived back at his seat his neighbour was rising from her seat once more.

"Hello. I'm afraid I've got a very weak bladder" she said as she squeezed past. Mr. Noble found himself replying in singularly ungallant style, as he trod on his reading glasses.

"Bully for you, dear" just somehow slipped out.

The Grand Hotel had been finished and opened by the mayor just three days before the O'Durrs arrived in Silencio de Mar. It overshadowed the Palacio Grande next door by approximately two hundred feet. The stretch limo that collected George and Dolly O'Durr from the airport, together with a box containing Filfy was similarly enormous, but then it

49

had to be. The Grand this week was full of happy competition winners who all read the Bum newspaper, and they were landing at regular intervals from all parts of the UK throughout the day.

The O'Durrs were one of the first families to book in, and were given a magnificent suite (The Alhambra Suite) on the 23rd floor. It boasted an extensive flower-bedecked balcony, a sea-view, and a gold-plated Jacuzzi. When the porter arrived with two large suitcases and a hysterical dog in a container, George O'Durr said "Thanks mate" and gave him the equivalent of £5 when he thought he was giving the man 50p. After Dolly had pointed out his mistake, he found it difficult to forget, and spent the rest of the holiday muttering "Cor, you'd think I was made of money" under his breath and tipping everyone with the equivalent of 2p.

Mr. O'Durr also lost out on the container, on which he had saved £10 by buying it from Sean Lift. After it arrived with its over-excited and dehydrated contents at the Grand Hotel, he realised he had forgotten the number of the combination lock, and he destroyed his wife's hair curling iron in trying to force open the box.

Reluctantly he called a blacksmith (cost £19.71 call out plus £8.87 weekend bonus). Sean Lift's handiwork was impressive. Even Filfy O'Durr had been unable to make much of an impression on the inside of the container. Dolly O'Durr was clearly distressed, and Filfy no less so as the blacksmith set to work. George O'Durr twisted his stubby fingers and prayed silently.

"Oh Gawd. Don't let him die now. It cost bleeding 500 quid to get him here."

In the much smaller and lower hotel next door, Mr. and Mrs. Noble were sitting quietly in a small, rather dark room with no balcony.

"Sweetener dear?" The lightwood chair creaked as Mr. Noble turned to address his wife.

"No dear. I'll have sugar today."

Jennifer Noble frowned to herself. "And have we got any chocolate cake? Or chocolate?"

Mrs. Noble rummaged in the suitcase that was lying on her

small bed, and came up triumphantly with a Sparks and Mincers Deep Chocolate Sponge. It was badly squashed. She transferred it to the cramped worktop and cut two shapeless lumps and put them on two plain saucers. She then poured the boiling water from the small plastic kettle on to the unidentified teabags she had found waiting for them, and stirred in the sugar for her husband. Mr. Noble had already tried Spanish television, but it seemed just like English television, only he couldn't understand a word they were saying on a reality show where a young woman was pouring the contents of a yellow watering can down the front of a thin man's bathing trunks and screeching with laughter.

So he had already switched it off, and was catching up with his copy of this month's "Accountancy Today." Charles Noble stirred his off-white cup of tea thoughtfully.

"I don't suppose you remembered to bring the Lapsang Souchong, did you dear?"

"No. Are you tired, dear?"

Jennifer Noble sounded very solicitous, although all she really wanted to do when she had finished the unpacking was to go out and take a look around the town. And of course to find a decent hairdresser.

"I think I'll have an early night. I think it would do you good, too, dear. We've still got some sandwiches left haven't we?"

"Yes, dear."


Twenty storeys above that dark little room, and just a few yards away, really, George and Dolly O'Durr were tucking in to a full room-service menu of seafood gratin, fillet steak, and well-soaked rum babas, washed down with a vintage Cava. The steaks were so big that there was plenty for Filfy who was hoovering the marble apartment floor to make sure he hadn't missed any of the delicious juice, and ingesting some delicious squashed flies at the same time.

As the sun set on the little town of Silencio de Mar, and the evening sky was streaked with garish red, George and Dolly O'Durr walked hand-in-hand out on to their balcony, where they were greeted by the scent of oleander and jasmine, and followed by the uncut claws of Filfy. Clip, clop, clip. They leaned on the brass balcony rail, and looked down on the rather shrivelled looking building next door.

"Is that a hotel?"

Dolly O'Durr shivered inadvertently, and her husband put his arm around her shoulders. She liked that. Way below, a curtain was pulled across a small window, and a light went out. "Must be, Doll. Look down there. Someone's having an early night."

The sun was just rising again when Charles Noble left his wife fast asleep in bed and descended to the shimmering outdoor pool wearing a pair of long swimming shorts he had bought in Sparks and Mincers' sale. The shorts were in navy blue and had a red and white 'speed stripe' running down the side. They made a startling contrast to the pallor of his skin.

After spreading his beach towel carefully over a plastic sun lounger, Mr. Noble noticed a young lady with long black hair swimming powerfully from the far end of the pool. She was deeply tanned. And she looked very attractive. Mr. Noble waited for her to come close and then performed a neat dive into the deep end, swallowing a mouthful of chlorinated water as he did so. When he rose to the surface, coughing and spluttering, the young lady was half way back down the pool with her back to him.

Mr. Noble climbed to the ten metre board as his co-swimmer reached the opposite end of the pool, and Mr. Noble coughed loudly as he tested the spring of the long board. The young woman stopped swimming, and trod water for a moment.

"Oh! Das ist verboten!"

Mr. Noble held his slight pot belly in, and answered in an unusually deep voice for him.

"I certainly am." He flashed a smile.

"Nein! Nein!!"

Charles Noble performed a little jump at the end of the board, and as it took his full weight, he felt the sisal matting that lined the end of the board slip from under him. Instead of sweeping down to the water in a graceful swallow-dive, he slewed sideways and flew through the air, turning over and over rather like a Formula Three racing car that has hit the tyre wall at 200 miles per hour.  An enormous untidy splash greeted his arrival at water level, and all the air was forced from his lungs.  As he rose slowly to the surface he found himself making strange inhuman sounds as he desperately tried to find his breath.

"Ach!  Donner und Blitzen!"  The young lady sounded worried.

"Yes, I'm fine."  Mr. Noble forced the words out and then made a noise as if he was vomiting.  His legs were trembling beneath him, and he felt himself sinking again.

"Help."

Gerda Guntrum caught Mr. Noble under the arms and swam on her back, powerfully, and in textbook lifesaver mode, to the edge of the pool.  If there had been any spectators present, they could not have failed to notice Gerda's fine physique, honed by regular visits to the Freiburg Gymnasium, nor Mr. Noble's extraordinarily unhoned and spare frame.  Nor indeed the discrepancy in their respective skin colouring.  He was still shaking when Gerda called for a doctor who noted the marked differences in skin pigmentation.  They made him think of London Gin and Jamaica Rum respectively.  Called from her bed, Mrs. Noble was shocked to see her husband so pallidly horizontal.

"What were you doing, dear?"

"Just getting fit dear.  Uurrgghh!  Hic!  Have you met Gerda?"

The first day improved after that.  The Nobles walked down to the old town after a light lunch in their room, and Jennifer Noble purchased some castanets and a straw hat. They bumped into Gerda Guntrum outside the London Disco Bar, but she didn't seem to notice them as she took a close interest in a toy donkey offered to her by a small boy with dusty knees.  They stopped for afternoon tea at the Donbelle English Tearooms, where the owner's bloodhound tried to make friends with Mr. Noble.  But dogs had difficulty making friends with Mr. Noble, especially when he was trying to eat. In fact Mr. Noble looked quite paranoid as he tried to protect his fruit meringue from the great dripping jaws that hung open by his left ear.

"Good boy" was all he said, as he forced the confection into his mouth, with his elbows stuck out awkwardly in the form of outer defence bulwarks. The meringue was very dry. Mr. Noble started to choke for the second time that day.

As he doubled up in a paroxysm of swiftly expelled air, the bloodhound, with one stroke of his enormous tongue, licked the plate clean.

There was another very happy dog abroad in Silencio de Mar that afternoon. Filfy O'Durr had actually been taken for a walk, and he was enjoying every moment. The container had been a nightmare for Filfy, and since he had been let loose, he had destroyed most of it. But now he was free, and there were Mr. and Mrs. O'Durr taking the airs on the Great South Beach of Silencio, seemingly oblivious of their charge. Filfy ran hither and thither. He was in Heaven. He had never felt happier, as he sprinted this way and that across the beach. He found towels to steal, sandcastles to knock over, smells of dead fish and sewage to investigate, unidentifiable objects to eat, and even knickers to run off with. Gerda Guntrum's mother, Griselda Guntrum wasn't too amused at this latter trick, as it occurred just as she was balancing on one leg and the towel wound around her ample midriff was starting to slip beachwards.

"Good afternoon." Mr. Noble stared, fascinated, at the cumulus buttocks as he passed. Luckily, no-one seemed to notice him. Filfy was off at the water's edge, dropping the knickers into the water, and Mr. and Mrs. O'Durr were tucking into multi-coloured ice creams next to the effluent outlet. It was only Jennifer Noble who noticed the episode at all.

"Keep your eyes to the front, dear" was all she said, as in the far distance an old dog raised his sandy nose in the air, and detected a scent that reminded him of home. But he was so excited by his adventures that he just couldn't make the connection between that characteristic smell of yogurt and fear. And Charles Noble.

It was inevitable that the O'Durrs and the Nobles should meet, but the circumstances could have been happier. Mr. Noble had complained to the manager of the Palacio

Grande about the less than grand little room he had been allocated, and he had been upgraded to a larger room with a proper balcony. Unfortunately the balcony which did have about half an inch of sea view was completely overlooked by the more generous balconies of the hotel next door, which was filled to bursting with jolly readers of the Bum newspaper, all intent on having a really good time.

Dolly O'Durr scraped a generous helping of Brahmaputra Vindaloo Doggie Chunks from the tin into Filfy's bowl, and carried it out on to the balcony, where the penetrating aroma would hopefully be dissipated in the wind that was starting to rise. Filfy followed his mistress outside and started to eat as Mrs. O'Durr lay down on the kingsize bed, donned a hairnet to keep her new coiffure in place and switched on her i-pod. She loved Vivaldi. It always made her feel so peaceful. And Enrico had been great. Such a sure touch. And those eyes!

Down below, Mr. Noble had ordered an evening meal served on his new balcony, where he had already pruned the geraniums and tidied up the hanging baskets. The young waiter, who was wearing an i-pod, wheeled in the trolley, and Mr. Noble looked up from the crossword in "Accountancy for Everyone" in which he had entered one answer, which later proved to be incorrect.
"Put it out there, would you?"
"Eh?"
"Out there."
The waiter removed the earpiece. "What, senor?"
"Put it out there." Mr. Noble indicated the balcony.
"Can't do that, senor. Not allowed."
"Not allowed? What the devil are you talking about?"
"Not allowed. Health and Safety regulation, senor."
"Health and Safety?!"
"The hotel next door, er…sometimes, senor they throw."
"They throw. Throw what? Throw up?"
"They throw things. At our balconies. Last month a customer receive a fork in the head."

"Good God!  A fork in the head, you say?"

"Si, senor."

"Good lord.  What sort of people are in that hotel?"

"English tourists, sir."  The waiter replied with barely concealed relish.

"Oh – we'd better keep this quiet.  I don't want Jennifer worried.  That's my wife."

Mr. Noble handed the waiter a much bigger tip than he had intended.

"We'll just keep this between ourselves, shall we Pedro?"

"Philippe, senor."

"Ah.  Philippe.  Yes.  It's a pity.  It's our anniversary.  It would have been nice to eat outside.  More romantic, you know."

"So you eat inside, senor?"

"Yes, I suppose so. We'll eat inside.  Now will you open the Champagne?"

"It's not Champagne, senor.  You order the Cava.  The cheap one."

Mr. Noble turned his head in the direction of the bathroom and raised his voice.

"Darling!  Come and have some Champagne!  Come along now!"  He turned to the waiter.

"She doesn't have to know that, does she?"


Upstairs in the Alhambra Suite of the Grand Hotel, Filfy O'Durr was having a grand time chasing a bouncing Christmas pudding that Mrs. O'Durr had bought him in the hotel gift shop.  He barked in happy abandon as Mrs. O'Durr threw it across the room, and it bounced off George O'Durr's new shiny Spanish riding boots.  Mr. O'Durr, who had only played with Filfy once before in his entire life, bent down and picked the Christmas pudding up.  Filfy was so surprised and happy that he threw himself at his master's feet and turned on his back for his tummy to be tickled.  Mr. O'Durr pretended to throw the toy out on to the balcony and Filfy leapt to his feet, barking loudly.  Mr. O'Durr laughed when he saw Filfy rush outside and fail to find the pudding.  Filfy barked and barked in delight and sheer anticipation.

"Here's to us, dear." Mr. Noble raised his glass. "Here's to us, dear. And to a wonderful holiday."

As Mr. Noble sipped the wine, he seemed to hear, in the distance, a very familiar sound. No, it couldn't be. That would be ridiculous. It couldn't possibly be that awful dog. He was safely back in England. No it couldn't be.

"I thought we might go and look at the temple of Frigidus tomorrow, dear."

"Frigidus?"

Jennifer Noble pursed her lips. "Ooh, That wine's very sharp. It's not going to do my cystitis any good at all."

She picked up the bottle from the dented ice bucket.

"Oh" she said in deep disillusion. "Cava. You said we were having Champagne."

As her husband chewed on a tough olive and couldn't think of anything at all to say, he seemed to hear that sound again. The heckles on his scrawny neck rose, and his Adam's apple did a little shimmy in his throat as the distant, excited barking reached a crescendo.

Mrs. Noble enquired.

"And who's Frigidus, anyway?"

She looked at her husband, whose nostrils were twitching and whose head was raised as if he were listening to the sound of distant drums.

"Charles! Are you all right, dear?"

Mr. Noble returned. "Yes, dear. I'm just fine", he said, with a slightly haunted look.

"Frigidus was the God of food preservation in Ancient Greece."

"That's enough now, Filf!"

Mrs. O'Durr had just thrown the bouncy Christmas Pudding once more, and Filfy had retrieved it from the balcony outside, and come back sliding across the marble floor like a toboggan, and crashed into a fake majolica aspidistra.

Mr. O'Durr had found a television programme featuring a group of pneumatic cavewomen defending their cave against an army of pterodactyls. Their brief leopardskin costumes kept slipping, and George O'Durr's mouth was hanging open. The

57

poor quality of the Spanish dialogue was totally lost on the man on the gold framed sofa.

"Now, settle down, Filf!"

Mrs. O'Durr tempted Filfy to calm down by putting another large helping of Brahmaputra Vindaloo Doggie Chunks into his bowl. But Filfy wasn't interested. He didn't want the game to end. It was such a very rare thing in his life. So he continued patting the pudding around the Alhambra Suite, and trying to unearth it noisily when it disappeared under the grand furniture that filled the apartment.

It was a lovely evening outside. The sweet scent of mimosa was born upward on a gentle breeze, and it finally tempted the Nobles to move outside on to their cramped balcony. They had finished the main course and dismissed Philippe and they were sitting opposite each other as the sun set. Mr. Noble kept casting uneasy glances in the direction of the upper floors of the Grand Hotel.

"Won't you please take that ice bucket off your head, Charles? It makes you look silly."

"No, dear. I'm quite comfortable, thank-you. And you never know what might come flying through the air. I might not be covered if somebody, say, dropped a fork from the 22nd floor!"

Mr. Noble had been quite shaken by the waiter's warning, but Mrs. Noble had been insistent on moving outside. It was, after all, her wedding anniversary. Mr. Noble stretched out from the little table and retrieved a large dish with a silver cover from the side table.

"Now, dear. Here's a very special treat for you."

He lifted his head and looked up at the building opposite, and the sudden movement caused the ice bucket to fall with a crash to the balcony floor.

"Confound it!" he said as he looked uneasily upwards to listen more carefully to the unmistakeable excited barking of Filfy O'Durr.

"I think perhaps we should be going inside now dear. You're looking quite cold."

"No. I'm not cold at all. What's the special treat then,

Charles?"

Mr. Noble replaced his helmet, and removed the silver cover from the dish with a flourish to reveal a highly coloured and delicious looking confection.

"Food for Lovers", he said, registering another flurry of barking from above.

"This is the Head Chef's special recommendation for honeymooners! I won't tell you how much it cost!"

"Oh! Charles!"

Jennifer Noble looked lovingly into her husband's eyes, and thought how close-set they were. In doing so she realised that it had been a very long time since their eyes had met. She dropped her gaze to the plate in front of her.

Up on the O'Durrs' balcony, Filfy had worked himself up into a frenzy, as totally ignored by both master and mistress, he charged backwards and forwards after the bouncing Christmas pudding. He patted it this way and that through the great rooms, and then with an inadvertently muscular swing of his paw, he batted it out at high velocity on to the balcony. He could see he was going to lose it unless he moved fast, so he launched himself across the floor, and tried to reach the balcony rail before the pudding did. He failed by a split second, and the pudding flew out into space in a lazy arc as Filfy's forepaws skidded across the slippery balcony floor and crashed into the half-full bowl of dogfood. The bowl slid smartly under the railing and followed the Christmas pudding. Like twin satellites, the pudding and the Doggie Chunks flew out in perfect synchronicity across the space dividing the two hotels.

"Oh. Do take that ridiculous helmet off, Charles. You have a fine head, and I'd like to see it."

As Charles Noble removed the helmet, a Bouncy Christmas Pudding hit him between the eyes before bouncing merrily away into the shrubbery below.. And it was to a cacophony of barking that the Lovers Food in the silver dish before his wife was joined by a generous and fast-moving portion of Brahmaputra Vindaloo Doggie Chunks.

# CHAPTER SEVEN
## May

## THE BIG SNIFF

George O'Durr was distracted. He bit the end of his pencil, and suddenly his mouth was full of bits of wood and a length of lead. He spat the offending morsels out and spattered his bank statement with little splinters, some graphite, and a lump of grizzle from the burger he had consumed earlier in the evening. Filfy O'Durr appeared from under the table and, keeping a wary eye on his master, stretched his neck to consume the delicious titbit.

Things were not looking good, even before he had desecrated the statement from Snodgrass's Bank, "The Bank for the Working Man" (although this was something of a misnomer as far as Mr. O'Durr was concerned.) The new manager, Mr. Sadillac, had asked him to make an urgent appointment to see him, and Mr. O'Durr was not looking forward to the experience.

On his last visit to the bank, Mr. Sadillac, in his dazzling white shirt and perfectly knotted silk tie had made him feel very inadequate when he had withdrawn Mr. O'Durr's 'Snodgrass Platinum Card' and replaced it with a 'Snodgrass Conditional'. Mr. O'Durr had found the bank's conditions far too onerous, taking into account his tastes for losing horses and Buster's Lager, and had been smoking more heavily than usual since his wife, Dolly, had, for unspecified reasons banished him from the marital bed to the box room.

Mrs. O'Durr was at that moment sitting in the inflatable armchair, watching an episode of "St. Wilfred's" in which the Reverend Jim Manley was using a sniffer dog to test his congregation for drugs as they entered his church.

"He looks a shifty bastard" she muttered, as Jim Manley ejected an emaciated teenager with a very enthusiastic Christian shove in the small of the back. Mrs. O'Durr reached for her glass of Pernod without taking her eyes off the screen, and knocked it over on the dusty carpet.

"Bugger!"

She tried to rise from the armchair, but it seemed to follow her hips as she moved, and she eventually keeled over majestically on to the floor with the arms of the chair embracing her rather like the suckers of a giant squid. Filfy rushed to her side anticipating a rare romp, but he was disappointed.

"Get off, Filf!" she said as her skirt rode up and she rolled, frustrated and voluptuous, into the wet aniseed patch on the carpet.

"You look like a bloody beached whale!"

Mr. O'Durr welcomed the distraction from his Snodgrass statement.

"Some husband, you are!" His wife's voice was shrill.

"If you didn't spend all our lolly on booze and fags we could have a decent lounge suite!".

Mrs. O'Durr managed to extricate herself, mortally squashing her packet of High Tar cigarettes with the "These are Your Death Warrant" logo, and flung the armchair into the corner of the room, where it landed with a modest "pop!" on the still extended aerial of a long defunct ghetto blaster. As she levered herself up from the floor, pulling down her skirt primly, the armchair quietly expired.

Next morning at nine o'clock, Channelle arrived unbidden for breakfast, wearing her Pinchley Substance Abuse Vigilantes (P.S.A.V.) uniform.

"Oh! Oh! Here comes the Hitler Youth."

Mrs. O'Durr had never really bonded with her daughter, and it had once made her feel very guilty. But she had now given up on the idea of any such intimacy.

"What you doing here?" she asked. Mr. O'Durr was more welcoming.

"Oh, hello, Nell. All right?" he asked, mopping up the grease from his plate with a piece of fried bread, and wondering if

'Dead Cert' would be running in the 2.30 at Haydock.

"You look awful, Dad! When did you last have a shave? And that vest!"

"Shut up girl, will you! Leave him alone. He's got worries."

"Worries? Who ain't got worries? You gotta be dead not to have any worries."

"Just shut up and park your arse!!! What'll you have? You can't have much. We're skint. What d'you want? A full fry-up?"

Channelle glanced at her father, who was looking inexplicably diminished.

"Yeah. A full frontal fry-up… What's the problem, Dad?"

She stood behind her father in her tight black uniform, and playfully twiddled with Mr. O'Durr's thinning hair with her short fingers.

"Ouch!" Mr. O'Durr flinched away from her.

"Cor! Your hair comes out easy, Dad!"

George O'Durr saw a tuft of his own hair float down before him and land neatly on his remaining fragment of fried bread.

"I got a job for Filf."

Filfy O'Durr, who had been waiting under the table for breakfast debris, arose from his lair, and leapt up at Channelle, dislodging a medal from her breast in his adoration, and whacking Mr. O'Durr with his uncontrollable tail.

"A job? What sort of job? Not one that pays some dosh?"

"Oh, yeah. It pays all right. Hard cash. The real thing."

Channelle savoured the moment as she pinned the New Anti-Sleaze Green Republican Multi-Arrest Medal back on. Mr. O'Durr was hooked.

"What? What sort of hard cash?"

He scarcely dared to hope. He had tried to get Filfy to earn his keep in the past, but his stint as a security dog had ended shamefully when the police had arrested him in the back yard of Ed's Supergrill as he tucked into a Vindalooburger and Fries, and a local master criminal disappeared down the expressway with a boot full of out-of-date sausages.

"Yeah! Real money, Dad. You know when Filf came down to my passing out parade at the scout hut?"

"You mean when he went all funny?"

"Yeah! Well, afterwards Hairy Musseldyke found out why. She found a bag of white powder round the back of the guides' loos, with toothmarks in it."

"What? You mean some kind of loo cleaner?"

"No, Dad! Drugs! Drugs! D'you see? And Filf took some! That's what made him go doolally like that."

Mrs. O'Durr looked down at the attentive and panting dog, as she passed a plate of fried breakfast to her daughter. A blackened chipolata fell off the side of the plate and was bound for the greasy tile floor when a flying muzzle intercepted it.

"You see that?" Channelle pulled down her tight black skirt and sat down.

"Filfy's quick as lightning when he wants something. Old Musseldyke says he's got the taste for heroin. He'll be perfect for our 'Clean Up Pinchley' anti-drugs drive."

George O'Durr took a chip off his daughter's plate.

"What sort of money?"

Mr. O'Durr lit up an expensive cigarillo, filling the room with the unmistakeable aroma of dried alpaca dung. Suddenly Filfy O'Durr was at his master's knee, his face pressing toward the cigarillo, his black nose quivering, and a strange and rather distant look in his eyes. He took a very deep breath, and rested his head on his master's thigh. Channelle stepped forward, and without ceremony snatched the cigar from her father's lips. She held it up, and looked at it hard in the light filtering in through the kitchen window, as Filfy followed her hand, and leapt up like a deranged highland dancer and tried to breath in more of the oddly distinctive smell.

"What the?! Show me the packet, Dad. Where did you get this stuff?"

George O'Durr looked even more shifty than usual.

"Oh, I dunno. Down the supermarket, I should think."

"You never got this down no supermarket, Dad. You been to Colombia lately?"

Channelle O'Durr had been educated  the previous evening about the South American "shit" entering this country by an intoxicated Myra Musseldyke at the Chardonnay Wine Bar in Ernest Bevin Way.

"Colombia? What do you think I am? A bleeding pervert?"

"Well, you been somewhere, Dad. This shit's what we been looking for. Where d'you get it ,Dad?"

Channelle turned to her mother, who was trying to restrain a very excited Filfy O'Durr from burrowing his nose between her thighs.

"Mum; I got to report this. Dad's breaking the law. He could get ten years. Ten years in the slammer. You better talk to him, Mum."

Mrs. O'Durr had got Filfy in a painful looking throat-hold. He was whimpering passionately and his eyes were bulging, but Dolly O'Durr didn't seem to notice.

"Ten years, you say?" It was hard to tell what she was thinking.

"What? You'd shop your own father?"

Mr. O'Durr looked disconsolately down at the mug of brassy brown tea in which his cigarillo had been dunked.

"Oh, yes! You bet she would! She's already grassed up her own boyfriend."

"Yes; I would and all."

Channelle stuck her chest out, and a button flew off her black shirt on to the table.

"This is Government business. I'm their eyes and ears in Pinchley, so don't you go messing me around. I got a thousand nicker for reporting that tosser Darren, and I can get more than that for you if you don't co-operate. Where did you get it, Dad? You'd better tell. If you know what's good for you."

Mr. O'Durr knew when he was beaten. Indeed, he had considerable experience of the condition. He looked up at his daughter's black shirt, which now had a white crevasse in the middle of it.

"It was Lifty."

"What? That muppet? Shaun Lift? What? Down the High Street? That geezer who sold you the jogging bottoms with one leg? No!! He's not bright enough to get into this sort of shit....is he?"

Mrs. O'Durr had by this time returned a disoriented Filfy to his basket under the table.

"Don't you believe it, girl! Old Lifty's as fly as they come.

They can't put a finger on him, but everyone knows he's bent."
Channelle dropped her voice.
"But I tell you who will finger him, and put him behind bars, where he belongs."
"And who's that, when he's at home?"
"Him!" Channelle indicated the unrequited form under the kitchen table. She looked down at her untouched and fast-congealing breakfast.
"Oy! Filf! Come on!" She emptied the contents of the plate on to the floor. "Have some grub! And then we got work to do!"

"Good morning sah!"
Myra Musseldyke snapped a smart salute, clicking together her heavy brogues, which made a noise like a cricket ball hit for six. The man with the lined face and the trilby looked up from his newspaper in the shade of the trolley park as Colonel Sadillac spoke.
"Good morning, Musseldyke. No need for formalities here. You know what I told you about having to blend in."
He looked across the Painsburys car park with narrowed eyes, but saw no-one he recognised. Colonel Sadillac was wearing a broad-brimmed leather hat, combat fatigues, and Plinkin Uremma shades. He was also sporting a row of medals, which included his late father's Burma Star, a Military Cross he had bought for £50 in The Precinct, and a Snodgrass's Bank Bronze Award. He looked down at his adjutant with distaste.
"Well, Musseldyke? What exactly do you want with me? I am a busy man, and I like to have my weekends free."
Had Myra Musseldyke possessed any idea of what Colonel Sadillac liked to keep his weekends free for, she would have left the car park that morning without a backward look. But she had never been invited to one of Mr. Sadillac's parties.
"You said something about a dog. A wonder-dog? 'A dog who can net us a fortune' were your words, I think".
"He certainly can, sir."
Myra Musseldyke clicked her heavy heels together, bruising her ankles.
"And that's him coming now if I'm not mistaken."
She reached into her khaki webbing handbag for the bag of

white powder, as a rusting Datsun Gooseberry that sounded like a tractor parked in front of them. A plump man with a crew-cut and wearing a singlet, stained jogging bottoms, and trainers got out, accompanied by a big smiling dog. There was a fearful glimmer of recognition in Mr. O'Durr's eyes as Channelle introduced him to her superior.

"And this is Filfy."

Colonel Sadillac looked down his aquiline nose at the scruffy but powerful looking mongrel with the challenging eyes. It seemed to be fascinated suddenly by the area of his upper thigh.

"I'll just go and hide this, and you see if Filf don't sniff it out."

Channelle disappeared in the direction of the landscaped Painsbury's shrubbery, leaving Filfy to continue his local investigations, and Mr. O'Durr to wonder where he had seen this oddly dressed man before.

"Down, Filf!"

Mr. O'Durr lit up a high tar Coffers Number One, and threw the empty packet into the shrubbery. The dog did seem to be more belligerent than usual, but then Mr. O'Durr had decided he didn't like the man anyway. There was something unnervingly familiar about him.

Suddenly Filfy was baring his teeth.

"Call him off!" There was a note of panic in Mr. Sadillac's voice.

"Call him off!"

Myra Musseldyke yelled "Get him off!" and clicked her heels painfully.

"Down, Filf'.

Mr. O'Durr didn't sound very enthusiastic. Colonel Sadillac's distasteful expression changed to one of terror. The dog still seemed to be smiling, but the smile had become strangely fixed and the animal was clearly out of control. Its jaws closed on Mr. Sadillac's trouser pocket, and the head jerked back violently. The medals on the colonel's chest jingled together as he tried to pull away, and magnetic brown eyes locked with his own.

"Get him off!"

But it was too late. Filfy removed the entire pocket with

almost surgical precision, and dropped both the patch of camouflaged material, and the lining of the pocket, on to the tarmac. Together with its contents..

It was at this moment that Channelle O'Durr arrived back, breathless, from the shrubbery.

"All right. I've hidden it" she said, excitedly, her bosom rising and falling like the heavy swell generated at the Pinchley Wave Pool when the controls were set to "max". The deep rhythm of her breath was suddenly arrested as she took in the scene.

Major Musseldyke, arms folded across her chest and her mouth open, stood staring at her superior's ruined trousers. Colonel Sadillac was very pale, holding himself where the white skin showed through the camouflage. Filfy O'Durr looked deliriously happy, and lolloped like a spring lamb as he repeatedly tossed a punctured bag of white powder in the air, and caught it precisely in his teeth each time it descended. Mr.O'Durr could also be very quick on his feet when he needed to be. His right hand shot out as the bag began to fall once more into Filfy's jaws, and he swiftly pocketed it.

Channelle's eyes met those of D.C. Cadwallader, his trilby at a jaunty angle, as she bent to retrieve her bag of heroin from the shrubbery. His hand tightened around her wrist, and as Mr. O'Durr bent to pick up the unread newspaper, a slow, beatific smile spread across his countenance. He helped Mr. Sadillac to his feet, and whispered into the bank manager's ear. The detective approached with Channelle O'Durr in tow. His cheeks were quite pink. George O'Durr smiled broadly.

"You two know each other? Detective Constable Wally. This is Mr. Sadillac from Snodgrass's Bank. An excellent bank, if I may say so. Very helpful with overdrafts, eh Mr. Sadillac? My dog Filf's just been getting a bit too excited, but no harm done, eh, Mr. Sadillac? And what's that daughter of mine been up to now, constable?"

# CHAPTER EIGHT
## May


## THE VIDEO


It was Emma Montgomery's needs that sparked things off. She had been alarmed to discover a window in her hectic social schedule on a Wednesday morning, after the wine appreciation classes under the tutelage of the late Piers Portley had suddenly ended with his premature departure from the "Au Revoir" ward at the Cheeseman Clinic for Excellent Habits. Emma had moved swiftly to fill the window upon meeting a charismatic yogi with volcanic eyes on the top deck of a number 17 bus.

Emma Montgomery didn't drive, and was usually to be seen chauffeured around Pinchley by her husband in their mature Jaguar Elite. On this particular day, however, she had taken the bus back from the flower arranging group in Silvers Green, and had been amazed to be offered a seat by an Asian gentleman with a quiet voice and a tortured expression. After she had settled herself, with the awkward and slightly imperfect flower arrangement on her lap, she raised her eyes and saw the stranger looking down at her. Although Emma Montgomery looked after herself, and had indeed in her younger days, been voted "Miss. Walton-on-the- Naze" it was a long time since a man had looked at her quite like that.

"Very lovely" he said gently.

Mrs. Montgomery coloured and looked down, and gripped her Gnocchi handbag a little more tightly.

"The flowers, dear one. The flowers."

She looked up. His eyes were very dark. Dark and red. They seemed to smoulder. Rather like the wall-mounted flaming torches she had admired the previous night at the "Medieval Eating Experience" at Bendon Castle Ruins, where her husband had been installed as "Chief Dragon."

"I think you have a hole."

Mrs. Montgomery grasped her handbag even more tightly and looked out of the window. It was steaming up, but she could still see the skinhead running out of the Amir 24 Hour Shopper clutching a sheaf of banknotes and a claw hammer and wearing a tee shirt saying "Screw You!"

She looked up once more, feeling a deep sadness.

"I think you have a hole inside you, and I can show you how to fill it."

Emma Montgomery had never done anything like this before, but before she knew it, she had invited the stranger home, and was offering him a cup of tea. The visitor removed his shiny leather shoes, and sat on her settee. His back was very straight and she saw he was very thin. Some would have said emaciated. He seemed to hover like a wraith above the luxurious cushions of her handcrafted "Superfine Windsor" settee, as he drew up and crossed his legs. He wiggled his tiny toes and looked imperiously around the room. And then he spoke. The authority in his voice was unmistakable, and the corncrake timbre was arresting.

"Yoga is the supreme blending of the spirit, mind and body into the One. The letting go of the self, the acceptance of eternal bliss. You, dear one, look like you could benefit from some bliss. Are you willing to accept eternal bliss now, today, dear one?"

"Mmm. Yes, I might be. How much do you charge?"

The visitor's eyes rolled upwards. All they saw was a reproduction French Empire chandelier with a bulb missing.

"I make no charge, dear one. No charge whatever. How could I charge anyone for this divine gift of realisation? But I will accept donations. Most people give £25 per session. If they want to give more, who am I to argue? The money goes to a charity."

The visitor looked down and studied his perfect little fingernails.

"Oh, and what's that?" Mrs. Montgomery felt she was on firmer ground here. She already made donations to Cancer for All, the Irritable Bowel Syndrome Fellowship, the Swollen Brain Foundation, and the Senior Dignity Oasis.

"Er. The … er … Rangoon Children's Refuge.   Actually."
The eyes were hooded.

Emma looked up at her favourite antique, a Georgian carriage clock, as it chimed the hour.  Her husband would be on the fifteenth tee by now.

"So you'll come here on Wednesday mornings at 10, Mr. Bandi?"

"I'll come on Wednesday mornings at 10, yes.  But not here, dear one."

The visitor made an expansive gesture that took in the palatial room, and his eyelids dropped suddenly over the smouldering eyes like a well-oiled safety curtain.

"Not here.  And please call me Ram.  Uh.  How many friends do you think you can get ?"

Ram reared up, flicking his tongue over his pale lips, and for a fearful moment, Emma thought she saw a coiled cobra on her best settee.  She swallowed and felt her heart make an unscheduled beat.

"About fifteen.  But what's wrong with this room?"

"It's too big.  Far too big for that number. How many people can you fit in here?"

His host thought for a moment.  There must have been at least a hundred invitees last year when her husband had celebrated his first forty years with International Pharmaceuticals.

"A hundred and twenty….  Ram."

"Well, there you are, dear one.  This room is too airy.  It's too cool. Too furnished.  It's too green.  My yoga is intense.  It needs a red room.  You have to leave behind your individual comfort zone.  You have to feel the heat.   You have to feel the heat and do it anyway.  You have to melt into divine stress, to be dissolved into the rampaging waters of the One, or you don't get the experience.  You don't experience the divine. The bliss.  And you want to experience divine bliss, don't you, dear one?"

Emma Montgomery looked into the hot eyes.

"Er.yes," she said, and her heart fluttered out of control, like a newborn Cabbage White taking its first flight.  Or was it a Painted Lady?

"Do you perhaps know someone with more modest quarters?"

70

For one agonisingly uncomfortable moment, Emma Montgomery, who had been a keen horsewoman with an excellent seat, felt the blood rising to her cheeks.

"With a much smaller front room. Good central heating. And a noble spirit?"

Emma hesitated. She knew one person with good central heating and a much smaller front room. But she had never thought of Jennifer Noble as a noble spirit, exactly.

Jennifer Noble stood at the kitchen sink. She was wearing a pink pinny and yellow rubber gloves and was quietly humming Tom Jones's "Delilah" as she washed up the breakfast crocks. She felt happy for the first time in some months. Her husband had been particularly busy, after his employers, Proods Educational Books, had taken over a failing magazine called "Healthy Burgers Monthly", and he had been arriving home exhausted. Indeed he had barely been summoning up enough energy to eat the delicious organic meals that had been prepared so lovingly for his return.

Jennifer Noble's married life had revolved around her husband since their marriage at the Pinchley Register Office some ten years previously, and although she had become used to his occasional lateness, Charles Noble was extremely punctual by nature and could become quite testy with those of a more relaxed habit. He was not a man to stay later at his desk than he had to, and he really liked to arrive home at a pre-arranged time to enjoy the food his wife had prepared for him.

But these last few months it had been hard. There had been powdery nut roasts, leathery, yellowing Brussels sprouts, and chewy dried-up salmon steaks, and Mrs. Noble had been reduced to watching "St. Wilfred's," "Are You a Genius?," and "Name That Celebrity" on her own. Well, almost on her own. Filfy O'Durr had started to pop by in the evenings. He liked Jennifer Noble; she gave him nice food, and sometimes she even played with him.

Mr. O'Durr also liked Jennifer Noble, even though he loathed her husband. He had trained Filfy to bring round the evening paper when he'd finished with it (which was after he had extracted the racing pages.) Jennifer Noble was touched, but didn't like to tell her neighbour that her husband always brought home the late edition with him after work. Filfy had also learned to deliver the odd video from one house to the other. Although Jennifer Noble's taste was generally for romantic or redemptive movies showing the power of the human spirit triumphing over evil, and George O'Durr's was of a simpler, more violent ilk, they sometimes enjoyed the same things. They had both recently appreciated, for example, "The Vikings" and "The Murders in the Rue Morgue." George O'Durr had bought these for 50p each at the Swollen Brain Foundation Shop in The Precinct, and had dispatched them to number 26 via Filfy.

"Take it to Jennifer!" he had said, and the dog had happily effected the deliveries and welcomed the Doggie Treat that had awaited him at the hand of his neighbour on each occasion.

George O'Durr had just taken a luxurious swig of Buster's Lager and rearranged his bare feet on the dog when he heard the key in the lock.

"Out the way, Filf!"

Mr. O'Durr could move very quickly when it was necessary, and it was certainly imperative now, as he moved like a rotund panther across the space between him and the television. Filfy had heard his mistress coming down the street for some time before she arrived but George O'Durr had missed all the warning signs. The raised head, the pricked ears, and the trembling expectation had all gone unnoticed as the man had sat staring in incredulity at the events on the screen.

Filfy raised himself up, pleased to be free of the weight of his master's hairy calves, moved to the door, and listened appreciatively to Mrs. O'Durr's movements in the hall. After tripping over his glass of lager George O'Durr staggered forward and nearly lost his balance as he lunged for the 'OFF' button. The door opened and Filfy was pushed to one side. A mass of highly-piled blond hair appeared round the door. It was so big indeed that the face beneath it looked rather like a shrunken head.

"D'you like my new hairstyle, George?"

George O'Durr's hunted expression gave way to one of excited admiration. He had a high colour.

"Cor! That's real glam, Doll!"

His wife saw he really meant it, and blushed.

"Desmond did a good job didn't he? He says I've got the hair of a twenty-one year old."

Her husband glowered.

"You can tell that poofter to keep his opinions to himself. A twenty-one year old what?"

Unknown to Mr. O'Durr, he had been about to be offered a cup of tea, but his wife had swiftly changed her mind.

"You can clean up that beer before you come out of my best room! And you can switch the bleeding video off too!"

After the door closed and Filfy and the blond head had both left the room, George O'Durr bent down and pressed the eject button on the video player. Nothing happened. He pressed it again with the same result. He got down on his knees, and tried again. Then he switched the machine off and on again at the wall, but nothing happened. He tried pressing each button, one after the other, but all to no avail. He felt a panic rising in his breast. Sean Lift wouldn't be at all pleased; he had a waiting list for the video, and some of his customers were people you just didn't say "no" to. George O'Durr scrabbled in the cushions of the new settee delivered by "Christian Faction" the previous week, and found the box. Just as well he hadn't left it out for Dolly to see. "Danish Discipline at the Convent of Sin" had a rather lurid cover.

Whilst Mr. O'Durr was busy shaking his video machine Mrs. Noble was sitting in her G Plan armchair consuming a Danish pastry, and watching the latest episode of "St. Wilfred's" on her high-definition flat-screen Wasabi. The pastry hovered just outside her open mouth, as the Reverend Jim Manley addressed his congregation.

"Are you ready for the Lord? Are your lamps lit?"

The close up of the minister played around his square jaw, and the crinkles at the corners of his dark eyes. Then it homed in on his mouth, in which white teeth twinkled like stars.

"Are you ready for the Lord?" he repeated, as the camera panned back to show a young woman having problems with her breathing. The church goers all around her were showing their concern as the young woman, who was very beautiful, collapsed into the aisle. The Reverend Manley sprang down the pulpit steps three at a time and was immediately at her side. There were reaction shots of the shocked fellow worshippers, as the vicar looked up at them and thundered "Are you ready for the Lord?!" before rearranging himself to administer the kiss of life to the recumbent parishioner, who looked like she was indeed more than ready.

Mrs. Noble's grip on herself and on the Danish tightened, and flakes of buttery pastry dropped on to her chest and stayed there. There was a knock at the door.

"Good morning, dear lady."

The Reverend Cyril Downmouth doffed his Panama, as the cat disappeared out of the catflap. The vicar's eyes dropped not very discreetly to Jennifer Noble's chest, where a Lord Mayor's chain of pastry flakes still rested on her bosom. Jennifer Noble felt the old familiar stirrings in her motherly heart, together with the old familiar conflict between a desire to watch the excitement of "St. Wilfred's", and to support her ageing vicar in another moment of need.

"Oh. Good morning. I suppose you'd better come in."

Then she saw the flowers.

"I mean please come in, Cyril."

Mrs. Noble took her visitor into the kitchen; she knew he didn't like his flock to watch 'St. Wilfred's'. And she wanted to show off her new cooker. The vicar put the wilting bunch of tulips down on the worktop.

"Would you like a cheese scone, Cyril? They've just come out of the oven. It's a new one."

"I'm not sure if I've got time. I'm due at the hospital shortly."

Then Cyril Downmouth saw the tray of scones. They were a lovely golden brown, and smelled like his mother's kitchen, long ago.

"Oh. Go on, then, Jennifer."

Mrs. Noble placed the largest and most magnificent scone on a Crown Derby plate, using a pair of silver-plated tongs, cut it in

74

half, and buttered it with a mother-of-pearl-handled knife. The Reverend Downmouth took the high stool offered, and tried to balance the plate on his knee as his hostess buttered a scone for herself and poured a cup of tea for the visitor from the Wedgwood teapot.

"I'll not keep you long today," Cyril Downmouth said, regretfully. "I have to be at the hospital shortly."

Mrs. Noble frowned. "Oh dear. Nothing serious, I hope?"

"Oh, no. Nothing like that. It's old Mrs. Tidings. Again."

He took an avid bite from the scone, and as he replaced the remaining portion on his plate, he dislodged the other half, and it fell to the floor and rolled under the cooker.

"Oh. Goodness me!" he said, descending from the stool and getting down rather stiffly to the floor to peer under the cooker. Mrs. Noble looked discreetly down at the dark shiny bottom, and experienced a strong sense of 'déjà vu', as she recalled the time the Reverend Downmouth had attempted to perform the kiss of life on a member of the congregation. They had just finished singing "Through the Night of Doubt and Sorrow" when Mrs. Chipchase had collapsed into the aisle at the Church of the Dead Martyrs, and the vicar had sprung forward to help her. He was unpractised, however, in the kiss of life technique, and had moreover been fitted with a new and ill-fitting National Health plate for his upper jaw earlier that week. An ambulance had had to be called after Mrs. Chipchase's windpipe had become blocked.

By the time Cyril Downmouth had consumed his second cheese scone, he was late for his appointment.

"I have to be at the hospital," he said plaintively, looking at his watch, and then looking at Jennifer Noble's impressive bosom, from which the pastry flakes had now disappeared.

"But I'd much rather be staying here." The words escaped his lips like birds from a cage, that rose and fluttered joyously round the room. But the experience to Cyril Downmouth felt more like opening Pandora's box.

"Oh! Goodness me! What have I said?" The voice was thinner and even more strangled than usual.

"You've said you like being here, Cyril. That's all."

Mrs. Noble was purring and primping her dark hair.

"Better than being at the hospital."

Suddenly her hand was gripping his. He slid down from the high stool, and trod on her foot.

"Ouch!"

The koala bear slipper gave some protection, but not much, and it had taken the full weight of an orthopaedic boot. The spell was broken. Mrs. Noble limped to the letter rack on the olive green work surface next to the cooker.

"I wanted to ask you about this, Cyril."

Her tone was suddenly more businesslike as she handed him a purple leaflet headed "Home-Style Yoga for Housewives."

The vicar grimaced, and asked in a stony voice "What did you want to ask me?"

"Well, Mrs. Montgomery, you know Mrs. Montgomery?"

"Yes."

"Well, she's been asked to host a Yoga group, this one, at her house. But it's difficult for her- her husband's home all day, you know, and he's not at all interested…"

"What is it that you want to ask me?"

"Oh. Have you heard of this man? Ram Bandy."

"No. Can't say I have."

Cyril Downmouth picked up the wilting tulips and turned for the door.

"And, my dear, if you're asking me if I like Yoga, I don't."

He suddenly turned to look Mrs. Noble in the eye for the first time since she had raised the matter.

"Yoga is the devil's work."

"But Mrs. Montgomery … "

"And now, dear lady, I really must be going."

Retreating to the kitchen door, Cyril Downmouth produced a sheaf of papers from his pocket.

"I really only called to give you this. It's about our new group for housewives starting next month. I've called it 'Matrons for Christ.' I really must go now. I'll let myself out."

Before Mrs. Noble could speak, her visitor had disappeared. As she heard the front door close behind him, she looked down at the leaflet in her hand.

"ED'S SUPERGRILL. SPECIAL OFFER. 3 PIZZAS FOR

THE PRICE OF 2.  BUY WHILE STOCKS LAST!"

It was on the following morning that Dolly O'Durr, waiting until her husband had left with Filfy for the betting shop, knelt down and switched on the video.  Finding an unmarked videotape still inside, and realising it must be the one George O'Durr had been watching surreptitiously the previous day, she stuffed it into the nearest empty cover she could find, which bore the message, scrawled in black marker pen "The Divine Experience."  She recalled with a pang of pleasure how she had once thrilled to the liberating music and pelvic thrusts of Joey Divine and the Hod Carriers.  Then she reloaded the machine, pressed "Play" and settled back in the settee to watch "The Best of I Married a Washing Machine."

In the modest quarters next door, preparations were being made for the arrival of Ram Bandi, and Jennifer Noble was spending even more time than usual on the telephone.
"Yes; you have to wear very loose-fitting clothing."
"What; a tracksuit, that sort of thing, sweetie?"
Sue Grinder had just purchased a very flattering Jaeger Thistledown Exercise Suit in Arctic Blue, which she hadn't yet worn in public.
"Well, yes.  But a lightweight one.  He says we will get very warm."
"Oh.  I think I've got just the thing, darling."
Jenda Steamwell took some persuading to attend.  She explained at length how her heart had been broken in Sioux Falls some years previously when she had fallen in love with an Indian yogi, who had taught her to chant at the sun at dawn, to climb the highest trees in the forest, and to mimic the cry of the Levitating Banshee.
"Was he a Red Indian?"  The words just spilled out.
"A what?!!  He was a Winnebago.  A Native Indian."
Jennifer Noble felt the reproof.
"Oh.  How very interesting, dear.  Well, Mr. Bandi is a real Indian.  A proper Indian.  At least I think he is.  From India.  Rangoon, I think he said.  Is that India?  And he..er..supports the Rangoon Children's Charity.  And he offers the experience

of.. er.. divine bliss."

"You sure Rangoon's in India? How much does he charge?"

"He doesn't."

"Oh?" A hint of hope could be heard in Jenda Steamwell's voice. Her partner, Randy Breed, hadn't had many bookings of late, and his last performance of 'Nashville Giant' at the Bendon Working Men's Club had barely paid for a new front tyre on the pick-up.

"But he accepts donations." Jennifer Noble needed more takers to get up to the fifteen promised, so she didn't mention the "suggested donation" of £25.

"Did you say I've got to dress lightweight?"

"Yes; that's right, dear one."

Emma Montgomery called round on the Tuesday about the time her husband was driving into a bunker on the seventh. She was wearing Plinkin Uremma shades and a pencil line woollen coat from Dave Popoudopoulos. It had a less than discreet "DP" monogram on the lapel and a length of purple wool hanging from the hem.

"All set, then, Jennifer?"

There was a hint of excited conspiracy in the voice, which faded somewhat when Jennifer Noble showed her into her front room.

All furniture had been removed for the morrow, and there was a strong smell of lavender furniture polish in the air.

"He won't like that."

"What?"

"The smell. Chemicals. He's very pure."

"So's my polish!"

Mrs. Noble picked up the can from the spotless mantelpiece. "Painsbury's Organic Furniture Polish."

Her visitor took the can, read the label carefully, and replaced it on the mantelpiece.

"It will have to be warmer than this. 75 degrees, he said."

"Don't worry, dear. I haven't forgotten. I'm turning up the heating to full blast after Charles goes to work in the morning. You know what he's like."

"Yes, dear one."

Emma Montgomery suddenly looked disinterested. She stood

in the middle of the stripped room and her mouth turned down at the corners.

"Can't imagine why he didn't want it at my place."

"I can." Jennifer Noble rose to the defence of her front room.

"This is cosy, and warm, dear. A nice space for joining."

The glistening lips were pursed.

"But it's so, so, infradig. Dear one."

That morning, the visitor was not offered a chair. Nor was she offered the customary coffee in a bone china cup with an amaretto biscuit in the saucer. As she was ushered out, her husband was searching for his ball in the formidable rough on the ninth.


"Breathe, ladies, breathe!"

The room was very warm. The heating was turned up and Ram Bandy had sealed every crack, every aperture, with duct tape. Every possible entry point for fresh cool air had been denied, and the room was becoming very uncomfortable. Everyone was sitting on the floor, facing the teacher who was balancing perfectly on a miniscule cushion.

"Breathe, ladies, breathe. And gentleman. Backs straight! I said straight, dear one! Keep it hard! Hard, I said!"

Ram Bandy fixed his glowing eyes on Brenda Goering, who had subsided into her voluminous green tracksuit like a melting pistachio ice cream.

"Are you okay, dear one?"

He was looking at the elderly Mrs. Nipp, who looked as if she was dead. Her head lolled on her chest, and her arms hung at odd angles as if dislocated. Jemima Nipp looked up. Her grey eyes were very clear.

"Yes, I'm fine. Just doing a little relaxation."

Mrs. Nipp didn't look like a founder member of the Pinchley League for Health and Beauty, but she was.

Filfy O'Durr couldn't see too well through the misted-up window, but he liked what he saw. He saw Mrs. Noble, whom he loved, with a beatific smile on her face as a small man with dark hair lifted her arms above her head. Filfy adjusted his position, and his claws scraped the dried paint on the window sill. Mrs. Noble looked so happy, and Filfy smiled in sympathy.

Suddenly he heard a harsh barking voice, and saw the little man, who seemed to be soaking wet, approaching the window, gesticulating wildly.

"Go away, dog! Go away!"

Filfy held his ground and smiled at the man. Ram Bandy thought for a moment about opening the window to frighten the confident animal away, but it would mean unsealing the room. So with an athletic sweeping movement he simply pulled the deep red velvet curtain across the window. The curtain careered off the end of the tracks like a train and crushed into a heap on the floor.

Filfy continued to watch Mrs. Noble stretching out her body and smiling. Her classical Greek robe flowed sympathetically around her, and at one point Filfy thought she was mimicking him, as she stretched her raised back in the "Dog" pose. On the other side of the glass, the hectoring voice continued.

"Keep your knees locked! Straighten your back! Nice asana!" (Ram Bandi pronounced the word "Arsena"). Then Filfy saw the man, perspiring heavily in his very short khaki shorts and miniscule waistcoat, hit Mrs. Noble with a ruler at the back of the knee. Filfy growled. The sound came from deep inside him, and he bared his teeth.

"Knees straight!" the man shouted, as he looked over his shoulder in the direction of the alien sound.

Arthur Brick was the only man present. Mrs. Nipp had persuaded him to accompany her, as her husband had refused to forego his regular Wednesday short mat bowling session at the Pally Alley. Arthur Brick's eighty-year-old legs protruded from his green and gold sateen shorts like pale fingers, and the white basket ball singlet bearing the number seven that he'd borrowed from his brawny grandson hung like a discarded parachute from his narrow shoulders. Every time he tried to stand on one foot and raise his other foot in the direction of his neck, his perspiring neighbour Jenda Steamwell, next to him, would overbalance and send him crashing to the floor.

"Artha! Artha! Artha!" (Purpose! Aim! Meaning!") the teacher shouted, as Arthur Brick struggled to rise, and looked

80

hopefully in the direction of the clock on the mantelpiece. The teacher caught the look and turned the clock face to the wall.
"Now! Asa! Through Asmita to Isvarah! Satya in the dharma megha Samadhi and now on to pranayama!"

Mrs. Noble had descended from her golden cloud and was starting to feel quite exhausted. She had propped herself up under the window, and disappeared from Filfy's view. As the perspiration ran down her nose and dripped on the carpet she noticed for the first time that Emma Montgomery's diaphanous smock actually became transparent with the light in the wall mirror behind it, and she watched as Ram Bandi helped her with a particularly challenging asana.
"More! More!"
Emma Montgomery's shimmering lips parted with the strain as she tried manfully to touch one heel to the back of her head, and she looked into the guru's eyes.
"Good! Good!" he said. "Excellent!"
Then he whacked her on the back with his ruler "Straighten your back. And go take that disgusting chemical concoction off your lips!"
Jennifer Noble found herself smiling covertly and wondering what time Charles would be in tonight. Should she prepare a nut loaf or a brown shrimp salad for his return?
"Stop smiling! You! This is not funny! And get up! Let's see that asana! No slacking! We're out of time!"
A wave of relief swept around the bare room.
"We're out of time. But we have all the time in the world. We're in eternity. No vasikara. Beyond all bodily concerns except the focus on the joining of the one with the all. We are out of time. We are one with the divine consciousness!"
The momentary wave of relief exploded in a million droplets on the pitiless rocks of eternity.

"What are all those bleeding cars doing out the front?"
George O'Durr had just arrived back from the betting shop where he had wagered the £6.50 in the piggy bank on a very slow horse at Uttoxeter. "Thunderbolt" was so slow, indeed, that it had arrived home at about the same time as George

O'Durr.

"It's that cow next door. And all her mates."

Dolly O'Durr was at the upstairs window, and shouted down the stairs.

"They just had an ambulance for Arthur Brick. Poor old bugger. He didn't half look pale. I dunno what's going on in there, but I don't think they're up to any good."

George O'Durr shuffled through the mixed heap of videos in the front room. His wife had clearly removed "Danish Nuns at the Convent of Sin" from the machine, because it now contained several episodes of "I Married a Washing Machine." Sean Lift had been at the betting shop and had passed on to him a very graphic warning about the painful penalties of a further delay in returning his video. As this warning had come from none other than Alf 'The Scalper' Bellchamber, Mr. O'Durr was not taking it lightly. Bellchamber had made it clear that the video was required without fail for a 'Boys Night' at his home in Nelson Heights on Saturday. And Bellchamber could call on quite a lot of 'Boys' if the need arose.

"Danish Nuns at the Convent of Sin" was nowhere to be found. He found "Bambi" and "Scarface" which Jennifer Noble had recently returned, and "The Hound of the Baskervilles", and even an old favourite of Dolly's, "The Divine Experience". George O'Durr shouted up the stairs

"Oy!"

"Oy, what?!" "I found that old video what you was looking for."

"What?"

"Joey Divine and the Hod Carriers!"

"Oh."

She didn't sound very interested.

"I'll leave it out for you."

George O'Durr leaned "The Divine Experience" up against the front of the fireplace, and continued his increasingly anxious search. There was no way he was going to ask Dolly about the disappearing video. He would rather face the wrath of Alf Bellchamber if push came to shove. Then he thought of the soft and womanly Jennifer Noble next door, and her clear liking for both George and Filfy O'Durr. She would like "The

82

Hound of the Baskervilles."

"Oy! Filf!" George O'Durr projected the sound softly but urgently so as not to alert his wife, and almost immediately a scruffy head poked around the corner of the door. He held the video out for Filfy, and the latter reached out and gripped it softly in his velvet jaws.

"Take it to Jennifer."

Filfy O'Durr understood. He turned and his unclipped claws could be heard pitter pattering down the hall into the laundry room. George O'Durr heard the crash as the dog exited the broken dogflap, and then there was silence.

"Keep going! Straighten your back, dear one. Straighten it!"

Sue Grinder felt the ruler strike her back for the umpteenth time that day, and she snapped, as she turned to her emaciated tormentor.

"Fuck off, you little twit. Just fuck off, will you?"

Everyone turned. It didn't matter whether they were in the sea of tranquillity at that moment, or even the hiranya garbha; they all turned. Ram Bandi seemed quite unabashed.

"Look, dear ones. This lovely lady has attacked me. She is hanging on to her personality. Hello, Asmita. Anyone in there? Come, bathe with me in the dharma megha samadhi, the raincloud of virtue. Dear one. Is it not eternal bliss you are wanting?"

"No, it's not!"

Sue Grinder was beside herself. "It's a large Bloody Mary!"

She moved to the door, her long blond hair darkly plastered to her head and neck, and started to rip the duct tape from around the frame.

"She is leaving us. Returning to her world of pain and narcissism. Hold her in your consciousness with love and compassion."

Sue Grinder pulled open the door, took one withering look back at the dripping assembly, and left. As she slammed the door shut behind her, she heard that excruciating voice.

"Santa Samadhi. Goodbye, dear one."

Sue Grinder was too preoccupied in reaching the front door

and escaping from the house to see the middle-aged dog that was waiting patiently outside the front room with a video clutched in its jaws.

Jennifer Noble left the room, embarrassed for her friend and guest, but by the time she reached the hall, Sue Grinder had left. But there was Filfy O'Durr sitting looking up at her with those glowing unfathomable dark eyes. She reached down and patted his head, and took the proffered video.

"Oh. The Hound of the Baskervilles. How nice. You tell that nice master of yours thank-you, won't you."

Suddenly Mrs. Noble felt the drop in temperature, and shivered as a rivulet of perspiration ran down her back. She found she didn't really want to go back inside. Instead she walked into the kitchen followed closely by Filfy O'Durr, whose tail was performing an asana all of its own.

"Now, I think you deserve a little treat, dear one." Mrs. Noble opened a drawer and produced a dried pig's ear.

"Sit!" Filfy sat.

"There. What a good boy!"

Out of sheer force of habit, Jennifer Noble put the kettle on. But Ram Bandy was not to be denied. His five feet four inches suddenly towered in the doorway. His little khaki waistcoat was stained with sweat, and his eyes were suddenly cold.

"Come, dear one," he said icily. "Come back. This is no time for refreshment. Come back, dear one."

He whacked the metal ruler into his palm, and Filfy O'Durr growled deeply.

"And what is this dog doing here?"

"Er, he's visiting. He's a friend of mine."

"Seek your friends in the ranks of the divine, dear one. Not in filth."

Filfy O'Durr growled again. He didn't like the man at all, which felt strange. He usually felt a deep inexplicable connection with humankind. The man was talking very sharply to Mrs. Noble. And his smell was unnerving, too.

Jennifer Noble bent to stroke Filfy. A drop of sweat dropped from the end of her nose on to his. He tried to lick it off.

"Better go home now, dear one, I mean dear. Home!"

Filfy took one more sideways look at the interloper and padded out of the back door.  The pig's ear was still clamped firmly in his jaws.

On his way home, Filfy stopped to enjoy his treat in the sideway where no other could dispute his ownership of the gristly object.  As he sat by the O'Durrs' overflowing dustbin, he saw the little man from next door walk out of the front door with a bunch of keys and open the boot of a Fiat Tadpole.  He returned carrying a cardboard box under his arm.
"Now, ladies. You can relax.  We are back in time."
Ram Bandi turned the clock around.  It said three o'clock.  He turned to Jennifer Noble, who was starting to feel faint.
"Now, please bring in your television and your video machine."
There was some whispering and shuffling and sighing in the hot room, as the guru put down his box on the parquet floor, and clapped his hands.
"Come!  Come!  Don't drift off now!  I am going to show you a video.  It's only two hours.  And then we'll have lunch."

Filfy O'Durr had by this time finished his ear, and returned to the front room at number 27, where he found his master lying on the floor, snoring.  Filfy was still hungry, and craved some more attention.  Then he saw the video propped up against the fireplace.  Without a second thought, Filfy picked it up and clicked down the hall, crashed through the broken dogflap, and went round to number 26, where Mrs. Noble, with a little help from an exhausted Jenda Steamwell was just delivering the television and the video machine to the front room.  Ram Bandi was sitting erect on his tiny cushion seemingly in a trance.  His back was very straight, his eyes were closed, and he was breathing very loudly.  He didn't notice Filfy O'Durr enter, drop a video in the box and raise his head to Mrs. Noble, who with a guilty look behind her at the absent guru, accompanied the dog into the kitchen.
It was some minutes later, after Filfy had left, that Ram Bandi awoke.
"What's that smell?" he asked.  There was no reply.
"Ah! Now. The video.  Is everyone sitting comfortably?"

He looked around the room at the agonised poses on the damp parquet. He had the protagonists in the palm of his hand.

"Now, just relax, dear ones, and let the spirit of divine bliss enter your very souls. He looked at Emma Montgomery, very pale in her classical white robe.

"Turn on the machine. What you are about to see will change your consciousness for ever."

As the cat o' nine tails cracked across the naked back of Sister Angelina to the accompaniment of a tolling bell, several of the backs in Jennifer Noble's front room straightened more readily than they had done all day. But it was when a naked monk, well-tonsured, hung like a horse, and chained to an iron grille, was flogged with a heavy bamboo cane by a frenzied, topless nun who looked just like the late Dolly Parton that the room came fully awake.

Jennifer Noble didn't host any more Yoga days, and Ram Bandi was not encountered in Pinchley Park again. As for Alf "The Scalper" Bellchamber, he smiled crookedly when the long-awaited video was delivered in time for his "Boys Night." But the smile had frozen long before the end of the first episode of "I Married a Washing Machine."

# CHAPTER NINE
## June


## MIDSUMMER EVE


"I'm just off to the meeting, dear."
Mr. Noble opened the front door, hoping against hope that his wife would remain in the kitchen, where the electric mixer was whirring away. There was no response. He adjusted his oakleaf bandana and closed the door silently behind him.

Filfy O'Durr was in the doghouse. He was sitting disconsolately at the entrance to the legless rabbit hutch that Mr. O'Durr had rescued from the Pinchley Municipal Tip that spring, chewing an irritable paw. The scruffy box had been placed in a position where Filfy could monitor activities both in Hillside Close and next door at the Nobles. His master knew that Mr. Noble hated Filfy as much as he himself hated Mr. Noble, so much thought had gone into the placement of the accommodation.

The old dog was losing interest in the packaging of the contraceptives. He had been sent outside for the night after producing Mr. O'Durr's recently purchased pack of three French Tiddlers and dropping them at the feet of the visiting Reverend Downmouth when Mr. and Mrs. O'Durr were trying, without much success, to impress the vicar with their suitability as hosts for an inter-church exchange for young people. Cyril Downmouth had already made up his mind that two young persons from Boulder, Colorado would be more happily accommodated with a more God-fearing family, like the Barclays in Pinchley Drive, for whom the money would not be such an important issue.

Filfy dropped the ruined plastic, and looked up. The

door of number twenty-six was opened quietly, and a strange figure emerged. In fact it was so strange that Filfy's jaw dropped, and he did a sort of strangled bark. It was a very odd sight. Filfy could see it was a human, but it didn't look anything like Mr. Noble. It looked like a tree. A creeping oak tree. It climbed awkwardly into Mr. Noble's dove-grey Rover 200. Filfy managed another semi-bark, and blinked twice as he caught the unmistakeable scent of fear and yogurt that was Charles Noble.

The oak tree breathed "Damn!" and got out, leaving a broken frond behind on the driver's seat, and returned to the porch of number 26 for some interesting looking parcels. Filfy rose, unseen, sidled over, and stood behind the shiny car as Mr. Noble threw the parcels carelessly on to the back seat. Filfy's curiosity, to say nothing of his need for some human company, got the better of him, and as Mr. Noble returned to the porch for the last package, Filfy jumped up into the open door of the car. He pressed his belly to the floor and hid his head under the front seat. The last package was thrown on to the cushions and the door was slammed.

Mr. Noble carefully adjusted his seatbelt and started the engine as quietly as he could, turning the key gently in the ignition, and scarcely revving the engine at all. He reversed slowly out into a deserted Hillside Close, looking right and left all the while. As he changed into first gear, and accelerated gently away, Filfy thought he heard a woman's voice.

"When will you be back from the finance meeting, dear?"

Mr. Noble took a deep breath and relaxed for the first time that day. It had not been easy hiding his midsummer's eve outfit from his wife, but it had been worth the effort. This was a 'man' thing. It was a very warm evening, and as he drove past the speed cameras on the Pinchley Expressway at 20m.p.h. precisely, his nose started to twitch like a rabbit's. His car didn't usually smell musty like that, especially when he'd just hung a new 'Smello-Fresh Brick' from the driving mirror. Mr. Noble didn't notice the unmarked police car that was following him. Constables Okri and Cadwallader had been told to look out for "hippy types" as there was a rumour at the station that there was to be a drug-fuelled rave in Potteridge Woods that night. In the back seat sat a police photographer.

When Charles Noble arrived at the meeting place half an hour early, he switched his radio on and threw open the doors of the car for a little ventilation as he listened to his favourite programme, "Perfect Gardening." As the signature tune filled the little glade in the middle of Potteridge Woods, Filfy O'Durr slipped silently out and was swiftly swallowed up by the undergrowth.

"Is that you in there, Charles?"
Mr. Noble looked up to see the Solstice Master towering above him. Gregory Swainson-Batt was wearing a long green robe. Round his neck was a garland of St. John's Wort, and on his head perched a crown of thorns in which Mr. Noble thought he could make out sprigs of yarrow and vervain. Mr. Noble reached forward a little irritably to turn off the radio. He had been keen to hear how to remove brown patches from the lawn, but you didn't keep the Solstice Master waiting.
"Oh Gregory. I mean your lordship."
Mr. Noble got out, losing another oak frond as he did so. Gregory Swainson-Batt was even taller than Charles Noble.
"Have you got a dog in there, old man?"
The Solstice Master bent to look inside the car. He was a little late.
"A dog? Certainly not!"
Mr. Noble's nostrils quivered slightly as he momentarily caught the alien odour.
"Must be the forest. Some fungus or other, eh what?"
Mr. Noble sniffed again. "You must be right. Your lordship."
"Well, Charles, old man. We certainly have a magical night for it. You've brought the grail? And the silver? And the parchment?"
"I have, Lord."
"Then let us prepare. Help me unload, will you, old man?"
The solstice master rubbed his large hands together, and strode across the clearing with a long swinging gait. Mr. Noble followed close behind, noticing that the green robe fitted quite

tightly around his master's bottom. He dragged his eyes away, and found himself looking, with some envy, at the Solstice Master's silver Mercedes Zenith 4x4.

Filfy O'Durr watched the two men silently from behind a rotting log. As they opened the back of the big car, he thought he could smell food. He lifted his head and sniffed deeply. He watched them unload a quantity of wood, a large quantity of wood, and pile it up in the middle of the clearing. Then they wandered around picking up smaller bits of wood. They never stopped talking. Of course, humans didn't. When one human stopped talking, another would start. Or if they all stopped talking, it would be because someone had switched the telly on so they could listen to someone else talking. Filfy liked the music programmes best, when everyone stopped talking.

"Have you been doing this for many years, Lord?"

"Indeed. Indeed."

The solstice master lifted a can of petrol from the cavernous boot, and opened one of the boxes of meat pies to check the contents. Batt's Hearty Pies were well known in the area. A few yards away a black nostril quivered in the gloaming.

"Beech and Hazel should be here shortly. They've got the coffin and the knives."

"Sorry?" Mr. Noble's adam's apple did a little jump.

"Did you say the coffin? And the knives?"

"Yes, old man. Tonight's when we say farewell to the past, and cut it away. Now give me a hand with these, will you? Come on old chap. Are you all right?"

'Beech' turned out to be Mr. Sadillac, now stood down from his duties at Snodgrass's Bank. He looked quite unmanager-like in a lime green gauzy confection and a beard of copper beech leaves. He gave Mr. Noble a hard look as if daring him to laugh, as he stepped down from his Nissan Globetrotter Flashdrive 4x4 SRI into the one muddy pool in the clearing.

'Hazel' was one of Mr. Noble's best private clients. Rod Puttick had opened the 'Princess Di Health Club' in the precinct only three years previously and had immediately attracted a membership of health-conscious republicans who

90

were delighted to pay Rod's extortionate rates in the cause of beautiful bodies and planetary harmony for the underdog. After acknowledging Mr. Noble with his index finger, Rod Puttick stood admiring his two-tone Bentley Gilgamesh Fury 6x6, and admiring his spotted green features with the silver highlights in the vast wing mirror.

Gradually the glade started to fill up with large vehicles. Mr. Noble suddenly realised that his car was by far the smallest in the clearing. His Rover 200 saloon sat like a baby next to the solstice master's silver Mercedes 4x4. In fact, it looked very much as if the latter had given birth.

Gregory Swainson-Batt noticed that the clearing had become so full of vehicles that the bonfire would threaten the smart paintwork all around it. He also realised that recent arrivals had already made it impossible for those in the inner circle of vehicles to move away. He leapt athletically up on to the beechwood coffin and raised his voice.
"Gentlemen! Gentlemen, please! We need room! Space for the ceremony! Will those who have arrived most recently please reverse out and allow those like myself and- er – Mr. Nobis who arrived in good time to remove their cars. The ceremony cannot take place until all cars have been parked appropriately in marked bays in the pay-and-display car park at the end of Badger Lane."
There was a general murmur of dissatisfied assent, as men and machines were reunited, and the air reeked for a moment as engines were started, and large wheels started to roll. The retreat was carried out with some expertise, considering the breadth of the cars and the narrowness of the track. Mr. Noble found himself crawling down the track, feeling rather like a mouse in his modest Rover saloon, boxed in by the solstice master's slab-sided Mercedes and Rod Puttick's gargantuan 6x6. The only casualty was Pan's Porsche Peppercorn 4x4, which hit an ancient oak as Pan leant down to retrieve a Romeo y Julieta corona from the floor and his horns became ensnared in the spokes of the steering wheel.

Pinchley Council had recently increased parking charges in the area, and as most of the revellers had arrived in pocketless garb, there proved to be a cash problem. Mr. Noble was all right because he always kept a range of coins in the glove box to cover any eventuality, but others were less prepared, and were forced to leave their vehicles without purchasing tickets. They were not to know that a parking warden in a uniform reminiscent of the Waffen S.S. was hiding in the bushes. Nor that he had recently been passed over for promotion by Councillor Conn, (alias Mountain Ash) despite having made more profit for the Council than any two of his colleagues. As the oddly mixed arboreal procession returned to the clearing, Warden Voroshilov licked his thin lips and started writing tickets for all he was worth.

Sergei Voroshilov had won the title of "Traffic Warden of the Year" in 1986 after fifteen unchallenging years in Moscow Central. But following the fall of Communism the Traffic Department had been taken over by a group of businessmen, and Sergei's job for life had disappeared. He didn't have enough to eat, his wife had left with his two children, and his previously dull but satisfying existence had become a vodka-fuelled nightmare of survival at all costs. He had developed a hatred of the new profit-centred oligarchy, and of men doing things in secret and of men driving large cars. Not only had he learned to drink in those dark days, but he had learned to look after himself. When Councillor Conn passed him over for promotion to Chief Warden in the face of the man's remarkable record, he didn't know quite who he was dealing with.

Filfy O'Durr had followed the cortège up the track, and as the participants returned on foot to the clearing, he decided to stay for the moment at least near the vehicle that exuded the smell of meat. He knew that men would always return to their cars sooner or later, and he had plenty of time. He waited behind a brimming council dog waste bin as a man in uniform walked around the car park at great speed, sticking pieces of paper to the windscreens. Filfy didn't care for his smell. It was acid and vengeful. It quite spoiled his enjoyment of the meat pie aroma that was starting to prey on his mind. The old dog trembled. He really hated the uniform.

Filfy willed the man to go away, but when he had finished sticking bits of paper on the vehicles, his manner changed from the brisk and efficient to the downright shifty. He did a round of the car park, looking inside each car and every so often trying a door. When he came to the solstice master's giant conveyance, the rear door opened to his touch. A black nose reawakened behind the waste bin as the man reached deep into the yawning boot, and plucked out a shooting stick and a large meat pie. He sat down on the shooting stick with his back to the vehicle and started to eat the still-warm pie. He didn't see the dog closing silently on his prey behind him.

As a strangely unpractised baritone chanting rose like a barrage from the direction of the clearing, Filfy O'Durr's remaining teeth closed silently on a deeply savorous Batt's Steak and Kidney Pie, still warm, and Filfy entered paradise for the first time that day.

The Solstice Master, who would like to have been a great orchestral conductor if he hadn't devoted his life to manufacturing meat pies, waved his arms as the chanting reached its discordant climax, and with a final flourish, brought the choir to a stumbling halt. Every eye was upon him as he turned majestically towards the altar, and, putting his hand upon the beech coffin, signalled for Mountain Ash to ready the block and tackle for raising it on to the top of the bonfire. A great steel hook descended slowly, and leaping athletically on top of the coffin the solstice master attempted to attach it to the heavy brass bracket on the coffin lid. Hawthorn, alias Mr. Jones from The Caring Mobility Store, whose father had once sung in the Morriston Orpheus Choir, led the accompanying chant, "Oh Great One in the Sky" as the solstice master shouted "Right-ho! Lift away, Morgan, old man!"

The hook somehow slipped from the bracket on the coffin, and caught under the solstice master's underskirts as Mountain Ash pressed the button for "Express Lift". As the solstice master raised his hands heavenwards, his green robe was peeled upwards from his ankles to his crown and disappeared at high velocity into the treetops. He was left with his crown of thorns askew over his left eye and no covering whatever for his "Slim Boy" corsage and his Sparks and Mincers bagaloons. A primeval silence punctuated by strangled guffaws filled the clearing.

Warden Voroshilov was feeling very satisfied with his evening's work. He had issued a total of fifty-four parking tickets before he had run out of the forms. In addition he had consumed three Batt's pies and half a bottle of Pimm's. He had ticketed every one of the hated 4x4s, and indeed there had only been one vehicle unticketed in the car park by the time he had finished. It was a small dove-grey saloon, barely worthy of attention. He let out a little sigh of regret as he turned from Mr. Noble's Rover 200 Passé to the still yawning boot of the Mercedes, from which an old black dog leapt with a Batt's Pie grasped in its teeth, and a Batt's Pies baseball cap at a jaunty angle on its head. The warden stepped back in shock as the dog high-tailed it into the undergrowth. "Nyet!" he shouted. But the dog took no notice whatsoever as he loped in the direction of the baritone coloured sounds in the distance. The warden bent and looked in the box of Batt's pies. The top layer was empty.

"A bit tighter, old man." Mr. Noble pulled on the laces as hard as he could, and the Solstice Master gasped.
"Ha! You're stronger than you look, Oak!"
Mr. Noble blushed slightly as he felt a warm glow suffusing his being. He tied the bow at the back of the corset, and caught himself once again admiring the solstice master's muscular bottom. He swiftly looked away.
"I keep myself pretty fit, sir; I mean Lord."
"Now the golden robe. And then the chasuble, if you don't mind, old man."
Mr. Noble stretched up for the robe that was hanging on a "Star Dry Cleaners" hanger on the branch of an alder. They had found a very private little glade in the depths of the woods,

and it felt very safe and indeed intimate. The golden robe floated down over the corset, and Mr. Noble held up the ornately framed mirror.

"Most becoming, Lord" he said.

"Thank-you, Oak."

The solstice master suddenly looked at Mr. Noble and felt a rush of brotherly gratitude as he saw him for the first time. He placed his right hand on Mr. Noble's shoulder and looked him tenderly in the eye.

"No. Thank-you, Derwydd."

Charles Noble's hand flew to his heart as it skipped like a gambolling lamb in his chest.

"Oh, sir. I mean Lord."

Mr. Noble inclined his head in deference, and also looked down because he felt tears coming. Derwydd! Derwydd, the Oak Seer. Charles Noble had read for years about the ancient Celtic rites, and the worshipful hierarchy in which the Oak Seer played such a key role, but he had never dreamed of attaining this level within the Pinchley brotherhood.

"Come, come, Derwydd. The chasuble if you please, old man."

Filfy O'Durr was feeling very unwell. He stopped by a fungus ridden tree stump and parted company with several deconstituted Batt's Pies. The chanting was louder now. And there was a new, a higher sound. A high, reedy tenor voice echoed through the woodland. It definitely sounded familiar. Filfy raised his nose and sniffed the air. And there it was. The unmistakeable scent of Mr. Noble. Filfy forgot about his nausea; he loved terrorising Mr. Noble. He padded on until he reached the clearing. And there he was, standing on a rough dais next to a very tall man in a golden robe. Mr. Noble was chanting.

"Homoborus angelicus laudamus."

The congregation responded with a deep growling: "Homoborus angelicus laudamus." "Carne et Spiritus." "Carne et Spiritus."

The man in the golden robe put his arm around Mr. Noble's shoulder.

"Gentlemen! I give you Derwydd! Derwydd the Oak Seer!"
A great sepulchral choir chorused "Derwydd!"
The solstice master, with a grand gesture, addressed his protégé.
"Derwydd. The shinbone of St. Aloysius, if you please!"
Derwydd reached into a wooden box and retrieved a large grey bone and held it high above his head. The sepulchral choir went "Aaaaaah!" as a large black dog wearing a Batts Pies baseball cap raced into the clearing, and with an athletic leap, snatched the relic from Mr. Noble's hands, and swiftly disappeared into the undergrowth with St. Aloysius's shinbone firmly clamped in his jaws. Alder shouted "After him!" And the entire congregation followed the scampering dog and the rotund Alder in his long flowing robe of Lincoln Green.

Warden Voroshilov had filled a Fesco carrier bag with Batts Pies, and was happily approaching the glade to see what his former boss was up to, when a large black dog with a huge bone in its jaws loped towards him. It stopped, astonished, before him, and as he raised the almost empty bottle of Pimms to defend himself, the dog cringed away from him and dropped the bone on the forest floor. Filfy was a courageous dog, but if there was one thing that struck terror into his heart, it was dark uniforms. He whimpered, and dodging past the warden with his tail between his legs and flattened ears, he disappeared in the direction of the car park. The warden stooped and picked up the heavy bone as he became aware of a great shouting.

Alder, alias Dennis Buggins of Respect Mobility Services stopped, breathless, and breathed "Bugger!" as his tight fitting robe expanded and contracted around his contours like a giant green lung. Honeysuckle and Ash, Messrs. Conn and Stradivarius respectively from the Pinchley Council Planning Department, who were both members of Pinchley's Princess Di Health and Fitness Club, just managed to stop and avoid cannoning into their brother, who had never faced a man armed with a shinbone before. The three stood facing the warden as more oddly attired celebrants slowed to a halt on the

96

path behind them.  The Solstice Master pushed to the front of the queue, and grabbed the Fesco carrier bag. But the warden hung on.

"My pies!" shouted the Solstice Master.

"Derwydd!  Arrest this man!"

Mr. Noble, who had been bringing up the rear, because he had recognised Filfy and did not wish to confess any association with him whatsoever, struggled forward to the front of the gasping queue, fighting for breath, and cringing inwardly with the anticipation of a public reprimand.

"Derwydd! Arrest that man!" chimed the Solstice Master, his long thick finger pointing unwaveringly at the cornered warden.

"Yes, Lord" Derwydd replied, feeling a great sense of relief that once more the Solstice Master was making a very public demonstration of trust in him.  And also that it wasn't a dog he was called upon to detain.

"Don't try it mate!"  Warden Voroshilov snarled, as he struggled to look threatening whilst clutching a Fesco carrier bag, some Pimms and a shinbone.

"You don't scare me!"

Derwydd, called by his Lord to the apprehension of a common thief was not going to let him down now.  He grabbed the shinbone and snatching it from the warden's grasp, turned to the Solstice Master with a little bow and passed the relic to him.

"Lord."

Gregory Swainson-Batt didn't seem to know what to do with the bone.

"The pies, Derwydd!  Get the pies!"

Mr. Noble tried to snatch the Fesco carrier bag from the warden's grasp, but the man hung on, and the bag was torn in two, spilling pies on the pathway.  The warden snarled.

"Okay!"  The white crowns he had had fitted by a Polish dentist on his flight from his homeland flashed wolfishly in the setting sun, as he smashed the bottle of Pimms against a beech tree and turned with sharp shards of glass pointed at his oppressor's throat.

Everyone except Mr. Noble stepped back a pace in horror, but the latter stood his ground.  Someone helpfully shouted "Come on, Derwydd!"  This was echoed by the Solstice Master, who by this time had retrieved most of his pies from the forest floor.

"Come on Derwydd!" he called, in a voice that belied his extreme concern for Mr. Noble's health.  In the Solstice Master's bell-like tone Charles Noble, alone and unarmed, heard only his Lord's total trust in him, Derwydd the Oak Seer, to finish the job.

"Hand me the weapon."

Mr. Noble's reedy voice cracked a little.  The warden lunged forward, and Derwydd leapt backwards, but not before the wicked shards of glass drew a drop of blood from his nose-end. He felt the sting, and put his finger to his nose.  It was in that moment of pure shock that the last week's episode of "St. Wilfred's" flashed into his mind. The Reverend Jim Manley had courageously confronted an armed atheist from Rotherham in the belfry, and subdued him by the use of a simple judo move.  And immediately Charles Noble recalled, as if in slow motion, the judo throw that had made his reputation so many years ago in the freezing gymnasium at Pinchley Grammar.  And even the way the voluptuous Linda Round in her midnight blue bloomers had cornered him behind the vaulting horse afterwards.

"Come on, Champ!  Let's do it."

The remembered softness of her voice and the admiration in her eyes had not changed one whit down the years.

"Come on, Derwydd.  Let's finish it!"

The Solstice Master's tones were so reassuring; indeed, inspirational.

Mr. Noble carefully removed his tortoiseshell-rimmed spectacles and handed them wordlessly to the Solstice Master. He began to circle the warden, his knees slightly bent, his hands up, his eyes short-sightedly mean.  He suddenly looked as if he knew what he was doing.  Warden Voroshilov realised he would have to seriously wound this man to have any chance of escape.  This wasn't the softy he had expected.  The warden lunged once more, but this time Mr. Noble didn't retire.  He moved swiftly to the side, and before the warden could regain his balance, Charles Noble had executed a perfect, indeed spectacular Harai Goshi sweeping hip throw and Mr. Voroshilov was instantaneously airborne. His black cap with the Pinchley Borough coat of arms on the front and the motto "God Save Pinchley" flew off, and his head hit the beech tree with the sound of a coconut at a funfair, as the glass flew from his fingers.

Mr. Noble put his hands together and bowed to his unconscious opponent as he had been trained to do. The Solstice Master boomed "Well done, Derwydd!" He was still clutching the shinbone of St. Aloysius and some pies and was wearing his champion's spectacles.

"Well done, Derwydd!" called Alder.

"Well done, Derwydd!" echoed Ash as he lowered his exhausted bulk on to a log.

"Well done, Derwydd!" The chorus was taken up along the pathway and around the scene of battle as Mr. Noble suddenly started to tremble uncontrollably. His knees refused to hold him up, and as he leaned against the beech tree for support he found himself slipping slowly down the trunk. He ended up in a pale and shivering heap on top of a squashed stinkhorn.

"Gather him up, boys!"

Mr. Noble heard the Solstice Master's voice as if from a great distance, and then he felt arms lifting him up until he sat somewhat uncertainly on the shoulders of his fellow Pinchleians. He was carried back along the path to rippling applause, as his former adversary was bound with thick brown sticky tape and dragged back unceremoniously behind him.

Behind the long berobed procession on its way back to the clearing, and at a distance, padded Filfy O'Durr. The warden had given him quite a turn. It was years since they had rescued him from that cage in the yard at Clink Terrace, and the security man who had hated him so. But that dark uniform and the man inside it still haunted his thoughts sometimes. Filfy certainly wasn't a dog who held on to grievances, but somehow his treatment at that man's hands had made an indelible mark on his psyche, that no amount of running or jumping or chasing or just sheer joy seemed able to erase. It was more with insatiable curiosity than thoughts of revenge that he followed the bound and horizontal Warden Voroshilov, the triumphant Mr. Noble and their guard of honour through the forest.

The moon was rising above the trees as the procession re-entered the clearing. The still unconscious traffic warden was dumped at the foot of the great bonfire, whilst Mr. Noble was tenderly helped to stand on the dais next to the Solstice Master. The latter's crown of thorns was looking distinctly lopsided as he raised the shinbone high above his head and intoned "Aloysius, our patron; we greet thee this midsummer eve."

The congregation read from their service sheets "We greet thee, oh great one."

The Solstice Master continued.

"And as the great sun reaches its zenith in our English sky we thank you, Aloysius, for your continuing love and devotion to us, your faithful servants."

"We thank you, oh great one."

"Light the solstice fire, Derwydd!"

Derwydd stepped down from the dais rather uncertainly and from his underpinnings produced a box of Guy Fawkes Executive Matches which he had been expecting to pass to the Solstice Master at this point. He looked quickly at his service sheet, which said "S.M. lights fire," and then looked up at the Solstice Master.

"Me?"

"Yes, you, old man." The Solstice Master smiled.

Once more, Charles Noble felt himself start to blush. This was possibly the greatest night of his life. He produced a match and struck it, and read:

"With this light we welcome the light of the high sun, and the light within, and the light of Heaven."

Mr. Noble dropped the lighted spill into the wood shavings at the base of the great fire and they took immediately.

"I give you Aloysius!"

The Solstice Master raised the bone again as the flames started to embrace the kindling and lick up into the heart of the edifice. The baritone chorus read from their sheets once more; "We receive Aloysius!"

Everyone raised their hands and silence filled the moonlit glade, broken only by the snorting sounds of the gagged warden as he struggled to breathe at the base of the fire. No-one knew what to do with him.

Constables Okri and Cadwallader had followed a number of "hippy" types that evening after losing Mr. Noble, as he drove out of town on the Potteridge Road at exactly 30 miles per hour. Their car had been pelted with dim sum by a group of Chinese lager louts, some of whom had been caught on the police camera. By the time the constables had engaged in a fruitless foot chase through the town precinct, the dove-grey Rover 200 was already bumping down a woodland track some miles away. It was almost midnight when they entered the car park at Potteridge Woods. After switching off the engine and sharing a bag of chips with his colleague, Constable Cadwallader wound down the window.

"Listen to that!"

"I can't hear anything."

"Neither can I. But just listen to it."

Constable Okri gave him a sidelong glance. He had always found his partner a bit strange. Then his ears caught a sound. A baritone sound.

"What's that?"

"I don't know."

"Want another chip?"

"No. What is it? And look there. That boot's open. I'm going to go take a look."

"Be careful. I'll call for backup."

Constable Okri stepped from the car, and as he saw the great congregation of large cars around him, he heard two sounds; one a deep chanting from the direction of the forest, and then a much closer sound of gasping breath and scuffling. He melted into the shadow of a gorse bush as two hippies dragged a coffin out of the trees. They then lifted it, with difficulty, into the yawning boot of the Mercedes. The constable stepped from behind the bush and flashed his torch., just as the flash of the police camera lit up the scene.

"Good evening, gents.  And what's going on here?"

"HUMAN  SACRIFICE  AT  POTTERIDGE!"  ran  the Pinchley Gazette headline under a picture of the Solstice Master clutching a bone, and of Mr. Noble pouring petrol on the flames.  Inside the editorial asked "WHAT IS PINCHLEY COMING TO?" and under a photograph of Mr. Sadillac, still in his woodland confection, was a caption that read "WOULD YOU TRUST THIS ODDBALL WITH YOUR MONEY?"

As Mrs. O'Durr looked at the paper that week, she called to her husband.

"Hey, look, George!  Filf's got hisself in the papers!"

George O'Durr joined her on the blow-up settee and looked approvingly at the striking portrait of Filfy posing  on a log with a pie in his jaws.

.

But next door, Mrs. Noble, who had been hoovering up mysterious dried oak leaves for some days, remained in the dark.  Her request for a copy of the Pinchley Gazette that week seemed to fall on deaf ears.  And when Charles Noble did hear it, Pinchley News had mysteriously run out.

# CHAPTER TEN
## July


## SUMMER SUNDAY


The suburb of Pinchley Park had once housed bank clerks and small shopkeepers and schoolteachers, but time had moved on, and the neat little semi-detached houses were now home to aromatherapists, website designers, pharmacists and accountants, and their families. There was even one man, Heaven forbid, on state benefits. George O'Durr was not only unpopular, but positively avoided by the other residents of Hillside Close.

Such a lack of neighbourliness did not go unnoticed by the Reverend Cyril Downmouth, who felt called to join such disparate personalities in the safe and joyous haven of his church. The Church of the Dead Martyrs in Tomb Road opened its doors each Sunday (it was locked during the week) to a small congregation, which largely consisted of elderly people from Bishops Mead and the Sunset Sheltered Housing Development on Laurel Way. Not too many worshippers were to be found in Hillside Close, but Cyril Downmouth had its residents very much in mind, as he stood in front of the mirror one Saturday morning, impersonating his God.

"And if thou refuse to let them go, behold, I will smite all thy borders with frogs!" he declaimed from the old Bible, looking hotly into the full-length mirror on the dark wardrobe that had belonged to his wife's mother. He recoiled from the angry looking figure he saw glaring back at him. It really was quite frightening.

Cyril was looking forward to Sunday morning, when he hoped his half-hearted congregation would be shocked into some sort of Christian action when he hit them from the pulpit with the story of the Plagues of Egypt. His life, and indeed that of Mrs. Downmouth, had not been easy, and he felt some kinship with the ancient Egyptians, who had borne the agonies of plagues of frogs, lice, foot and mouth disease, hail, and locusts. He definitely felt he was the man to speak from experience of plague. Apart from bouts of chicken pox, asthma, measles, mumps, eczema, and even scarlet fever as a child, he had also contracted malaria whilst guarding ammunition trains during National Service in Egypt, and went down with the 'flu' each February. He was left with variable and unreliable energy and temper levels, and a rather tremulous air.

"And the Lord did according to the word of Moses, and the frogs died out of the houses, out of the villages, and out of the fields. And they gathered them together upon heaps, and the land stank."
A spray of spittle hit the stained mirror, as Dolores Downmouth entered the room with a migraine. She was inured to her husband's preaching rehearsals, and didn't acknowledge him as she moved to the window with a martyred expression and slowly closed the curtains, before falling decorously into her single divan with a faint moan, and a whispered "Thank-you, darling."
Cyril Downmouth took a deep breath, scrabbled around in the half light for his glasses, picked up the heavy black book, and silently left the room. His lips were tightly pursed.

Just around the corner in Hillside Close, Randy Breed's cherubic lips curled in pleasure as he checked the pile of acceptances for his barbecue on Sunday night. He ran a dark hand across his low, deeply tanned brow, and stood to admire the recently taken photograph on the grand piano. He had been in his all-white ensemble at Nashville, and had looked, and sounded, magnificent. No wonder the residents of Hillside Close, and some from beyond, had almost unanimously accepted the invitation he had issued. It had dropped on to Pinchley doormats accompanied by a glowing article from the Nashville Vibe that had included this very flattering likeness. It wasn't every day such folk were invited to dine with a celebrity. It didn't matter at all that most of the acceptors, if not all, had never heard his recordings of "Put me down Soft" or "Lay me down in the Old Corral" or "I'm Down; I'm Really Down." Had they done so, the acceptance rate would have been rather less impressive. Country Music was not big in Pinchley. Apart from a bit of Line Dancing featuring Veronica Hargreaves and her tiny partner at the Cheeseman Centre each Tuesday, and some live Irish music from Celtic Platoon at the Old Drill Hall, Pinchley wasn't generally a very musical sort of place.

Randy flashed a smile into the Georgian-style full-length mirror, which bore the message in spangly letters in the top corner "Love Thyself", and called "Jen!" Jenda Steamwell was his girlfriend, and secretary of his U.S. Fan Club. She too had designs on the London suburban market, and was delighted with the response when she examined the guest list, dressed in the new "Loving Karess" knickers she had found in a hotel room in Newcastle-under-Lyme.
"Gee, Rand," she breathed. "That's great! Maybe they'll stop grouching about the bird, now."
The "bird" was Randy Breed's beloved Ford Thunderbird pickup which had a perforated silencer, and only just fitted into the modest driveway. It stood out clearly from the other cars in the short quiet street, which were, without exception, modest family saloons in shades of white or grey. The Thunderbird was finished in scarlet and silver, with the head of a bald eagle on the front of the bonnet. Jenda Steamwell sighed, and ruffled the black highlights in her partner's cloud of grey hair, which caused its owner to feel the stirrings of unrequited love in his tight, stonewashed "Big Rider" jeans.

Filfy O'Durr had also felt the stirrings of true love in an almost forgotten part of his anatomy that morning when he had trespassed in the Downmouths' back garden at "Damascus," and, after eating a Wedgwood bowlful of Aristo Canine Titbits that had clearly been left out for him, he had come across the most beautiful bitch he had ever seen. Her owners had, somewhat distractedly, put her out to rest under a

105

drooping gooseberry bush because she was on heat. Filfy's heartbeat speeded up. He felt he was supposed to do something macho and exciting, but he couldn't remember what it was. Magdalena Downmouth was not at all turned on by his prancing and posturing, particularly after his front paws with their workman's nails got caught in the fruit netting. Magdalena, looking every inch the thoroughbred Saluki she knew she was, rose and cruised imperiously in the direction of a blighted apple tree, and sat down in its uncertain shade whilst Filfy growled horribly as he fought the netting in which he had become hopelessly enmeshed.

Upstairs in a darkened room, Dolores Downmouth was dreaming of the charismatic young man with whom she had fallen in love forty years ago at the Christian Endeavour holiday home at Llandudno Junction. Had you been in the room, you would have seen how the lines of her face had almost melted away as she re-experienced the joy of that far-off moment when his shining eyes had first looked into hers. A little tear rolled down her cheek on to the goosedown pillow, and a fleeting smile blew across her lips. Dolores looked almost young again.

Back in Hillside Close, Mr. Noble was feeling very pleased with himself. He had picked up a "Jardin-Niagara" for only £19.99 at the garden centre. The Griplock Garden Centre stood at the popular junction and accident blackspot where the Downtown Expressway regurgitated millions of tons of hurtling metal each day on to the old North Circular, and specialised in plants strongly resistant to lead and carbon monoxide poisoning.
For some years Mr. Noble had made do with an old thick green rubber hosepipe to water his perfect lawn and flowerbeds. His late father had given it to him when he had had to leave his little detached bungalow in Greenways and move into the Lengthening Shadows Nursing Home in Horizontal Avenue. "Look after it, son," he'd said. But the rubber, like his progenitor, had started to perish and would now automatically form into irritating kinks whenever it was

unwound from its rusty metal reel. And the pinhole punctures in the rubber would irrigate parts of Mr. Noble's garden like the greenhouse wall or the lily pond, whilst its operator was trying impatiently to unkink the most seriously contorted sections of piping.

Now, at last, Charles Noble was the proud possessor of a "Jardin-Niagara", which he had seen advertised over a period on the Mammon T.V. channel by a cheery, trustworthy looking man with white hair and a reassuringly northern accent. The bluff blunt tones of Greg Gross had become a fixture on Channel 210, and most people wouldn't have known their owner had once been head of the Vice Squad, had he not written a graphic book about his days in office entitled "Keeping Britain Clean." Now, everyone in Britain knew more sexual perversions and techniques than they had ever known before, to a point where a marital bedroom in Redditch, for example, was starting to bear a strong resemblance to Madam Whack's Punishment Rooms in Paddington, W2. But the advertising worked, and viewers deferred to this rather jolly, retired personage in the way that one might defer to a distant but affable uncle who performed experiments on rats. It didn't matter to Mr. Noble where Greg Gross had spent his evenings. Charles Noble was convinced that a "Jardin-Niagara" would furnish him with a more beautiful garden than anyone else in the street

The morning was hot. George and Dolly O'Durr were sunbathing on sagging sunloungers on their disintegrating patio, that had been built very cheaply by illegal immigrants that Spring. Mrs.O'Durr was challenging a bikini she had obtained from the "Little Beauty" catalogue, and never paid for. It was probably just as well that Greg Gross wasn't in the vicinity. (He was holidaying with the Primident and Arnold Schwarzenegger and their families on Capri). Greg Gross's smiling blue eyes would almost certainly have taken on a steely quality as he surveyed the O'Durrs' patio with its cargo of skin, alcohol, and sun oil. Behind the tinted glasses, his cold stare would have taken on the quality of the phobic as he looked down on the warm human flesh that offended him so deeply.

Mr. O'Durr, who was himself wearing some rather flashy shades that his mate, Sean Lift, had stolen from Hoots the Chemist, and a pair of very uncomfortable briefs that cruelly emphasised the size of his paunch, lit up another Casketts Killer Number One from the butt end of the last one, and threw the latter over the fence into the Nobles' garden. It was followed by the empty packet. It was only much later that Charles Noble would creep out into his garden with a torch and throw all the accumulated cigarette ends and packets, together with the empty Busters Lager cans and Pernod bottles back over the fence. Mr. Noble didn't care for confrontation, and was blessed with excellent night vision.

Filfy O'Durr had grown bored with sitting on the patio panting in the shade of his mistress's sunlounger. Mrs. O'Durr had nearly crushed Filfy's ageing ribs when she had adjusted her position during a dream involving Cliff Richard and a white rabbit, and so Filfy had padded out of the disintegrating side gate to investigate the noises in Mr. Noble's garage. He was still dragging around a length of fruit netting, which had got stuck between the toes of his left forefoot.

Filfy was feeling upset on two counts. He hated to hear a human cry. And the weeping he had heard from the upper room at "Damascus" had quite unsettled him, especially as he couldn't see who it was, and had been in no position, being entangled in the fruit net, to offer any consolation.

It was also much too hot for Filfy, and his stomach wasn't feeling too good. Earlier that week, Mrs. O'Durr had purchased a special bargain pack ("Fifty for the Price of Twenty!!") of Brahmaputra Vindaloo Doggie Chunks for Older Doggies, which contained a very small number of miniscule chunks and a very large volume of highly spiced sauce.

Mrs. O'Durr had been impressed by the garish display card at Fesco's, which had asked "Is your pet getting a bit long in the tooth? Does he have trouble chewing? Then Vindaloo Doggie Chunks O. D. is for you. LOWER ON SOLIDS!" Sadly, faced with the choice of "Medium," "Hot," or "Furnace Fiery," Mrs. O'Durr had selected the latter because she liked the colour of the label.

Of course, it wasn't for her to know that the automatic mixing and filling machine at Fleabys Petfood Factory in Smethwick had played up the previous summer, and that the resulting superheated gravy containing a few miserable shavings of cartilege and offal had even been turned down by Fleaby's best stockist in Calcutta as being too spicy. Nor that the retailer had bought three thousand pallets full of the offending concoction for a song.

As for Filfy, who had given up trying to remove the scrap of netting from his paw, he decided the sight of Mr. Noble trying to unpack a large cardboard box was really a bit of a bore, and after a few minutes of superficial preening, padded off to the garden at "Damascus." There, Magdalena Downmouth was busy scratching herself under the apple tree, and paid him no attention whatsoever. Filfy moved disconsolately to the empty Wedgwood bowl, and licked it across the lawn until it came to rest against a little block of polished granite bearing the name, deeply inscribed, "REX."

At that very moment, a slightly distracted Mrs. Downmouth, whose migraine had passed, opened the kitchen door to see the bowl's progress arrested by the headstone. It was as if the stranger wanted to give the late Rex a meal. Filfy suddenly felt a wave of Fiery Furnace nausea sweep over him, and sank to the ground with a moan as Mrs. Downmouth leaned on the door jamb for support and looked down at him. Filfy somehow managed to look quite soulful as he lay doggo next to the sad little piece of granite. Dolores Downmouth hesitated. She felt she may have seen this strange scruffy looking dog somewhere before. It was something about the eyes. Rex had had eyes like that, deep and soft and quizzical. Filfy wagged his tail, just like Rex, on her approach.

Mrs. Downmouth had missed Rex keenly these last three years, and had never really come to know the pedigree saluki her husband had insisted upon having in his place. Filfy's inexorable eyes looked adoringly up at her, as he remembered the delicious Aristo Canine Titbits he had enjoyed earlier in the day. He let out a pitiful whimper, and nudged the empty bowl in Mrs. Downmouth's direction.

The latter's soft heart opened. She bent down to pat Filfy's head, and as she knelt to make a real fuss of him, Filfy was suddenly taken with a serious scratching fit, and yelped loudly as he tried to ease the irritation on his belly. Mrs. Downmouth rose with the empty bowl and a distasteful expression and walked to the kitchen door. The itch subsided, and Filfy followed. He knew when he was on to a good thing, and, in any case, this woman needed help. And so it was that as Pinchley Park sweltered under a cloudless sky, Filfy O'Durr and Dolores Downmouth spent a few hours together.

The afternoon was being spent less fulfillingly by Mr. Noble. The "Jardin-Niagara" was by now largely unpacked, and was spread around the garage floor, whilst Mr. Noble swore under his breath. (His spiritual beliefs forbade the uttering of such words out loud). He was attempting to assemble the "Jardin-Niagara Mark 2" with a set of instructions for the Mark 1 written in what looked like Norwegian, Urdu, and Mandarin Chinese. Greg Gross had said on the T.V. that assembling the "Jardin-Niagara" was "easy as ABC," but as so many of the characters on the instruction sheet did not come into this alphabetical category, Charles Noble was in the event finding it very difficult indeed. His grasp of Urdu did not for example run to anything as technical as "Conjoin the lower baseplate with the oscillating arm shown in Figure 16, being sure to press button X as you do so."

There were an awful lot of separate parts to the "Jardin-Niagara." Mr. Noble had had no idea there would be so many bits inside the relatively compact box he had brought home with him from the garden centre, strapped into the back seat of his dove-grey Rover 200. He had managed to fit together the rotor-arm buttresses with the umbrella shield, and had spread most of the other components around his garage floor. The biggest item, which had unfolded to an awkwardly large size, had been the closed reservoir around which, as far as he could see, all the other parts seemed to move. This had taken up so much room that he had carried it outside and left it on the crazy paving at the rear of the garage.

As Mr. Noble ripped open the annoying seamless grey polythene bag stuck to the inside of the contraption's ingenious packaging, he noticed a flash of white from somewhere in the interstices of the box, and, tearing out the intervening cardboard whilst uttering a silent prayer, he triumphantly produced the English assembly instructions. Mr. Noble now started to work at great speed, as he first screwed the rotor arm buttresses into the baseplate support cones, and then turned the hydraulic volumeter to "MAX" whilst he attached the constant performance manifold to the integrated flow control cylinder. By this time the volume gauge was looking a bit cock-eyed, and as Charles Noble didn't care for things being cock-eyed, he attempted to straighten it and it came off in his hand, as a very small screw dropped, unnoticed, from the turbopower limiter into the turn-up of his fawn corduroy trousers.

"Damn!" he spat through his teeth, and then looked guiltily around to make sure no-one had heard his transgression. But no-one else in Hillside Close was silly enough to spend such a perfect summer's day stressing out at the back of their garage. Mr.Margulies at number 14, for example, was spraying his roses whilst listening to Test Match Special from Lords Cricket Ground, Siegfried and Brenda Goering were playing a very competitive game of doubles at the Pinchley Park Club, whilst Dave and Sue Grinder at number six were in their "Bathroom Niagara" shower enjoying some fantastic singles, after taking a mind altering substance.

It was towards evening that Filfy O'Durr left "Damascus." Mrs. Downmouth opened the French windows that let on to the garden, and whispered "Goodbye, dear." They had not been interrupted, as Cyril Downmouth had become totally immersed in preparations for his sermon the following day in his dark and rather cramped little study upstairs. The mirror didn't reflect too accurately where the spittle had landed, and pages from a scrap pad, covered in spidery handwriting in purple ink littered the floor. The vicar knew he had stumbled on fertile ground with the plagues of Egypt, and deep down in his soul he experienced a wonderful feeling of holy exultation as he anticipated his smug congregation's startled reaction to his words.

He had counted the plastic frogs he had purchased out of church funds, and selected the most horrific photo he could find of a funeral pyre from the previous month's foot and mouth epidemic. He also had a blown-up picture of a head louse he had obtained from the local health authority, and had found a little girl from Pinchley Woods Primary who was willing to stand up at the front of the church and say "I have head lice."

For the last week he had been swatting flies around the house, and scraping their corpses off the fly-paper with which "Damascus" was festooned. He had even borrowed a stuffed locust from the "Suez Nights" restaurant in North Pinchley. As for hail, this had been a problem until he had had a brainwave, and purchased a batch of ice-cube moulds that had been left in the deep freeze awaiting the great day, when transport to church by cool box would not present a problem.

Dolores Downmouth had long since ceased to react, overtly at least, to her husband's strange ways, and had made a point of failing to comment on the myriad flypapers and ice-cube containers that seemed to have taken over her nest.

"Have a good day, dear? Er..what's that smell?" he asked absentmindedly as he entered the kitchen where his wife was cooking some Painsburys "Cheap Basics" minced beef, and wondering if her husband had mad cow disease. She replied with fervency. "Oh yes, Cyril. I did." As she spoke Dolores Downmouth looked out of the window at the spot where she had last seen Filfy O'Durr. Preoccupied as he was with weightier matters, her husband could not fail to pick up something in her tone, and looked at her sharply. But her soft gaze was impenetrable.

After his three extra meals that day, Filfy O'Durr was feeling overfilled, and his stomach was bulging on his spare frame. His bottom was smarting because the "Furnace Fiery

Vindaloo Doggie Reduced Chunks Lower on Solids" had reached the lower regions of his stressed alimentary tract. It was all feeling very tumultuous in there. He tried trotting to ease the discomfort, and then running, and then rolled over and over in the middle of the road before having to take evasive action as a huge scarlet and silver monster with bull bars on the front came rending down the quiet street with its horn blasting. Filfy knew his master and mistress would now be lolling in front of the telly watching "Name that Recipe" on BBC2 or "Horny Witches" that followed, and he certainly didn't want anything else to eat, least of all that awful "Lower in Solids" stuff.   So he disconsolately pattered round to the rear of number 26's garage where he knew a comfortable spot for some shuteye.

Filfy had been mistaken about the television programme that George and Dolly O'Durr were watching. They had in fact tuned in to the BBC's new award-winning soap, "St.Wilfred's" and were sitting open-mouthed  as a dramatic scene was played out between Ben Brett and Janice Woolley, who had become engaged in a life-or-death struggle in the crypt.  As Ben's powerful hands closed around Janice's windpipe, a piece of "Kleeno-Kavity" chewing gum fell out of George O'Durr's mouth into his lager.
"You do that tomorrow night and I'll crown you, you old bugger" said Mrs. O'Durr, taking a swig of Pernod on the rocks, and without taking her eyes off the screen for a moment.

Next door, Charles Noble was trying to unscrew the constant performance sensors from the oscillating arm on his new "Jardin-Niagara" because he had just realised that they should have been first attached to the constant performance manifold before the latter could be slid via the dorsal freewheel into the outer whirlpool reservoir. As Mr.Noble struggled manfully with the contraption the sun started to descend imperceptibly in the direction of the old gasometers at Chokes Brow.  Filfy was asleep and dreaming of Dolores Downmouth scratching his distended stomach and telling him he was a very beautiful dog, and the shadows were lengthening, before Mr. Noble straightened with a heartfelt "Yes!" and realised his "Jardin-Niagara" was now ready for action.

. After attaching the built-in superflexihose to his garden tap he stood, washed by the sun's buttery early evening rays and feeling very complete. He took a deep breath, bent and pressed the "Power" button. After a stutter the "Jardin-Niagara" gradually started to spray water through its unique turbocharged hydropower system to an immense height and then as the oscillating arm began to turn, the water danced in great sparkling curtains across the entire extent of the lawn, and those of the neighbours on either side. Mr. Noble had great difficulty in reducing the power, as the English instructions were by this time washed away into the rose bed, and the "fingertip control trigger" had become jammed on full. The buckled sun loungers next door became drenched in moments, and on the other side Randy Breed's patio quickly took on the look of a giant angry puddle.

A crepescular figure wafted in through the French windows of number twenty-six, as dusk settled on Hillside Close, and Mrs.Noble dished up an organic lentil loaf with red pepper sauce. Mr.Noble felt quite exhausted, but he nevertheless produced his carefully written job list for the day, and with a sigh and a flourish, crossed off the first item, "Assemble Jardin Niagara."
After washing his hands, as instructed by Mrs. Noble, he took a mouthful of the lentil loaf, which tasted slightly odd, as if the lentils had been overcooked. It was very dry indeed and Charles Noble helped himself to some more sauce from the Royal Doulton sauceboat.
"Don't you like it dear?" his wife enquired accusingly.
"Yes, it's delicious" he replied, as he checked the list. "Accept Breed's Invitation."
Although he didn't care much for the look of his new neighbour, at least he and his fancy piece must be an improvement on the dreadful O'Durrs on the other side. And it was to be a barbecue, so he might get the chance of some

real food for a change. Mrs. Noble looked smilingly on her husband as he cleared his plate, and rose from the table.
"And just remember tomorrow night, darling – no meat!"
Damn the woman! It was as if she could read his mind.

Mr.Noble's list for Sunday read:
Set clocks (1)
Shower and shave.
Breakfast.
Meditate.
Clean car.
Church with Jennifer.
Move bowels.
Luncheon.
Mend lawnmower and service Dyson.
Bath.
Buy wine at Painsbury's (Max. £2.99).
Breed's Barbecue with Jennifer.
Set clocks.(2)

Mr. Noble had meant to note on Saturday's list "Turn off Jardin-Niagara at mains," but in his exhaustion, had forgotten. When Charles Noble put things on his list they got done, but when he didn't, they didn't. The "Jardin-Niagara" remained switched on, and the long auxiliary standpipe remained where he had left it, protruding from the murky liquid in the old water butt behind the garage.
The clocks were all synchronised, and Mr. Noble's dove-grey Rover with the A.A. badge and the National Trust sticker stood shimmering in the drive. It also displayed a sticker in the rear window next to the bowl of plastic tulips saying "How's my driving?" But the phone number had been heavily crossed out.

Charles Noble in white shirt, dark suit, and Old Pinchleians tie strode elegantly out of his front door, and trod in an offering from Filfy O'Durr.
"You should be more careful, dear" said his wife, sharply, as she recoiled from the distinctive odour.

"Oh, shut up, would you" Mr.Noble snapped, as he tried to scrape the offending material off his shoe on the edge of the doorstep.

"Don't do that!" shouted Mrs.Noble. I cleaned that this morning! If you're going to wipe it anywhere, take it back where it came from."

She knew, like her husband, exactly where it had come from. For a moment her partner hesitated as his wife settled herself in the passenger seat of the gleaming car and gesticulated wildly in the direction of the house next door. With a determined stride Charles Noble walked quickly up the footpath and turned in at number 27. On reaching the threshold, he started to scrape his shiny black shoe thoroughly on the edge of the doorstep, anointing it with a generous helping of poop.

A large scarlet and silver conveyance snarled majestically up Hillside Close, and Randy Breed and Jenda Steamwell gave Mr. Noble a strange look as they passed. When Mrs. O'Durr opened her front door to put the milk bottles out she gave him an even stranger look, and an earful of expletives as he retreated shamefacedly up the brick pathway that led to freedom; or, rather, his wife. Mr. Noble checked his watch. They were late. He started the engine and they purred up Hillside Close for their weekly encounter with the Spirit.

"Oh! That smell's making me feel quite ill" said Mrs. Noble.

Her husband drove at a processional pace down Bishops Mead, turned left at Prescott Boulevard, and joined the Downtown Expressway just as Randy Breed and his partner were settling in their pew at the Church of the Dead Martyrs. Cyril Downmouth was once more rehearsing his sermon in front of the vestry mirror where he had spent the morning. He knew that this day he had something truly important to impart. But he had to relax. He tried to recall a relaxation technique he had learned on the self-assertiveness training the Bishop had sent him on last autumn, but failed. So he just wiped the spittle off the mirror he had balanced on a small Sunday School chair. But the mirror fell off and smashed on the dusty floor.

"Oh, God!" he said as he started to pick up the bigger shards of glass and drop them in the yellow plastic wastebin. He cut himself and cursed, and sucking on the injured finger, opened the Red Cross emergency first-aid box on the vestry wall to find it contained nothing more than a copy of "Buck Matcho's Book of Campfire Songs," a paper clip, and a postcard of the stoning of St. Stephen. So he contented himself with binding the spotless white handkerchief he had brought with him that morning around the wound. Then he opened the vestry door a chink and peeped out into the church. Yes; it was starting to fill up. There were the Margulies, sitting ramrod straight in their usual pew, and there was Mrs. Brick, handing out hymnbooks and offertory envelopes with her usual aplomb. He could just make out the bowed, professorial head of Doctor Fell under the tablet commemorating those from the parish who had fallen in the Great War. And there, in a beam of bright sunlight that shafted in through the east window sat the Merry girls, with their distinguished parents. What a lovely Christian family, he thought, as Piers Merry scratched his bottom, and Melissa told her younger sister a rude joke she'd heard at the Boudoir Club in Jade Lane.

Cyril Downmouth felt gratified when he looked at the front row of expectant parishioners. There, unless he was very much mistaken, were Mr. Breed and Ms. Steamwell, whose barbecue he would be attending that evening. They were very tanned. Mr. Breed was looking down contemplatively, humbly almost, but Ms. Steamwell was looking brightly about her with neck movements resembling those of a happy chicken as she tried to discern if the people of Pinchley recognised the celebrity in their midst, and that she was his partner. No-one did, actually. And, good Heavens! Bless me! There next to them was Dolores. Dolores?!

She hadn't been to hear him preach for years, ever since he had compared her to Lot's wife in front of the whole congregation. The vicar peered out from his hiding place, straining his eyes behind the steel-rimmed spectacles. Who was that strange creature in a headscarf sitting next to his wife? A little shiver of apprehension went down his spine. It might have been a much greater shiver if he had recognised his wife's escort that day. It was the first time that Filfy O'Durr had ever been to church.

Cyril Downmouth peeped again in the direction of his wife, who was wearing a scarlet blouse she had really bought for the barbecue from the Eventide Hospice Shop in Terminus Road. Her companion was very still, immersed no doubt in prayer. Her head seemed a very strange shape. Immediately behind her, he could just about make out the Nobles, looking a little flustered as they had to excuse their way past earlier arrivals to a place directly beneath the pulpit. They had been further delayed by an encounter with a road enraged Mrs. Love who had been trying to reverse into a car park space outside when Mr. Noble had, at his wife's bidding, nipped smartly into it forwards. As Mr. Noble passed down the pew, the occupants looked up at him and wrinkled their noses and exchanged glances.

Cyril Downmouth began to register the sense of restiveness in the church and with a start he suddenly realised they were all waiting for him. He stepped forward, and mounting the pulpit steps he announced the opening hymn, "Through the Night of Doubt and Sorrow".

"Where's Filf?" enquired Channelle O'Durr as she revved up her Kawasaki 750 before switching off and lifting the machine effortlessly on to its stand on the mosaic of empty flattened sardine and Doggie Chunks tins that constituted her parents' front garden.

"Dunno" replied her father, scratching at something under his off-white singlet.

"You here for long?" he asked, giving his large daughter a perfunctory hug.

"Mum!!"

"What are you here for?" asked Dolly O'Durr as she descended the stairs in a rayon housecoat that was too small for her.

"And where's Filfy?"

"Cor, you look awful, mum. I dunno where he is. I only just

arrived."

Mrs. O'Durr gave her daughter a malevolent stare. "What do you want?"

"I want to watch St. Wilfred's. The omnibus edition. All right?"

Mrs. O'Durr walked past her daughter, kissing her with a loud sucking sound and an "mmm" from a distance of six inches, and went to put the kettle on. Outside, Mr. O'Durr was stamping hard on an upstanding sardine tin.

"No; it's not all right. We was looking forward to a nice Sunday morning down Fesco's."

"Well, that's all right, Mum; I'll just stay here."

Mrs. O'Durr switched on the kettle. "No you won't, my girl! Oh, no; I'm not leaving you here on your own. No sooner we'll be gone than you'll have that lightfingered spotty boyfriend of yours around!"

Channelle O'Durr lost patience. "Mum! Shut up, will you!? We've split up. He's gone back to Victoria."

Mrs. O'Durr poured some hot water on to a "Cheepo" teabag in a mug marked "Men? No,thanks!"

"I didn't know he was an Aussie."

"No! Mum! Victoria. His wife!"

The younger woman's voice broke, and for a moment she felt her mother's concern.

"Good riddance to bad rubbish; that's what I say. All right, then. You can stay and watch while we're shopping. You know where it is."

Channelle stepped into the musty living room with the brown paint and the picture of Ballybunnion, and switched on the television whilst her mother closed the door firmly behind her.

Ben Brett and Janice Woolley were sitting in their pew at St. Wilfred's when the Reverend Jim Manley announced the first hymn whilst behind Ben, in a very low-cut dress hovered the predatory Regina Swipes.

"Let us sing together hymn number 414, 'Angel Voices, Ever Singing' ."

The organ chirruped an introduction, and slowly the massed congregation took up the melody. Jim sang lustily as the camera closed in on the pair but Janice was clearly no singer and looked nervous that someone might hear her squeaky voice. But then, above both of them, and above indeed every other voice in St. Wilfred's there rose the most glorious and mellifluous sound of a practised mezzo-soprano in the full bloom of her womanhood.

Channelle gagged on the Blotcher's Kruncho she was absent-mindedly stuffing into her mouth as the camera, ever so slowly, moved from Jim and Janice to the source of the heavenly sound. There in inspiring close-up was the striking Regina Swipes, looking quite celestial, her dark eyes like pools of midnight focussed on something far, far above. The whiteness of her little white teeth was emphasised by the full dark red gleaming lips, and her remarkable breasts, barely confined in a dark silk blouse, rose and fell with the inexorable rhythm of a great ocean's tide.

The camera panned to Jim Brett, who was standing, wordless and transfixed. He looked around with an awkward sideways glance of adoration at the source of the sublime sound behind him, and there on the sculpted lips of Regina Swipes there appeared the very ghost of a smile as she continued her heavenly song without shifting her gaze by one degree in his direction. The rest of the congregation had, however, shifted their gaze as one to Regina Swipes. Everyone, that is, except Janice Woolley, who was looking hard at her distracted partner, and who had stopped singing altogether.

Inside the Church of the Dead Martyrs, the singing was much less spectacular. There had been a funereal quality to the rendering of the second hymn, "Let All Mortal Flesh Keep Silence". In fact, everyone had taken up the suggestion in the title with the notable exception of the Misses. Small and Frowde, Mrs. de la Mere, and Mr. Armitage-Shanks.

It was a small choir for such a church, but they tried heroically to fill the empty spaces with sound. There was a clear divergence in the notes issuing forth. The dissonant and febrile warbling drove Filfy O'Durr under the pew where he put his paws over his ears, which was just as well because the subsequent rendering of "Round Me Falls the Night" would have represented the most depressing sound he had ever heard.

Mrs. Old's last miscued notes on the organ tiptoed away into the rafters, and the modest congregation took their seats. There was a very long silence before the vicar rose to begin his address.

"My friends", he said, and looked around the place, stopping to search each blank face as he went. Everyone waited for something to happen but the speaker just continued looking around. People started to feel uncomfortable. "My friends," he continued in a slightly broken voice, modulated to communicate just the right degree of piety and resignation.

"Have you come here today to meet your friends, to sing a few rousing songs, listen to some other people's ideas, and to a very short sermon from the old boy, and then get down to serious business at 'The Gay Trooper' or 'The George and Dragon?' Or are you perhaps thinking more about the roast beef and Yorkshire Pudding that await you than the salvation of your own soul?"

Waves of emotion were injected into these last few words and eyes hooded up and looked away from the speaker's bi-focalled gaze that once more swept the assembly. Jenda Steamwell looked down at the brown hairy hand that was resting on her thigh, and Mr. Noble looked down at the spot where a piece of doggie poo stuck out like a wart from the welt of his shiny left shoe. He suddenly realised that his neighbour in the pew, Mr.Hussein, was looking at it too, and with a great effort of will, raised his eyes to the tablet in memory of the first Lord Delimere who had died whilst grappling with a lion in Basutoland. He had heard that lions had very bad breath.

Channelle O'Durr tried to throw the empty packet of "Smoking Will Probably Kill You" cigarettes into the fireplace and missed, as events at St. Cuthbert's started to get out of hand. Janice Woolley had just thrown a cup of scalding coffee over Regina Swipes who had called her a muppet and a bitch, and was now screaming for an ambulance. The Reverend Jim was holding her in his arms as if her legs had gone, but she just kept screaming.

"Calm down!" ordered the vicar in a deep masterful voice. But the woman became more hysterical. Jim Brett could be seen in the background wiping his face with a white handkerchief and acting very badly. Suddenly there was a loud "crack!" as Reverend Jim slapped Regina across the face. The screaming stopped abruptly and Regina looked, apparently for the first time, at the man in whose arms she sheltered. Her dark sensuous lower lip trembled, she closed her eyes, and she relaxed her lovely head contentedly on Jim's broad right shoulder. Everyone had stopped drinking coffee around them, and looked with undisguised interest at the entwined couple as the vaguely ecclesiastical sounding pop theme music filtered into the church hall, and the titles started to roll at indecipherable speed.

In a darkened room at Broadcasting House, a group of executives broke into spontaneous applause as the viewing figures for the previous week's episodes were flashed on to the screen. One of them rose to speak. He was black, tall, and wore an expertly tailored suit.
"Gentlemen,-and-oh-er lady" he added humorously. "Well done, everybody. This show has broken all records. Who says religion has lost its way?! Now, there's something you need to know. In total confidence, of course." He paused, and examined a carefully manicured fingernail.
"The D.G.'s told us we must have a gay on the show. It's to do with the quota system. He's going to be a psychotic drug pusher who's really a great guy underneath."
There was a generally contented sound in the room. The tall man continued, removing an invisible speck of lint from his suit.
"And he's not going to be a Christian." The contented sound suddenly abated. Everyone looked at everyone else. There was a dead silence.

In the real church Mrs. Brick had by this time helped the Reverend Downmouth to show a large picture of a head louse on the overhead projector, and a little girl had stood at the front of the church and announced that she had lice in her hair, which didn't go down too well with her parents.

"Well done, Isobel" chimed the preacher, giving Camilla a solitary round of applause as she returned to her family. "Next!" he said sharply, as Mrs. Brick struggled with the projector. The next picture was to have been a horrific image of dead cattle lying on their backs with their stiff legs pointing to the heavens, as clouds of black smoke attended their incineration. But as Mrs. Brick had put the slide in the machine upside down, the smoke was all at the bottom of the picture and the whole thing looked like a Victorian oil painting of cattle standing serenely in the clouds.

"Have you ever known a plague of flies?" enquired the Reverend Downmouth. There was no answer from the congregation, who were not enjoying this one bit. In fact some of them had already decided to leave their roast beef and Yorkshire pudding to another day. A swarm of black dots flew through the air. The vicar was throwing dead flies into the body of the church. Randy Breed raised his arms to Heaven and shouted "Alleluiah!" at the wrong moment, and his reward was a dried-up bluebottle under the tongue.

The Reverend Downmouth had so many late flies that he lost patience with his broadcasting technique and simply emptied a jar and a half of the corpses on to the front two rows. Randy Breed's mouth was by now firmly closed, but women screamed. Little rubber frogs which the vicar had obtained from the toyshop in The Precinct then rained down, together with sloppy lime jelly with which he'd mixed them for maximum impact. Worshippers were already leaving the Church of the Dead Martyrs as Cyril Downmouth turned to his pièce de resistance.

"Would you continue in the ways of wickedness if you knew you would be punished with a plague of hail?"

Ice cubes flew through the air. One caught Mr. Armitage-Shanks in the eye, and another knocked Dr.Nipp's glasses off. Panic gripped the congregation, and someone yelled "Call the police!"

Filfy O'Durr stirred momentarily under the pew whilst his distracted escort tried to keep him quiet with a good ear-tickling. Dolores Downmouth felt that she should really be at her husband's side. He had clearly lost his marbles. But, looking up at the windmilling arms and the staring eyes, she decided that, for her, discretion was, this morning at least, the better part of valour. As woman and dog cleared the rear of the church on a frightened raft of worshippers, Mrs. Downmouth stopped to look back.

"And you too, Dolores! You remember what happened to Lot's wife, don't you?!"

Being a Sunday, it was not easy to find a doctor, but Mrs. Downmouth persevered and was eventually put through to a Doctor Martini, who didn't speak much English and had been drinking for most of the morning. Rather than risk driving, he walked round to Bishop's Mead carrying a brand-new Gladstone bag, and enjoyed the birdsong, and colourful and carefully tended front gardens en route.

By the time he entered the front room at "Damascus," the Reverend Downmouth had recovered somewhat, and was propped up in an armchair watching a new episode of "St. Cuthbert's" in which a lady choir member had attacked her drug-crazed grandson with a hatpin in the churchyard. Doctor Martini noted the patient's shallow breathing, perspiration, and wild staring eyes, and introduced himself in a thick accent.

"Hi, padre. I'm Dr. Martini. How's it going?"
Cyril stopped pulling the limbs off the rubber frog, and looked up.

"It's very nasty. Very nasty," he said, as the close-up of a bloodstained hatpin appeared on the screen of the very small television.

"Ha! I see you English have not lost your sense of humour!"
Tears ran down Cyril Downmouth's cheeks.

"Now I am going to examine you, okay? Are you okay?"

Fifteen minutes later, Dolores Downmouth was hastening down Bishops Mead in the direction of the duty chemists, clutching a prescription for some very powerful tranquillisers, having left her husband in front of the television.

Cyril Downmouth flinched and the remains of the green rubber frog fell to the floor, as the Reverend Jim Shepherd punched an interloper viciously on the nose after finding him writing "Bottom" on the vestry wall.

There was no roast beef and Yorkshire pudding at "Damascus" that afternoon. Whilst Cyril Downmouth watched a remake of "The Greatest Story Ever Told", starring Ray Shunt of "St. Wilfred's" fame, and episode 37 of "The Great War", Dolores Downmouth was upstairs, reflecting on the morning's events. Her few friends in the congregation had been very supportive. Mr. Armitage-Shanks, despite the beginnings of a very nasty black eye, had helped her sweep up the fly corpses and the little green frogs with their attendant lime jelly, and the ever-faithful Mrs. Brick had mopped up the melting ice cubes from floor and pew and font. Now Dolores was alone in the stuffy room her husband used as a study. She reached across the old mahogany desk that had belonged to her father, and opened the little wooden window under the eaves, dislodging a grey woolly cocoon that was borne away on the breeze that was by now cooling the hot air of Pinchley Park. There was a birds' nest near the window somewhere and she heard the fledglings crying for food.

Dolores Downmouth felt her humiliation keenly. Not for herself, really, but for her husband. The trio of younger parishioners had been laughing amongst themselves and performing overdrawn impressions of Cyril after he had hurled frogs and flies into the body of the church. Most of those present had avoided her afterwards, and Dr. Nipp had told her curtly that he would be claiming for a new pair of spectacles. Someone had phoned the police, but by the time the probationary constables had arrived from the station at Bendon, the church had been cleaned, locked up, and abandoned. Now Dolores was alone.

She really didn't want to be here. She longed for another place; another time. She sat back in the wicker backed chair and began to relax for the first time that day. The birds were singing outside.. Dolores delved back in her memory, as she always did, to find those precious, happy moments when Cyril had supported and inspired her to break free from the iron grip inflicted by her parents. It was Cyril who had eventually stood up to them, who had faced them down, and fearlessly declared his love for their meek daughter. It was Cyril who had always been the life and soul of the party at the Forgiveness Mission Society where they had met, and it was Cyril, with his breathless love of life, with whom she had eventually eloped. Now it seemed she could do nothing for this dried up, demented creature sitting in front of the television downstairs. He seemed to blame her for his problems; it was as if he hated her. Dolores Downmouth had no answers. She felt abandoned. She picked up the framed photo that stood centrally on the desk. It was of a smiling young woman with curly blond hair, looking challengingly into the lens, and screwing her eyes up slightly to protect her from the bright Llandudno sun. Yes; she had been pretty.

After replacing the old photograph and giving the desk a quick dust with the pinnie, Dolores bent down and picked up a pink rubber frog and a dead wasp on a piece of Inland Revenue brown envelope, before quietly descending the stairs to make herself a cup of tea. She looked in on her husband, but his head had fallen on to his chest in sleep, and he was missing the grey and black and ancient shots of men sitting in trenches and smoking, and being blown to bits. Almost exactly a hundred years ago. She closed the door soundlessly, and went into the kitchen. Filfy O'Durr was sitting in the corner. He looked pleased.

Dolores smiled for the first time since she had decided to take Filfy to church that morning. It seemed so long ago now. If she was honest with herself, she had to admit she had wanted to discomfit Cyril by taking an animal to sit in her pew when her husband wanted to impress people with his oratory. There was something more to her strange action, she knew, but she couldn't explain it at all. It had been futile anyway; it all seemed so illogical to her now as she bent down and stroked the tufty head raised in welcome.

Dolores boiled the kettle, talking to Filfy in a "doggie" voice that simply puzzled Filfy and made him wonder if Mrs. Downmouth was going the same way as the old man.

"Who was a goody-woody-doggy-woggy in the church, then?"

Filfy loved to be talked to, even in this juvenile way, because Mr. and Mrs. O'Durr rarely addressed him, or each other, come to that, except at the top of their raucous voices. More often than not, they only screamed at him when he had committed a misdeed. But this was different. This lady really talked to him. But she did seem so sad. It was a pity, he thought, that she was so sad.

He had been very sad, once. Before Dolly O'Durr, after half a bottle of Pernod, had crashed her car into the gates of the Pinchley Dog Refuge where he had been confined, and then decided that a dog who would worship her might make life with Mr. O'Durr more bearable. Filfy had been there for months, because he wasn't small or cute or handsome or even sweet-smelling, and his self esteem had been very low. When people had taken an interest in him, he had appeared embarassed and looked away or moved to the other side of the small concrete enclosure. But when Mrs. O'Durr had arrived, she was not going to take no for an answer, and had barged into the enclosure before Mr. Barkeley-Lupin could say "Jack Russell," and gathering Filfy up in her arms had announced "This one'll do."

Filfy had never "done" for anyone before, so he felt a curious sort of loyalty for the loud blond woman who seemed sometimes to hate him.

The phone rang in the hall, and Mrs. Downmouth rose, giving Filfy a comforting pat on the head en route, and went to answer it. The ensuing conversation was hushed. Filfy was not a stupid dog, and realised it had something to do with the man who had been shouting in church, and giving off odours of fear. Filfy could smell it now. He padded to the living room door and pushed it open to find Cyril Downmouth looking blankly at the television screen. When he'd gone to sleep, which seemed only a moment ago,   he had been watching a religious epic, but he was now tuned in to the BBC's new surefire winner, "Celebrity Underpants." He looked awfully sad to Filfy, and watched with mournful eyes as the dog tiptoed across the Wilton carpet and sat at his feet.

"Dolores!" he called. There was no answer.

"Dolores!"

"I'm on the phone, dear."

"There's a dog in here! And it's not Magda."

"I won't be a minute dear, I won't be a minute."

Filfy O'Durr put his chin on the floor not far from Cyril's shiny built-up shoe, and looked gravely up at the vicar. Cyril Downmouth looked down at the unkempt visitor. He didn't appear threatening. The vicar found himself looking into Filfy's deep, soft, wise brown eyes, and looked away. No human had ever looked at him like that. Humans had a different way of looking at you, when they looked into your eyes. It was as if they were always looking for something from you. They were always looking for your weak points, where to strike next, something they could use. He looked back at the dog, and held Filfy's soft enigmatic gaze for a few moments. Filfy moved forward a couple of inches, and rested his chin on Cyril Downmouth's foot. His eyes were still on the man. Were things really so bad? The dog wagged his tail. Was he really such an ineffectual louse? Had his sermon really been so humiliating for him? And for the woman outside in the hall?

Filfy exerted gentle pressure on the shiny black shoe, and the Reverend Downmouth felt himself, ever so slightly, begin to relax. He reached down and patted the shaggy head that was raised in acknowledgement. Filfy sat up and looked again into the man's eyes. He barked softly. The sound was deep and amiable. Filfy pushed his blunt wet nose into the vicar's crotch. Cyril Downmouth flinched, and pushed him away, but the dog homed in on him once more and climbed, quite uninvited, on to his knee. Despite the distinctive odour, the man found himself hugging the animal to him. Filfy turned and started to wash Cyril Downmouth's face with an insatiable tongue. The man laughed. The dog really liked him! Oh, the contact! That contact!

Dolores Downmouth entered the room looking distracted, with the intention of announcing that her brother, who was a mortgage broker, recommended an early visit to a psychiatrist. But when she saw the look on her husband's face and heard his laughter flow so uncontrollably, she said nothing at all.

"Celebrity Underpants" had finished with a flourish when Dolores Downmouth sat down on the little red pouffe next to her husband's chair, and took his hand gravely in hers, as Filfy O'Durr allowed himself to slide to the floor.   Magdalena Downmouth was giving them a baleful glare through the window.
"Would you like a nice cup of tea, dear?" she asked, as Filfy's head reappeared resting on Cyril Downmouth's bony thigh. The vicar tousled the head with one hand, and reached for his wife's hand with the other.
"I'm so sorry" he said, as a frog was produced from the floor.
"I think I'll be all right now.  Yes".
The dog dropped the frog into his lap.
"By the way," he added.  "Who was that in church with you this morning, dearest?"

# CHAPTER ELEVEN
## August

## THE FLOWER

In the closing years of the 20th.century, on a cold winter's day, a great tit flew over Pinchley. It was returning from the big gardens in Nelson Acres, where the residents all stood for "God Save the Queen", and put out high quality birdfood in cold weather. The bird grasped a black sunflower seed in its powerful beak, and turned for home in the Cheeseman Crescent shrubbery.

As the bird flew over the smoking chimney of number 27 Hillside Close, it sneezed and lost its grip on the seed, which flew to earth in a lazy arc, and landed in George O'Durr's front garden. It bounced on an empty tin of Vindaloo Doggie Chunks. It ricocheted off another, and, rolling across one of the few spots not totally covered by tinplate, it disappeared from view in the shade of an empty sardine can. The bird looked down at the unnatural garden below, coughed, shivered, and decided that the food was lost. With a deep sigh he performed a smooth about-turn and with his beak in the air, returned whence he had come.

Mr. O'Durr stood up straight and grunted. His back was hurting. It was very warm. He wiped the sweat from his forehead with the back of a hairy hand, and admired his handiwork. His lawn looked good. Better than ever. The shimmering multicoloured surface reflected back at him in shades of silver and red and ochre and mud.

His mate Sean Lift had come by the roller down at the Grammar School playing fields and heavy as it was, it had done a good job. The red and silver livery of the empty "Mercury Sardines" tins shone in the afternoon sunshine and the more earthy colours of those that had once contained "Brahmaputra

Vindaloo Doggie Chunks" contrasted well. The surface was very smooth.

George O'Durr read the Government logo on his cigarette packet "This is Suicide!," and lighting up a Caskett's Killer Number One, inhaled deeply. There was still at least half the front garden to do, and according to his imitation Rolex, it was almost time for "Tunbridge Wells Vice." He left the roller where it was and made his way across the still rough portion of lawn to the front door. Open sardine tins snapped at his heels and one of them took hold of his boot. Mr. O'Durr swore under his breath, and kicked it off into the air. It flew over the hedge and landed on the manicured neighbouring lawn, next to a small specimen gingko.

"And take those bleeding boots off before you come in here!" Dolly O'Durr had become bored watching "Are You a Genius?" and had been spying on her husband through the off-white lace curtains.

George O'Durr had done enough for one day. Not only was he hot and exhausted, but he had grown tired of the persecution he had had to suffer. He should have left the job for a weekday, but on a Saturday, of course, all the local busybodies were about.

The lawn had somehow grown up. He had never intended it, but he had suffered from an ingrowing toenail after they had moved in to number 27 some ten years ago, now. The back door lock had jammed, and the kitchen waste bin had melted and its remains had become fused to the kitchen floor after a conflagration involving a discarded cigarette. So he had taken to throwing the empty tins out of the front in the hope that someone else in the family would collect them. But neither Dolly nor Channelle O'Durr had done so. Indeed, they had both enjoyed the game of throwing tins out into the front garden, particularly as it caused their next-door-neighbour so much distress. And so it had gone on. Despite bitter complaints from neighbours about the smell, and representations from Councillor Conn and the Pinchley District Council, the layer of tins at the front of number 27 had deepened, and together with the attendant armies of

131

scavenging rodents, seagulls and pets, had become a more-or-less accepted part of the Hillside Close landscape. Gradually the spaces between the tins had been taken up, the soil beneath had disappeared, and unlike the healthy specimens in the back garden, the weeds had actually stopped growing.

"Nice scrapyard," Mr. Bultitude had commented as he passed with 'The Guardian' under his arm.

"Why don't you try some grass?" was the best Dr. Nipp could manage as he stumped by on short legs with copies of "The Lancet" and "Hustler" protruding from the pockets of his Harris Tweed jacket. Mr. O'Durr had looked up hopefully at this request, but the doctor had continued on his way.

As for Mr. Noble, he never said a word as he cleaned his dove-grey Rover 200 Passé with great vigour and athleticism in the next-door driveway. He just stopped what he was doing every few minutes and stared. Sometimes he shook his head, and sometimes he hissed through his teeth "Sshhhhhhhh!" But no word passed his lips. Last time he had baited his next-door-neighbour, Mrs. O'Durr had set the dog on him, and although Filfy had enjoyed the romp and all the vicious growling and pretend biting when his opponent had fallen over, Mr. Noble hadn't. He was convinced the dog had rabies, and had immediately persuaded Mrs. Noble to drive him to the doctor for an injection.

After George O'Durr had gone inside, Mr. Noble plucked up courage and walked round to the front of the neighbouring house. He stood for a few moments with his hands on his hips, glaring at the partially rolled 'lawn.' Then the off-white lace curtains parted, and a grimacing blond head with red lips and sharp white teeth grasping a lighted cigarette appeared, accompanied by the head of a large dog. The mouth was open and Filfy was displaying his teeth too. Filfy was happy, but to his neighbour the smile looked threatening indeed. Charles Noble returned to his own property with long stretching paces that he hoped would make it look like he wasn't in a desperate hurry.

A black cloud blotted out the sun, and a few large drops of rain fell on the lawn."Ping! Ting!"

As Mr. O'Durr settled down with a glass of Buster's Lager on the blow-up settee and switched on "Tunbridge Wells Vice" and Mr. Noble regained the safety of his front door and called "I'm home, dear!," a black sunflower seed stirred in the middle of the tinplate lawn. Dislodged from its dream of hibernation between two long-empty Doggie Chunks tins by George O'Durr's roller, and lovingly cradled for a brief moment between hot sunshine and warmed soil, the seed found itself in a state of profound inner bliss. Then, as the music of a million raindrops rose to a crescendo, and a rich little puddle formed around the seed, it started to experience the beginnings of a rapid and inevitable transformation.

"You got a  weed out here!"
Dolly O'Durr called back into the house as she scattered a Fesco carrier bag full of empty Mercury Sardine cans over the reflective surface of the front garden. She stood over the 'weed', and looking down, was struck by the fresh loveliness of the leaves. It was a beautiful plant. She breathed deeply and felt gratitude suffuse her being. Then she remembered her husband had taken Filfy for a walk, and so he would now be at the betting shop, and her mood of peaceful wondering changed abruptly to one of angry resentment. "Bastard!" she mouthed, as Councillor Kevin Conn from Pinchley District Council cleared his throat.
"Good morning, Mrs. O'Durr" he called from the front gate. "May I have a word with your husband?"

The plant grew at a remarkable rate.  People started talking about it. Dr. Nipp said "Good specimen" to Mr. O'Durr as he passed one July morning. George O'Durr had recently had a urine test at the surgery, and said "Thank-you, sir" before he realised the doctor was referring to the sunflower. Randy Breed actually stopped his pick-up one day in a cloud of tyre smoke to admire Mr. O'Durr's handiwork, and advised watering. Mr. O'Durr watered the plant, and it responded graciously. On advice from the Griplock Garden Centre, he purchased a very lofty and expensive sunflower support. Carefully he raised the support around the plant, and carefully he buried the base of the support deep in the patch of soil he had cleared around it. By this time the thick stem had become a conduit for all kinds of liquid nourishment from morsels of sardine and Doggie Chunks sluiced from the empty tins by the summer rains. By August, when Councillor Conn returned bearing an official letter from Pinchley District Council, he was quite disarmed by the majesty of the enormous plant, crowned by a dazzling flower the size of a dustbin lid.

"How….how did you do that?"

The councillor craned his neck to look at the giant flower as a sardine tin snapped at his heels.

"Green fingers, I guess, councillor."

Mr. O'Durr looked over the councillor's shoulder at the little crowd of onlookers who had gathered to admire his plant.

"Oy! What you gawping at?! Push off! This is private property!".

He advanced menacingly on his audience.

"How did you grow that?" Mrs. Chin, who had been raised amongst stronger and more ruthless men than George O'Durr was not to be put off by a podgy man gesticulating in a dirty singlet.

"Green fingers, love", said Mr. O'Durr, extending two of them.

"We can make some dosh out of this. Have you watered it today?" George O'Durr leaned back in his chair and drew on a cigarillo.

"Course I watered it. You said you was going to. What do you mean 'make some dosh?' "

Dolly O'Durr was trying to force the packaging from a Fesco "Banger and Bean Casserole" into the new and already overfilled wastebin, whilst Filfy tried to lick the foil container as it moved through the air.

"Well. Everyone stands and gawps at the thing every time they go past. So we can charge them, can't we? Charge them for the privilege."

"Don't be stupid, George. You can't stop them walking past. And in any case, some of them are talking to me. Never used to."

"Can't stop them walking past, no. But I can stop them looking at Sunny. I can put a fence up."

"Put a fence up? That high?! George O'Durr; you must be out of your mind!"

Mr. O'Durr took a long luxurious draw on his cigarillo.

"And then charge them dosh to come in. You can sell them coffees and all."

Sean Lift came up with the goods the very next day, after overnight removal of the high fencing from the new Leisure Centre Extension site in Cheeseman Way before the Council could get the contractors round there. Dolly O'Durr was kept busy practising her role of hostess the following night as Lifty's friends kept up a constant demand for teas and coffees, and the fence, more or less soundlessly, grew higher.

Filfy O'Durr, who was a natural host, loved all his new friends, and was everywhere. When Scrubs Davis was trying to silently bury the foundations by the front gate, Filfy jumped in the hole and tried to deepen it by dint of frantic scratching. And then when he had loosened more soil and Scrubs was ready with the concrete, Filfy lay on his back in the hole and jiggled his whole body about in a frenzy of itch-alleviation. Scrubs gave him a long chilling stare. Filfy never knew how close he came to forming a part of the foundations.

The next morning, Randy Breed and Jenda Steamwell set off at dawn for an early morning cut-price recording session at the Pro-Twang Studios in Neasden.

"What's that, Rand?"

Randy Breed stamped on the brakes of the pick-up, wound down the window, and stared.

"Mother of Gaad! Where's next door's? Where's Dolly's house?"

A high solid fence stretched from the front perimeter of the garden all the way around to the front corner of the house. The fence was so high that it was impossible to see the first floor windows. Randy Breed got out, and studied the large rough sunflower painted on the heavily padlocked door in the fence.

"Ha! See this, Jen!"

Next to the picture, there was a typewritten notice in a wooden frame.

"SUNFLOWER VILLA. OPEN 7 DAYS. 9 to 5. ADMISHUN £2.75 INCLUDING TEA/COFEE COME AND SEE THE BIGEST SUNFLOWER IN THE WORLD WILE IT'S STILL HERE!"

By ten o'clock that morning, Councillor Conn had received seven phone calls, all complaining about the giant fence in Hillside Close. Mr. Hussein from number fourteen had said "It's obscene, and a curse on the landscape."

"I don't want to see walls like that ever again" said an agitated Dr. Nipp, who had spent two years confined in Colditz during the second world war.

When Charles Noble had left home in his shiny Rover Passé, his mind focused on the illustration budget he had that day to present to the board at Prood's Educational Books, he had reached the top of Hillside Close before the great structure registered on his radar.

He stopped the car with a jerk and then reversed carefully back down the slope to see if it had been his imagination. But no; it hadn't. A vast wall of timber hid his neighbour's house and garden from view, and totally overshadowed his own. He phoned Councillor Conn, whom he knew hated Mr. O'Durr, and made an anonymous complaint, putting his handkerchief over the receiver as he'd seen them do in so many movies, and assuming a version of a cockney accent. At the other end, the councillor simply noted 'C. Noble v. unhappy', and thought to himself "What a creep!"

By the time Councillor Conn's list had grown to twenty-five names, and he had enjoyed lunch with local developer Lance Grabbett in the gracious restaurant of The Lawns hotel, he decided he should pay George O'Durr a visit.

"What you want, Adolf?"

Channelle O'Durr was on the gate (or, rather, the door that allowed access through the great screen, into the O'Durrs' front garden.)

"I am here in an official capacity. To see your father."

"£2.75. Mind out the way. There's plenty more who want to see Sunny."

As she spoke a chattering family group paid £13.75 for the privilege, and as the door in the vast barrier was opened, Councillor Conn espied a crowd of people milling around inside.

Unknown to him, Pinchley Television had featured the story on their lunchtime news. Then the BBC itself had used the story as a lighthearted finale to their own bulletin which had been particularly heavy that day on death, financial collapse, and disaster. Even as the news reader was injecting herself with morphine to ease the pain of her work, heartwarming shots of Filfy O'Durr personally fertilising the remarkable sunflower were beamed into homes across the land.

Councillor Conn looked the young woman up and down, and decided he wouldn't wish to tangle with her. Or, indeed, do anything else with her. For one thing, she weighed roughly twice as much as he did, and for another, she obviously didn't feel pain like ordinary folks. The nose ring was the biggest he had ever seen, and the tattoos seemed to go on for ever.

"Excuse me!" Another very large woman pushed past urgently. "I'm from the Express" she said, waving a card. Channelle O'Durr opened the gate.

"Welcome, darling."

Then Channelle O'Durr pulled a mobile from the pocket of her sleeveless waistcoat. There was a badge on the pocket saying "Get Stuffed!"

"Dad. The big bitch with the dyed black hair's from the Express. Get Mum to give her a raspberry muffin."

Then she shrieked with laughter at the reply, and returned the phone to her pocket.

"Look what we're doing for you, Adolf. We're putting Pinchley on the map. That's £2.75 if you don't mind."

Councillor Conn looked at the bulging money bag attached to the young woman's belt. It was almost full.

"As a representative of Pinchley Borough Council, I feel I should receive a discount."

"You'll receive a punch up the bracket, sunshine. It's £2.75. Or else piss off out of it!"

The councillor was used to this sort of treatment from the O'Durrs, and he didn't really feel like tangling with the girl's ebullient father that afternoon. Neither, under any circumstances, was he going to pay to enter the O'Durr compound to issue an official warning. But somewhere in his mind, the germ of an idea was forming, and rather like that little sunflower seed, it would have its brief moment of glory. As would he.

Returning to his rather grand office at the Town Hall, the councillor called his secretary.

"Matilda. Bring me the O'Durr file."

It was one of the most exciting times of Filfy O'Durr's life. Day after day, new friends arrived from all over England to stroke him and give him treats. They also stood looking up at the sunflower, and chatted amiably with his beloved mistress. Dolly O'Durr had once had a dream of running a transport cafe, and this came very close to it. She was a skilled baker, and the crowds drawn to Hillside Close appreciated her talents as both a cook and a hostess. Indeed some of the male visitors took quite a shine to her. She had, after all, been a very attractive woman.

"Your blueberry patties remind me of my darling late wife." James Mc.Gillivrock, the celebrated wildlife artist looked into Dolly O'Durr's eyes, and she felt like a teenager again. She primped her blond curls and pushed out her chest.

"Well, you'd better have another one, then, James."

Randy Breed was similarly enchanted, although his approach was more familiar. And more predictable.

"Is your husband at home?"

Dolly O'Durr's husband was very much at home. He had turned the utility room into an office and attached a piece of card to the closed door.

"CHAIRMAN, SUNFLOWER ENTAPRIZES. KEEP OUT."

When he wasn't fielding enquiries from the media, he was counting his money. He loved sorting it out into piles of notes, and sorting the coins into piles of the same denomination. He didn't want to bank any of it. It was such a thrill to see it all mounting up like that. He was so impressed with his own ingenuity that he didn't even take one penny

138

down to the betting shop, but exulted in his daily growing hoard.

At Pinchley Town Hall, Councillor Conn's office had taken on the look of a market garden. There were pots on every window sill containing sprouting sunflowers, and the mayor wasn't too impressed.

"These have got to go, Kevin. How much did they cost? When are you moving them out of here? Hope you haven't forgotten about the fifteenth."

"Not long now, Jim. I'm planting them out next week. Not much at all really. The fifteenth? What about the fifteenth?" The councillor caressed a leaf.

"For God's sake, man. Don't say you've forgotten! Her Majesty! We're commandeering your office for lunch. Remember?"

The mayor swept out of the office and Kevin Conn returned to the O'Durr file on his desk. Then he picked up a little plastic spoon and took a dollop out of a can of "Mercury" sardines, and a dollop out of a can of Brahmaputra Vindaloo Doggie Chunks and stirred them into the contents of a plastic watering can. As he applied the brew to the serried ranks of sunflower plants that sat on his window sills, he happily hummed a tune to himself that sounded a bit like "Come into the Garden Maud." The councillor was so focused on his work that he didn't notice the whiskery figure at the open French window, nor the ardently twitching nostrils.

"Your Majesty!" George O'Durr bowed so low that the seat of his shiny and only best suit split open with an embarrassing rending sound. Queen Elizabeth looked quite pained and moved on to the man's wife.

"Your Majesty!" Dolly O'Durr curtseyed gracefully.

"Cor. You're looking lovely. I hope I look as good when I get to your age."

Queen Elizabeth looked even more pained and signalled for her attendant to move the wheelchair outside so she could see the giant sunflower. She gazed upwards at the remarkable bloom, and under her breath, she said "Hell's teeth!"

Suddenly a remarkably spruce looking Filfy O'Durr appeared from the kitchen where he had been watching his master's welcome. Filfy bent low before the visitor, and then put his head on her lap. A beringed hand stroked the dark head, and Filfy O'Durr and the visitor bonded in delight.

"Sweet animal."

Filfy had fallen in love with the beautiful stranger, and after she had taken leave of his master and mistress, he followed Her Majesty out to the Royal Mitsubishi. As the Queen was helped into the back seat, Filfy climbed aboard too.

"Oh, you lovely thing."

The Queen thought for a moment, chewing her underlip.

"I don't suppose they would mind if I borrowed you for a bit?"

She put her hand to her brow.

"I'll make sure you're taken home afterwards. Drive on, Bywaters. The Council Offices."

And then she started to sing quietly and sweetly "How Much is That Doggie in the Window?"

The speeches and toasts were over. Queen Elizabeth drained her glass of mineral water and yawned behind her hand. She had made a good job of feeding Filfy who was now fast asleep under the table, but she hadn't remotely enjoyed the sardines nor the hot curry dish served up by liveried Town Hall staff. All she wanted now was to go home. But the mayor had a final treat in store.

"Your Majesty. You are invited now to join me and Councillor Conn and the Council members in the Town Hall gardens."

"Oh." The Queen looked pained.

"And we would ask your gracious Highness to cut the ribbon to open our new Municipal Sunflower Garden. Now the Borough of Pinchley has celebrated its five hundredth year, we are adopting the mighty sunflower as our emblem of hope for the future."

"Oh. Yes."

Then, under her breath, Her Majesty hissed "Make this quick,

Bywaters" as her wheelchair was pushed down the slope on to the freshly mown Town Hall lawn where a recent shower had freshened up the sardine and vindaloo perfumed air.

"Round here. Your  Majesty!"

The mayor turned the corner of a shrubbery accompanied by the short-striding Councillor Conn.  And then he stopped abruptly.

The pair looked aghast at the scene of desolation that greeted their gaze.  Not one sunflower plant was vertical, and many were not even intact.  Canine pawmarks crossed and recrossed the beds, and the smell of sardines in tomato sauce blended with the unmistakeable odour of Brahmaputra Doggie Chunks created a truly nauseating miasma that seemed to cover the entire municipal garden.  The Queen turned very pale and scrambled to turn her wheelchair around.

"Get me out of here, Bywaters."

As the mayor and corporation stood staring at the devastation, Filfy O'Durr awoke in the rear of the royal limousine, looked up at his monarch, and burped.  The National Anthem rang out in a reedy electronic timbre, and Her Majesty Queen Elizabeth fumbled in her handbag, and produced her  mobile phone.  It was pink.  She carefully pressed a button, and put the instrument to her ear.

"Yes, dear.  I'm in the car.  It's been a frightful day."

There was a loud shouting from the other end.

"No. I won't be able to watch 'Big Bugger' with you tonight.  I won't be home in time.  No, I haven't forgotten about you. As if I could, dearest.  And I've met the most heavenly dog.  Just wait till you see him!"

# CHAPTER TWELVE
## August

## A QUESTION OF IDENTITY

Pow! "Grrr"! Yeow!! Bop!!! Filfy O'Durr's head hit the stonework of the misused municipal dogs' fountain in Pinchley Park with a terrible thump. The other dog was just too strong. The fountain had long been out of use, and the trough at the base, intended for thirsty animals, was no longer filled with water. It contained empty crisp and cigarette packets, acorns, needles, and the dried oak leaves of many summers. Filfy's vision was blurred, and he was barely conscious, as he lay looking at the verdigris on a faded brass plaque saying "Donated by Cllr. Henry Cheeseman, B.A., 1913".

Above the heavy odorous breathing next to his torn ear, Filfy heard, as if in a dream, a familiar voice.
"Oy! Filf! Where are yer?"
The other dog turned with a low hateful growl as an unshaven Mr. O'Durr appeared from the direction of Witless Road and the bookmakers, in his trademark singlet and trainer pants.
"Filf?"
There was concern in the tone, as Mr. O'Durr first saw Filfy spreadeagled and bloodied at the feet of a strange dog with dripping jaws and a mad expression. Mr. O'Durr, thoughtless of his own safety, stepped forward.
"Oy! You little shit! Get off him or I'll do for yer."
Filfy's heart filled with gratitude for the man who loved him, but he was still feeling very groggy and remained grounded. The aggressor's heckles rose all along his broad black back, and he lowered his head ready to spring.
George O'Durr's experience of mortal combat had been confined to the car park of the White Horse in Old Pinchley

after closing time, and he had learned that his lack of stature could be more than compensated for by the use of an appropriate weapon. Looking from the reddened eyes of the savage creature before him, he saw a 2"x2" municipal stake supporting a dried up creeper, still bearing the Gridlock Garden Centre label "Half-Price". Mr. O'Durr tore the stake from the ground, and with a fearsome whoop, advanced upon Filfy's attacker, waving it around his head.

The bully looked up and his ears went back. He had never seen anything like this. He retreated with an uncertain growl that swiftly turned into a pitiful whimper. Mr. O'Durr, who was by now feeling both pleased with himself and terrified that his show of strength might be rumbled by the aggressor, ran ever faster on his short legs, waving the timber around his head, with his breath coming in increasingly urgent gasps, as the dog accelerated from a trot to a canter.

Unlike the cats who spent their time sleeping, and killing things, and yowling in the night, and spitting at each other, the multicultural canine community of Pinchley was quite sociable, and generally got on very well together. Owners like Quentin Cruft and Charlie Stadium had their own ideas about breeding, of course, but even their animals were, given the opportunity, delighted to play with one another indefinitely, sublimely unaware of the strictures put upon them in their owners' manuals.

There was, admittedly, some holding back by the surviving handful of Bulldogs and Old English Sheepdogs when Schnauzers and German Shepherds and Weimaraners started their exercises in the park, and the appearance of the odd Pekingese or Afghan or Chihuahua caused slightly raised eyebrows, but as a rule it was a happy community. It was the owners who were anti-social.

Filfy O'Durr had friends and playmates from every walk of life and from all over the planet. They all smelled different, of course, which was part of the fun, and they all survived on different diets, although as far as he knew, Filfy was the only customer in Pinchley for Brahmaputra Vindaloo Doggie Chunks. Unlike Filfy, who had the run of the house and of the neighbourhood, some of his pals spent their lives indoors on laps, some in gardens whilst their owners were at work, trying to find shade in summer and seeking shelter in winter. Some spent all day in a kennel outside, or a basket inside. Then there was the occasional thin dog who walked the streets. But there was one dog, and one dog only in the suburb, whom Filfy always avoided. His name was Gripper. Gripper Butt.

As Gripper Butt careered out of the side gate of Pinchley Park, pursued by a screaming little man in a singlet, waving a stick around his head, Elspeth Parker stamped on the brakes of her Nissan Miniscule. The dog shot out from under her front wheels and disappeared in the direction of the Church of the Weeping Virgin. Mr. O'Durr was so carried away with the passion of the chase that he had difficulty stopping as the little blue car with the elderly and startled driver barred his way. The driver's window was wound down.
"And what do you think you're doing, young man?"
The voice was schoolma'mly and the tone was frosty, but the "young" went down well with Mr. O'Durr who had been experiencing a crisis of some sort in recent weeks. Mr. O'Durr was out of breath, and leaned on the roof of the car as he bent down to talk to the driver.
"And what gasp do you think gasp you're doing gasp you silly gasp old bat?"
The breath reminded Ms. Parker of her cat's after Dinky had eaten a plate of faggots. Her heart was beating unnaturally fast.
"I shall be reporting you, young man," she said as she swiftly wound up the window, engaged first gear and stalled the engine.
Filfy was by now feeling more himself, and was following the distinctive scent of his master's trainers to the side gate, where a threadbare privet hedge clung to life in the dust. He moved slowly and uncertainly, looking this way and that to make sure Gripper had not returned. He had been very lucky that day, and he knew it. Mr. O'Durr had been less fortunate in that, unbeknown to him, Ms. Elspeth Parker had only recently retired from the R.S.P.C.A. She had been forced to leave after

a 20foot python had taken a special liking to her, but still had live contacts within the organisation. As she had jerked away from the kerb, she had looked in her rear-view mirror at the nasty little man in the singlet and shuddered. Then she had looked again. Another dog, very similar in size to the first, had slunk up to the man, in a distinctly lopsided manner. It was very unsteady on its feet. And it seemed to be bleeding. Ms. Parker's pale lips turned down at the corners as she mounted the kerb.

Darren Butt came from a very unfortunate background, which partially explained his anti-social record since arriving in Pinchley. His father, who had made money in the early days of Sku Television, and who now drove a Mercedes 696 Turbo Automatic and a 5Litre Buick Wanderer with a naked woman on the side, had moved to the respectable suburb of Pinchley after making dangerous enemies in Hackney. Mrs. Butt had left him for an Ethiopian long-distance runner some years previously, and had not been heard of since emigrating. Meanwhile, revelling in his new-found fortune, Mr. Butt had sent his son to an expensive school, where everyone else, especially those of Asian descent, was very much brighter and spoke better English than he. It had left Darren with an eating disorder, a hatred of foreigners, and a deep desire to revenge himself upon the world.

The "Pinchley Patriotic Party" met at the crumbling drill hall in Church Street on a Thursday night, despite angry opposition from some members of the local council, particularly Councillor Bert Cheeseman, who claimed young Butt didn't know what patriotism meant. But Darren Butt still had the key to the building, and spent his Thursday evenings honing his oratorial skills in front of a small group of slightly defective patriots. This group included Mr. Reich from the Co-Op, Mr. Hunwick from Hunwick's Army Surplus in the Precinct, and a group of anonymous red-faced males who didn't seem to have anywhere else to go. Occasionally they would be joined by Mr. and Mrs. Bultitude, who both felt that something should be done about the state of their country, but weren't very sure what.

When they looked at the posturing Darren Butt and listened to the disaster he made of their language, they were left with the vague feeling that although something had to be done, it wasn't this. But at least, submitting to a haranguing from the leather-jacketed Mr. Butt was marginally more entertaining than the Thursday television schedules. "Are You a Genius"?, "The Oestrogen Factor", "I Married a Washing Machine, and "Naked Volleyball" did not figure very high in their ratings.

"Old Cheesey Cheeseman says I don't know what patriotism means."

Darren Butt's face was very dark, as he removed the black leather jacket he had stolen from the back seat of a Honda Vertebrate. His singlet displayed the cross of St. George, and "Rule Brittania!" and "England for Ever!" featured in the complex tattoos that weaved themselves around his muscular shoulders. Darren Butt moved around so all present could admire his decorations. Unlike a true mannequin, he moved with a not altogether attractive strutting grace, reminiscent of a teenage wild boar.

"Well, whatcha think of that then?"

A general murmur went around the dusty room. Mr. Bultitude leaned forward. He was not mistaken. Below the "England for Ever" characters, there were more. "SOUTHEND UNITED!"

"What made this country what it is today.." Darren Butt stood, hands on hips, glowering at his audience, "was geezers like you and me. Not bastard Frenchies or wops or Pakkies or Chinks. It was us Brits what....made it what it is today. It was us what paid into the National Health. To look after our own kids when they was sick, not to accom.....accomma....put up Johnny Foreigner in the Chandos or the Talbot and claim the bleeding sick. Yeah! Think about it. And when you go home tonight, think about it again. Think about King Arthur and his knights. And Robin Hood. And Lord Nelson. He saw off the froggies, didn't he?!"

Darren Butt struck a dramatic pose as he raised one

camouflaged leg on to a chair and leaned forward conspiratorially towards his audience. With a stabbing motion of his right forefinger, he spoke quietly, but with great intensity as the black dog under the chair stirred in its sleep.

"You go home tonight and you think of those men. Arthur. Hood. Nelson. Sinatra. And then think of me. The name's Darren. Darren Butt. Yeah."

An embarrassed silence filled the drill hall. Nobody moved.

The speaker retrieved his jacket from the table and stumped towards the door.

"Come on, Gripper. We're going home."

Bert Cheeseman's stuffy editorial office at the Pinchley Gazette was a very lived-in room. Bert's grandfather had started the paper just before the outbreak of war in 1914, and had then marched away to be gassed and dismembered on the Western Front. He had left behind him a newspaper that aspired to changing things for the better, but now, nearly a century later, his grandson espoused few causes, and contented himself with reporting as accurately as possible on local matters. Council affairs figured largely, and there was an excellent market in Pinchley for the reportage of petty crime and road accidents, the more gory the better. Bert himself had an aversion to dogs, and there was usually an article or two about the dangerous fouling of footways, and stern entreaties to the public to always go walkies armed with a pooper-scooper.

Although Mr. Cheeseman espoused few causes, he espoused his own as a councillor very enthusiastically, and never lost an opportunity to score a point or two in his editorials against his fellow councillors, or indeed, against anyone of whom he personally disapproved. It was only the previous year that he had launched an investigation into the state of the kitchens at the Naff Tikka Restaurant, and had publicised the scandalous state of George O'Durr's front garden, where squashed "Mercury" sardine tins and Brahmaputra Doggie Chunks cans far outnumbered the few blades of grass.

The editor took a sip of cinnamon coffee from the

polystyrene cup that his secretary had just fetched from the Baghdad Big Apple Coffee House next door. It tasted revolting but it was better than nothing. You couldn't get actual plain coffee in Pinchley any more. In fact, most people had forgotten what it tasted like. Bert rose to his feet and lit a Carcinoma King Size. He looked out of the window and saw a big black dog pooing in the precinct below, whilst its tattooed owner admired his reflection in the window of the Pinchley Building Society. Mr. Cheeseman saw red. He strode to the window, yanked up the sash, and hurled the remains of his cinnamon coffee at the offending animal.

"You disgusting beast!" he shouted, as a gust of wind took the coffee and deposited most of it on the person of Elspeth Parker.

The lady was already in a very bad mood. After that unpleasant meeting with the nasty little man and his dogs in the park, she had just emerged from the Pinchley Building Society where the cashier had first sent her back to the "Wait Here to be Called by a Cashier" sign, and had then coolly informed her that her last deposit had gone into her Super Senior Long Stay Graveyard Account instead of the Instant Access Motivation Executive Advantage Titanium Gold. Now to be showered by a seagull was just too much. She looked up and shook her fist, and found she was shaking it at a middle aged man in braces leaning out of a first floor window with one hand gripping a polystyrene cup and the other pressed hard to his mouth.

"And what exactly did you mean by calling me a disgusting beast, Mr. Cheeseman?" Ms. Parker coughed ostentatiously.

"Will you kindly put that cigarette out?"

Her grey eyes roamed around the room with distaste. Dusty files and boxes were everywhere. Ms. Parker looked down at her lavender coat as if it might already have picked up some of the dust. The editor put out his cigarette in an ashtray that had once been a howitzer shell casing, and raised his eyes.

"It was a most regrettable mistake. It was that disgusting dog I was talking to. And aiming at."

Elspeth Parker appeared mollified.

148

"You will of course be paying for the dry cleaning of my coat".

"Naturally, madam".

"Then let us agree on that. And if you find yourself able to make a donation to the R.S.P.C.A., then I think we can say that is an end to the matter".

"A donation?"

"Yes, certainly. Shall we say £50?"

"£50?"

"Yes. I think that would be very acceptable. A small price to pay to avoid going to court on a charge of common assault. My brother is a practising barrister, you know."

Despite unpromising beginnings, it was in that stuffy little editorial office that a powerful alliance was forged that morning. Bert Cheeseman in his creased white shirt and braces and Elspeth Parker in her lavender coat and turquoise silk scarf made an unlikely campaign team, but that is what they became. They probably only had one thing in common apart from a love of the place where they had lived all their lives, and that was a hatred of those who abused animals. Although the editor's bête noir was actually the fouling that was becoming a feature of Pinchley, and Elspeth Parker's concern was for the welfare of the animals themselves, they came together powerfully that day in a mission. It was a mission to clean up the dog owners of Pinchley.

"PRECINCT FOULER CAUGHT IN THE ACT" ran the first headline, which was accompanied by a very poor photo, taken by Bert Cheeseman himself from his window of a hazy dark dog squatting outside the Dollar Shop. Below this was a more graphic close-up of a sausage with a booted foot next to it to give an idea of scale. It was either a very small boot or a very large sausage.

"DO YOU KNOW THIS DOG?" accompanied another photo of a crouching black dog of indeterminate ancestry in the next week's edition. This was followed by "LOCAL LADY'S FASHION SHOE WRITE-OFF!" (accompanied by a full-length picture of Ms. Parker holding a lace hankie to her retrousse nose and pointing disgustedly to a brown object stuck to her shoe), and "WAR ON FILTH!" under a photograph of an overflowing bin marked "Dog Waste Only". Bert Cheeseman had himself penned the editorial that accused local dog owners of a total disregard for hygiene, and had indeed taken the photograph on page three of a group of local children staring disgustedly at the overfilled bin from the front page.

"We at the Observer" Councillor Cheeseman boomed, "are proud of our historic borough of Pinchley, and we will not give in to the filthmongers. Today we declare war on the stink brigade, and mark our promise well: we will use every weapon in our armoury, both spiritual and temporal, to clean up Pinchley for the generations to come.

And please, if you are a dog owner, ask yourself – 'Is my Rover part of the problem or part of the answer?'"

This confused some of the car owners of Pinchley, including Mr. Noble, who had rather enjoyed the "spiritual and temporal" reference. He found, however, the last hardhitting paragraph less than transparent "If your god loves you, he won't want you to have an A.S.B.O. slapped on you. But if he continues to foul our manor, then he's got another thing coming!"

Despite the rantings of the Gazette, the campaign against careless dog owners might well have petered out, but for the introduction of another factor into the Pinchley equation. The headline "RACE FILTH ATTACK!" sold more newspapers for the Cheesemans than had been achieved since Armistice Day in 1918. The editor never knew how much the nebulous nature of the words contributed to these extra sales. But the facts were simple enough. Young Sachin Khan (10) had been attacked by a black mongrel wearing a Union Jack waistcoat, as he sat on a swing in Pinchley Park, doing his English Literature homework. He had arrived home in a state of great distress minus his Manchester United shorts and with a bitten bottom. Later in the day, the pages of his book, "The Sonnets of William Shakespeare" (with a foreword by Prince Philip, Duke of Edinburgh) were found torn and scattered to the four winds.

The police were, of course, immediately informed, and a search for the delinquent dog and its owner was put in train. Detective Sergeant Ray Allwight had been on a "Race Discrimination is History" course, and a workshop entitled "Understanding Islam", and had boys of his own, so he was understandably quite rabid about finding the culprit at the first opportunity. "There's no room for Race in Pinchley," he told his investigation team.

Probationary Constable Mel Mangold and Community Policeperson Eartha Supreme looked at each other, puzzled.

"Everyone here has the same rights, right? It doesn't matter who their parents are, or where they were born, everyone's equal now, right? Some may be more equal than others, but that's not the point, is it? No it's not, right? Right, you two pandas. Let's get on the case, right?

I want a report on my desk Friday. Right.... Right; what are you two dummies waiting for? I want to know everything about the black dogs in the area. Just the black ones, right? I want to know their habits, their locals, who their mates are, what they have for breakfast, what their owners do that they shouldn't be doing. Especially their owners. I want to know all about them. I want to know when they go to the pub, if they beat their wives, what they drink, if they've got car insurance, what time they go for a crap, if they're on the sick. And, of course, if they're on our files. I want to know everything about them. Mr. Khan is not a happy man. And Mr. Khan's got friends. Friends in high places. And I'm not a happy man either. In fact right now I'm very unhappy indeed. Make me happy. Get me a cup of coffee on the way out, Eartha. A proper coffee. None of that flavoured muck."

"RACE HOUND ATTACKS AGAIN" sold a lot more newspapers the following week. Skateboarder Jazzbert Soames-Windsor had been attacked by a big black mongrel in the park as he had attempted an impossible jump over a rhododendron, and landed on the beast as it was eating a rat. His Manchester United shorts had gone the same way as the previous victim's, which led to some speculation about the attacker's footballing allegiances, and he had been rushed to

Pinchley General Accident and Emergency, where he had waited for six hours for treatment, quite unable to sit down. Jazzbert's skateboard was never seen again, despite a photograph of Ms. Soames and Mr. Windsor standing looking disgusted next to an overflowing bin marked "Dog Waste" appearing in Mr. Cheeseman's inimitable style in the Gazette. Indeed, the parents were also featured on an inner page, each with a hand on a pair of torn red shorts, asking what was being done about catching the offender, and what was being done about the service at Pinchley General. The answer to the latter question was easy: Nothing. But the article praised the police for their new Park Patrol consisting of Mr. Mangold and Ms. Kitt, and showed a picture of "ex R.S.P.C.A. manager, Elspeth Parker on vigilante patrol." The latter was featured looking through a pair of opera glasses at what looked like a hedgehog.

Mr. O'Durr didn't read the local paper. If he hadn't spent so much time with his nose in "Betting Weekly," he might have seen the problem coming. Similarly, Dolly O'Durr shunned the Gazette, preferring to spend her money on "The Daily Insult", "The Bum", and a range of magazines including "The Larger Woman," "Sex Secrets of Hollywood," "Goodbye Cellulite," and the free magazine from Fesco entitled "The Miracle of Food." So in the O'Durr household Mr. Cheeseman's sensational headlines, and indeed his campaign against irresponsible dog owners went quite unheeded. For a while, at least.

Bert Cheeseman had never seen himself as a lady's man. But Elspeth Parker seemed to have taken a shine to him. They started to spend more time together in places like the "Copper Kettle" and "Beanz Coffee House", ostensibly discussing their campaign at length, but certainly getting to know one another much better in the process. Bert Cheeseman soon realised that Ms. Parker was younger than he had first thought. Her luxuriant head of hair had turned prematurely white after the Python Incident, but her hands were smooth and youthful looking. In fact Bert Cheeseman found himself wondering one morning in the "Copper Kettle" how they would feel caressing his long-abandoned erogenous zones. A piece of fruit scone lodged in his throat, and Ms. Parker's young right hand gave him several muscular slaps on the back to dislodge it. She was no weakling, he noted.

The editor had once intended to re-establish the Gazette as a reforming, campaigning organ of the borough, but had found that it was more profitable to report what people wanted to hear, and that this policy left him with more time for council business and the long lunches that went with it. He had, in a word, become lazy. But clearly, Elspeth Parker didn't see him in this light at all. She made him feel much younger as she exhorted him to greater efforts in the battle for the hearts and minds of the animal lovers of Pinchley. He found her fervency very sexy, and she somehow made him feel extremely male.

"You can do it, Bert," uttered in that low dusky voice, with a flash of the blue-grey eyes, or even a squeeze of the hand, made Bert Cheeseman feel quite certain he could do it. And phrases like "a man like you" and "what made Britain great," and "you'll show them, Bert" lodged in his heart like arrows, and kept him awake at night, thinking about the words she had spoken and the lips that had spoken them. It was a long time since Joy had left.

Although Elspeth Parker didn't care much for the braces, she knew that in time she could change that outdated image for Bert and help him become more of a twenty-first century man. He clearly didn't have any idea of his powerful male attraction. Mind you, he could afford to lose a couple of stone, and some aloe vera would help those patches of dry skin. Ms. Parker suddenly awoke to her train of thought and shuddered. She had had one journalist in her life, and that was surely enough. What was she thinking of?! Then she looked across the table at Bert, as he outlined his plan to engage the council in their campaign. She saw his wide masculine jaw, and his kind sad eyes, and the flash of his whiteish teeth as he smiled fleetingly or took another bite of scone. And as she cast her eyes down to the bone china cup, and stirred her coffee, she found herself melting inside. Like a sugar cube in hot cappuccino.

In subsequent weeks, various people were attacked by the vicious predator in Pinchley Park. Matts Ericsson, a young man from Stockholm on a foreign exchange trip lost his shirt and his English phrasebook. Jacques Fournier, an onion seller from Carcassonne lost his onions and his dignity, and Winston Mbogu, a security guard from Fesco had to buy himself a new pair of blue-grey trousers with a yellow stripe down the side. All the victims suffered bitten bottoms, and all the victims described a big black mongrel with immense energy and yellow teeth. In one case the victim reported a scruffy looking little man shouting from a distance "Go get him, Tiger!" or words to that effect.

When Darren Butt read in the Gazette about Gripper's mistaken attack on a white English child, he knew he had to act quickly. The little girl had a sun tan because she had just come back from a holiday in Provence, and wore her hair in a sort of Afro style, but that had been enough to make Gripper see red. He had fortunately left the little girl alone, but savaged her black doll.
"BLACK BABY SAVAGED IN PARK!" roared the Gazette.
That very night, Darren borrowed a Vauxhall Viagra from his mate, Mervyn Dome, and delivered a desolated Gripper, together with a couple of cases of Fesco's "Cheapo" dog food to his grandma in West Ham. Darren's grandma, who suffered from Alzheimer's, thought Gripper was a present, and couldn't recall who Darren was.

It was on the day that "RACIST BUM-BITER STRIKES AGAIN!" was displayed on every news stand in Pinchley that George O'Durr decided to take Filfy with him to the betting shop in Witless Road. After frying himself up some Fesco streaky bacon rashers with eggs and potato wedges, he sat back on his rickety kitchen chair and burped opulently. "Oy! Filf!" he shouted at the ceiling. Upstairs, Filfy O'Durr, who had been dreaming about becoming a heroic police dog, opened his eyes and noted that his mistress was still asleep and snoring gently next to him.

154

"Filf! Walkies!"

The golden sound of his master's voice floated up the stairs, accompanied by the smell of fried bacon. This was going to be a good day! Filfy rolled out of bed on to the floor, taking the duvet with him, and padding to the door, prised it open with a practised paw, and rushed downstairs. The reclining nude slept on.

Filfy O'Durr always enjoyed visits to the betting shop, where he usually met some of his friends, who were to be found sitting disconsolately around the room whilst their owners greeted Mr. O'Durr, studied form, swapped jokes, watched television, and kept going back and forth to a window. Filfy really had no idea what his master was doing, but whatever it was, it seemed to bring him some happiness. Some days, Mr. O'Durr seemed extra happy upon emerging from the shop, and made straight for the White Horse and then took a taxi home. The White Horse was okay, because Filfy also knew most of the canine regulars there too. But there were other, better days, when Mr. O'Durr emerged from the shop with a long, sober face.

"Well, Filf," he would say conspiratorially; "there's nothing for it. It'll have to be a walk in the park. And it's a walk home and all."

On this particular day no-one greeted Mr. O'Durr, and even the dogs gave Filfy a less than enthusiastic welcome. The manager, Leroy Williams didn't look at Mr. O'Durr as he accepted a losing bet on Mr. Tortoise in the 3.30 and an unnecessarily complex losing treble. The strangely muted atmosphere seemed to have no effect at all on Mr. O'Durr, who wasn't a very sensitive sort of man, but Filfy felt it keenly. After an hour, Mr. O'Durr had spent all his benefits, and moving to the door, followed closely by an expectant Filfy, he turned and addressed the room.

"Well; see you miserable buggers later."

Leroy said "Watch that dog of yours, friend."

No-one else bothered to reply.

After doing her mother's washing at the launderette, and dropping it off at her bungalow in Sundown Close, Elspeth Parker decided to get a sandwich from Healthy MacShambles for her lunch, and eat it in the park. The children were on holiday from school, so she certainly wouldn't be on her own. Bert Cheeseman was on the golf course. Since meeting Elspeth, his game had deteriorated somewhat, as he kept finding thoughts of her eyes and her hands and her hair affecting his concentration. As Elspeth Parker paid for her Stilton and sun-dried tomato baguette, Bert was less than a mile away on the sixth hole, driving a second ball into the ornamental lake.

Elspeth parked her car by the memorial gates of Pinchley Park, and walked gracefully through, pausing to look at the list of names of those who had not returned to Pinchley after two world wars. It was a long list, and Elspeth noted it included a Captain Henry Cheeseman of The Middlesex Regiment. Ms. Parker's stomach rumbled like a distant barrage, and she looked guiltily around her to make sure no-one else had heard. No; there was no-one near. A little way off, a group of youngsters were playing a riotous ball game, and Elspeth sat down on a bench to watch while she ate her lunch and thought of Bert.

Elspeth took a deep, grateful breath as she looked around her. The cries of the children reminded her of her own days of motherhood, and the warm summer air was still and sweet. She sat against a little metal plaque, darkened with age, which said simply "Dedicated to the Memory of Mary and Ernest Cheeseman."

She took a sip of mineral water from the bottle she carried everywhere, removed her opera glasses from the yellow handbag, and put them on the bench beside her. She could hear the song of a blackbird somewhere near. She opened the polystyrene container and took out the baguette, and became aware of a change in the quality of the sound coming from the children.

The laughter had stopped and little shrieks had taken its place. She looked up, and almost dropped her lunch. A big black mongrel was bounding towards her. Elspeth grabbed the opera glasses and her yellow handbag, and ran, panic-stricken to the car. Filfy O'Durr thought this was great fun, and he ran alongside her, leaping up and barking his head off. Suddenly Elspeth Parker's baguette was no longer in her youthful hand, but in the dog's jaws. She reached the car, breathless. She fumbled with her R.S.P.C.A. key ring before throwing herself into the driver's seat and slamming the door.

The camera! The camera! The camera was in the glove compartment. Elspeth moved quickly, if shakily, and put the viewfinder to her eye. Then she took off the lens cap, and took a close-up of Filfy O'Durr in mid air, as he leapt up next to the driver's window with jaws agape, and a piece of MacShambles expanded polystyrene packaging impaled on a long yellow tooth. Suddenly a dumpy little man with a crew-cut, trainer pants and an England football shirt appeared, puffing, through the park gates.
"Oy! Filf! Oy! Filf!"
Elspeth Parker, although of a nervous disposition, was not one to shirk her responsibilities. She raised the viewfinder to her eye once more, pressed the "zoom" button to maximum, and took a picture of George O'Durr.
"Oy! Filf!"
Elspeth heard the man, but she had no intention of hanging about. She started the engine, and before George O'Durr could get near, shot off up Cheeseman Road with shrieking tyres.

Bert Cheeseman guiltily put out his cigarette in the "Coffers' Number Ones" ashtray, as Elspeth Parker entered the room clutching a camera.
"I've got him! Oh, Bert, I've got him!"
She collapsed gracefully on the new visitors' chair, and started to cough.
"Have you been smoking again, Bert?"
Bert Cheeseman was still smarting after the heavy defeat on the golf course. He didn't mind losing, but please, not to Councillor Conn. And not ignominiously.

"No, I haven't," he lied, throwing open the window, and looking once more at his visitor.

"Are you all right?"

He noticing for the first time the breathlessness, the pallor, and the marks on the lavender coat. Elspeth Parker put the camera on the desk.

"No, I'm not all right, Bert. I'm very not all right. But thanks for asking."

Bert heard the irony and twanged his red braces against his creased white shirt. He put out a hand across the desk, but it was ignored.

"Cup of tea? Coffee?" Elspeth handed him the camera.

"I want you to see these. Just a glass of water."

"Coffee anyone?" Detective Sergeant Ray Allwight didn't really want to see the visitors who had turned up without an appointment, because he thought he knew what to expect. When he had joined the force and been first attached to the Pinchley Police Station, he had found Ms. Parker and her animal passions hard to deal with, particularly after he had been made the R.S.P.C.A. liaison officer, (a job that none of his seniors wanted to do).

"No, thank-you, Sergeant."

"And for you, councillor?"

Sergeant Allwight pressed the button on the new machine and watched a scummy fawn liquid with lumps on its surface fill his plastic cup.

"No thanks" said Bert. "We thought it was time we met the officer in charge of the manhunt. Or shall I say the doghunt? Ha! Ha!"

Ray Allwight's miserable lips didn't move. He wasn't a happy man. He had no leads, and was being pressured from all sides, particularly since the latest attack involving an English girl. He had been trained to catch criminals. Murders, bank robberies, serious assaults; they were his bag. Not some piddling racist dog.

"He stole your baguette?"

Sergeant Allwight's eyes glazed over. Elspeth Parker leaned

forward.

"Yes, he did. And I've got him on camera."

"On camera?" The policeman looked from one visitor to the other.

"You mean … like Candid Camera?"

"On this camera!" Elspeth raised her Canon Multipixel Macroranger A1000 in triumph.

"Just look at these!"

Ray Allwight appeared confused.

"Look at what?" he asked.

Mel Mangold and Eartha Supreme picked their way across the sea of squashed sardine and Vindaloo Doggie Chunks tins that constituted the O'Durrs' front garden. Someone had removed the knocker by force, and the bell didn't work. Probationary Constable Mangold hammered on the door with his knuckles, and stepped back in alarm as a body threw itself against the inside of the door. Filfy O'Durr loved to guard his home, and started to bark in the most frightening way he knew. It had the desired effect on the two police officers.

As the deep throated barking reached a crescendo of "Get off my doorstep!" Probationary Constable Mangold had a very brief peep through the flapless letter box, and satisfied himself that the leaping dog was indeed big and black, before dropping the letter through. The letter was an invitation from Ray Allwight for Mr. O'Durr to attend Pinchley Police Station with his dog that afternoon. Filfy O'Durr had eaten it before the two police officers had reached their Vauxhall Teeny.

"Good morning, officers!" Mr. Noble rose from cleaning the inside of the exhaust pipe on his Rover Passé.

"Anything I can do for you?"

Community Policeperson Supreme looked at her colleague who was having trouble with his radio.

"No, I don't think so, sir."

But Charles Noble persisted. It was about time the police knew about his neighbours.

"I expect it would help you to know where they are, officer?"

159

Eartha Supreme looked at her colleague once more. The radio seemed to have come in two, and was emitting a piercing whine.

"And I dare say you are looking for the dog."

Mel Mangold gave up on the radio.

"The dog? What about the dog, sir?"


Councillor Bert Cheeseman took a sip of coffee. It tasted like rubbing compound, and he was left with a piece of grey scum attached to his lip.

"The dog will clearly have to be put down."

"Yes; but we don't have the evidence, do we?"

Ray Allwight didn't like the councillor, and was not going to be bullied here on his own patch. Elspeth Parker was outraged.

"What about the photos? What about the photos I took of that dog? And the man?"

Ray Allwight took a sip of coffee, and winced.

"What about the photos, Miss? They don't prove anything. Just a dog jumping up at your car. And a little guy who could be anybody. And they were blurred anyway. No proof of any misdemeanour there."

Bert Cheeseman raised his voice. He wasn't going to have his friend talked to like that.

"No proof of any misdemeanour, sergeant? There's proof all over town. What's your investigation team doing, in Heaven's name? And who do you think you're talking to? I would suggest you don't sound so damned smug. We want this case closed."

Sergeant Allwight took a very deep breath. The phone rang.

"Yes?!" he snarled.

"Hello, sergeant. Sorry to trouble you, but I've got some information. On the dog."

The voice boomed around the room and the sergeant quickly switched the call to his handset, but the damage had been done. As Sergeant Allwight tried to hear the message, Councillor Cheeseman homed in.

"Right, let's hear it! Let's all hear it! Where is he? Let's have him in."

Probationary Constable Mangold was in fact in the building

trying to obtain a new radio and a hat that fitted him and it was only a matter of minutes before he and Ms. Supreme were standing before the sergeant's desk.

"Yes, Miss. It was a big black dog. And it jumped up. I put the letter through the letter box. Then I talked to this man next door."

Mel Mangold consulted his notebook.

"Mr. Noble, the next-door neighbour. He says the dog is always causing trouble, and it bit him on the bottom last year."

"Bit him on the bottom, eh?"

The councillor looked triumphant, and Elspeth Parker put her hand to her mouth and said "Oh."

Constable Mangold continued.

"The place looks a mess, sergeant. You should see the front garden. No path. No grass. Just a load of squashed tins."

Bert Cheeseman sat forward in his chair.

"Squashed tins, you say?"

"Yes, sir; squashed tins."

And, consulting his notebook; "Mercury Sardines in Tomato sauce, and Brahmaputra Vindaloo Doggie Chunks."

The councillor banged his fist on the desk.

"Got him. That the fellow with the disgraceful front garden I had trouble with last year Yes! I couldn't nail him then. But with your co-operation, sergeant … "

The councillor gave the sergeant a sickly, dangerous grin, "….we'll really nail him this time."


Neither Raj Patel, Li Ho Nam, Basil Hussein, nor Pedro Ochoa had ever stood in a police identity parade before. Come to that, neither had George O'Durr. Nor Filfy. All but Filfy were wearing England football shirts, loaned by "Big Boy Sports" in the precinct. The men were of similar height, but Filfy was the only dog present. When Councillor Cheeseman had first looked through the window to see Sachin Khan pointing to Filfy, he had raised his fist the way he did if Pinchley United ever scored a goal, but he found he had some misgivings. Sergeant Allwight, however, was very clear.

"We're all equal here, councillor. They were the first people of the correct height I could find. And remember, sir, there's no race in Pinchley, as you say yourself."

Bert Cheeseman couldn't quite grasp the argument, and found himself saying "Oh, no", and squeezing Elspeth Parker's hand without really thinking, as Matts Ericsson pointed with great certainty at Filfy O'Durr.

Gripper Butt had been terrorising West Ham for some three weeks before his master visited for the first time. The postman, the meter reader, and the milkman had all refused to call after being attacked by Gripper, who had put on a lot of weight after Darren's grandma, on account of her short-term memory loss, had forgotten when she'd fed him.

"Where's all the bleeding dog food, Gran? I brought enough for a couple of months at least!"

Darren's Gran looked troubled.

"I really don't know, dear. He's looking well, dear. Don't you think?"

It was the article in the London News that had decided Darren to take his dog home. "BUM BITER IDENTIFIED!" A close-up of Filfy O'Durr bearing his teeth sat below the announcement, together with a piece about Pinchley and its recent problems, which had been lifted straight out of the Pinchley Gazette.

"The good folk of Pinchley can rest easy in their beds tonight. The racist bum biter has been clearly identified by three of his victims and is in police custody. His name is Filfy O'Durr, and his owner is low-life layabout, George O'Durr of Hillside Close. A case is being prepared against the latter, and court proceedings will be fully reported in this newspaper. So watch out for Her Majesty versus George O'Durr!"

There was nothing new on the case the following week, so Bert Cheeseman decided to feature his new friend.

The newsstands blared "NISSAN MINISCULE HITS ONE-LEGGED VAGRANT!"

Filfy O'Durr didn't know why his master was so upset, and he couldn't understand the whispered, worried conversations he was having with Dolly O'Durr when they thought he wasn't listening. The bail had taken their last penny and their daughter, Chanelle, had even sold her motor bike to help out. Mr. O'Durr started taking Filfy on really long walks, even as far as the grounds of Pinchley Manor, where one met few other walkers, and where Filfy could chase pigeons and rabbits and other forms of wild life to his heart's content. The fact that he never caught anything didn't interfere one jot with his fun, but he did find himself looking out of his eye corners at his master from time to time. Mr. O'Durr had never taken him walking like this before. He had even stopped going to the betting shop, and he scarcely ever went to the White Horse any more.

On the walks, Filfy would return from another unsuccessful foray into the undergrowth to find Mr. O'Durr standing looking into the distance, seemingly quite unaware of his surroundings. It would take at least a bark or two to bring him back.

And then there was the sudden affection. Filfy had grown used to his master's dictatorial ways over the years, and had come to respect them. Even though Filfy would have liked some physical affection, he still knew Mr. O'Durr loved him, and that was the important thing. But now, his master would suddenly bend down and ruffle up his coat, or tickle him under the ears, and he would for the first time even tickle his tummy if Filfy rolled over. And he seemed to be talking to him a lot more, even if the voice sometimes dried or became thick with emotion. Mr. O'Durr couldn't tell Filfy that he might soon be put down. Even if he wanted to.

Mr. Sanjay Singh, Secretary of the Pinchley Race Relations Committee always took his Old English Sheepdog, Elizabeth, to the grounds of Pinchley Manor for her walk. You tended to get a superior type of dog there. So it came as a nasty shock to Mr. Singh and Elizabeth to suddenly be confronted by Gripper and Darren Butt at the edge of the Old Pond. The Old English Sheepdog decided to go for a headlong run in the woods, leaving Mr. Singh with Gripper.

"Good Boy" was not the thing to say to Gripper under such circumstances, and turning tail and fleeing was even worse.

After Mr. Singh had lost his turban and the seat of his English worsted trousers, Gripper Butt noticed another black dog ineffectively chasing pigeons, and with a low growl, he tore off in its direction, leaving the Chairman sitting in the reeds, muttering into his beard.

"Oy! Gripper!"

Darren Butt took a shot at a passing kestrel with his air rifle and downed it.

"Oy! Gripper! Come 'ere!"

But, after seeing another dog, Gripper Butt was about as likely to return to his master's side as was the bird likely to return to life.

Once more, Mr. O'Durr seized a weapon, in this case the branch of a long-deceased elm tree, and waved it around his head as he advanced upon the aggressor. Gripper turned his attention from Filfy to the man who was today wearing a black singlet.

A scarlet mist descended as Gripper Butt charged. Once launched, the dog's extra poundage, courtesy of Grandma Butt, gave him a huge momentum, and indeed a force that Mr. O'Durr found irresistible. As he hesitated the flying dog hit him amidships, slamming him into the solid trunk of an English oak.

"Oof!"

Mr. O'Durr slowly slipped down the trunk into a sitting position, as Gripper Butt danced triumphantly above him and opened his jaws ready for the kill.

Filfy O'Durr had been skulking off, confident that his master would once more see off the aggressor, but when he heard Mr. O'Durr's expellation of breath he turned. His master was about to die; it was very clear. And here he was, Filfy O'Durr, son of Whizzbang the Finnegan of Blarney, about to run away.

Oh, no! Oh, no! Filfy turned, feeling once more a passion in his veins and a hatred in his heart and an immense primeval energy flooding his being. Forgetting his inglorious past in one wonderful moment of magnificent savagery, he leapt upon the slavering aggressor. As his master appeared through the trees, pursued by Mr. Singh and Sir Robert Pinchley himself, Gripper Butt was flying through the air and hitting his head with the sound of a perfectly timed cover-drive on an English willow tree.

"INNOCENT!" thundered the Gazette, which showed a picture of a playful Filfy O'Durr on its front page.
"We are delighted to announce that this dog is innocent. Mistakenly identified as a racially motivated pariah, Filfy O'Durr,(10) helped Race Relations Chief Mr. Amrit Singh (50) and local squire, Sir Robert Pinchley (64) to apprehend the real offender. Filfy's proud owner, local artisan Mr. George O'Durr (48) said 'I'm real proud of Filf, and I'm glad the nightmare's over.' "
As for the real racially motivated pooch, he is Gripper Butt (7) and we can reveal for the first time that his low-life owner is local fascist, Darren Butt (36), whose racist meetings at the Memorial Hall have now been closed down by Police Chief Ray Allwight and his team. Also detained for questioning is Mrs. Butt (96) of West Ham. Well done, our wonderful Police!"

It was a day or two later that Bert Cheeseman and Elspeth Parker were enjoying a quiet coffee at the Patel Motel, just off the Newtown Expressway.
Despite the double glazing, you could still pick up the constant deep hum of traffic, but otherwise only the whisper of the air conditioning broke the silence. At the light wood reception desk, a sign told guests they could pay using any one of seven international credit and debit cards, and another sign said "Ici, on parle Francais."
They were sitting on a black leather banquette under a giant rubber plant that had been shedding dry brown leaves on the parquet floor.
"There you go" said the waitress, setting a tray before them on the low teak table. It carried a stainless steel sugar bowl with sachets of sugar, a stainless steel milk jug, and two Chinese cups and saucers.    The small stainless steel teapot had a handle that was red hot and a spout that dribbled

Elspeth Parker poured two cups of very pale tea and

turned to her companion.

"This place means a lot to you, doesn't it, Bert?"

"Huh? Yes, it does. It does, Elspeth."

"Is it the place? Or the people?"

Bert Cheeseman twanged his braces, and looked out of the window, where the proprietor was pruning a rose. Mrs. Patel looked in at him, and gave him a flashing smile. Somewhere, Elgar was being played on a sitar.

"It's the people. It's the family. And friends. And tolerance."

"Yes. Tolerance. Bert."

Elspeth Parker rubbed away with a paper napkin at the tea-stain on her lavender coat, and then wiped the underside of the teapot.

"And caring about…about people. And - it's about having a place of your own in the world, really. We're so lucky here, don't you think?"

He ran his hand through his hair.

Elspeth Parker smiled, and touched Bert gently on the knee. She picked up the bill. £7.50 seemed a bit excessive, but she smiled.

"Yes, Bert" she said. "We're very lucky."

# CHAPTER THIRTEEN
## September

## SNAPDRAGONS

Charles Noble loved snapdragons. They surrounded his perfect front lawn in bright profusion. Sometimes of a summer's night he'd go out and sniff their sweet perfume. And then, checking that no-one was watching, he'd get down on one knee and press with finger and thumb on the jaws and smile happily as the mouth opened. His father had grown snapdragons, and it had been his father who had shown him the trick of opening their jaws. Walter Noble had not been a gregarious man, but he had always seemed happy in the garden, or when he was digging on an archaeological site for remains from past eras. It was only at these times, it seemed to Charles, that his father had spoken to him.

"It was God that made these flowers, Charlie. Never forget that, lad."

Or: "Look at this iron-age arrowhead. These men could certainly teach us a bit about engineering."

For Mr. Noble, snapdragons symbolised an age of innocence and warm security.

Jennifer Noble had dropped off on the G-Plan settee after watching an episode of "St. Wilfred's" in which the Reverend Jim Manley had been facing a rabid bloodhound in the belltower. Her snores were drowning out the 11 o'clock news which was being read by a member of the new Primident's staff.

"His Grace the Primident will today be opening the new Grimethorpe School of Political Correctness, previously known as the Womens' Institute, and will be giving a groundbreaking speech on the joys of non-Christian faiths, assisted by the Archbishop of Canterbury."

The snores continued. Mr. Noble let himself out of the front door, and was immediately assailed by the even louder sound of heavy metal music from next door. They seemed to be having a party. Against the deep electric throb of a base guitar, someone was singing "Give It to Me Baby Tonight."

Charles Noble caught the summery scent of his snapdragons as he fell to one knee and started pressing the corners of their soft velvety jaws. But what was this? A number of the heads had been removed and were now scattered on the soil, and even on the edge of the lawn. In the moonlight he scooped up handfuls of blossoms, as someone with a very gravelly voice started singing "You Get Me All Excited When You Move Those Hips of Yours."

He looked up at next door's front window as the sound of a dog howling could clearly be heard above the music "Confounded polluters!" he breathed as he looked down once more and saw that some of his plants had actually been uprooted, and were laying limp and sad on the dark earth. He took in a deep breath, sniffing the soft night air for the old reassuringly familiar snapdragon perfume, and caught the unmistakeably nauseating odour of fresh doggie poo. For a moment he thought of knocking on the O'Durrs' front door, but thinking better of it, he slipped back into his own house. His wife was still snoring. After a warming mug of Maltokup, he went upstairs to bed.

It was 2 a.m. when he awoke to the reverberation of a base guitar that found a deep echo in his breastbone. He thought for a moment that it was a heart attack. He knocked over the half-empty mug of cold Maltokup as he tried to switch on the bedside light and look at his watch. "London Calling" was crashing through the party wall, as he realised he had lost an earplug somewhere in the bed. As he threw off the bedclothes to find it, a little rubber plug flew through the air straight into the wastebasket.

Mr. Noble was no coward. He donned his white towelling robe over his plaid Sparks and Mincers pyjamas, donned his Donald Duck slippers, and stepped purposefully downstairs and strode with a long loping pace to the neighbours' front door. After numerous bell-ringings and hammerings on the door, it was opened by a young man wearing a tee shirt bearing the legend "I am Shit" and what appeared to be a miniature motor cycle dangling from his nose.

"Will you kindly turn down that music?!"

The young man's reddened eyeballs rolled up into his head, and the door was slammed in the visitor's face. Mr. Noble said "Stay calm, Noble" under his breath, and hammered on the door once more. This time the door was opened suddenly and very wide by Mr. O'Durr who was wearing a lambskin thong with the message "You're Only Young Once" and a leopardskin brassiere. His right fist shot out, and landed, hard, on his neighbour's nose. Mr. Noble gasped "Ouch!" and fell to the ground, where Filfy O'Durr attended him. Before Charles Noble could gather his wits, the old dog had removed one of his Donald Duck Slippers, and had disappeared with it in the direction of the shrubbery.

"What's going on out here?"

The blond head of Dolly O'Durr appeared at the door, and she looked down at the recumbent neighbour in horror. She was wearing an off-the-shoulder dress in scarlet satin.

"What you done now, George?" she screeched, and bent down to help lift the confused Charles Noble, whose nose was bleeding, to his feet.

"You better come in."

These were the first friendly words Mrs. O'Durr had ever addressed to her neighbour, and Charles Noble found his eyes watering, and not just from the pain in his nose. He found there was also a pain in his heart.

Dolly O'Durr took the visitor into her little kitchen after shouting into the living room.

"Turn that bleeding music down, George! Now!!"

She took some off-white cotton wool from a cupboard and put it under the tap and then insisted that Mr. Noble sit back while she bathed his nose. Her visitor noticed a foreign smell in the air, a mixture of old burgers and dog, that totally overcame the "Wickedness" perfume by Jacques Spotti that Mrs. O'Durr had recently applied. As the sound in the next room increased once more, his hostess suddenly stopped work on Mr. Noble's nose,

169

and clip-clopped in her four-inch heels to the living room door. She wrenched it open.

"Let's have a little peace, George, shall we?! Remember what I told you! Turn that bleeding music off!"

Mr. Noble was amazed how quickly silence prevailed, and wondered what hold Mrs. O'Durr had over her brutish husband.

"Now then. Let's get you sorted out."

Dolly O'Durr returned to her nursing, and Mr. Noble managed a little smile for the first time that night.

"That's better. Thank-you."

"You hold still. You've had a nasty blow."

"Yes."

The young man in the "I am Shit" tee shirt appeared through the kitchen door.

"Out!"

He turned tail.

"It's Noble isn't it? Mr. Noble? But I don't know your first name."

"Charles."

"I'm Dolly. Do you like decent music?"

"Well, yes. Yes I do."

Suddenly Charles Noble felt the warm feminine presence desert him as Dolly O'Durr moved once more to the door and shouted into the living room.

"About time you lot went home. Come on! Shove off! Come on George! Sort them out will you!? Or I'll be asking why not!"

Out of the corner of his eye, Mr. Noble saw the young man with the "I am Shit" tee shirt file out with a group of other youthful undesirables, not one of them wearing a suit. They were followed by a tall lady in a threadbare pencil-line coat clutching a small black dog and hiccupping, and a big man with bushy eyebrows wearing a reproduction Arsenal Football shirt who seemed to have difficulty in walking.

After the door had closed on the last of the revellers, George O'Durr leaned on the kitchen door handle and waving a half empty glass in the air, took a long look at the pale figure in the chair.

"What happened to him?"

"Piss off to bed, you old bugger! You're in the box room tonight."

"What, Doll?"

"You're lucky you ain't in a police cell. Now piss off!"

Dolly O'Durr put the kettle on.

"Want a cuppa?"

"I don't suppose you have any Lapsang Souchong."

"No, I don't. I got Fesco's Cheapo. Will that do for you, your lordship?"

"That'll do very nicely, thank-you."

There was a 'click' somewhere behind Mr. Noble's head, and the sound of an orchestra filled the small room. Mr. Noble closed his eyes and let the music play over him. As he listened, something in the music spoke to him of security and of peace and home and of....of … of his mother. Mavis Noble had disappeared from his life when he was very young.

The sound of a clarinet rose above that of the orchestra. It was a sound of joy. Like a brightly painted butterfly it rose and fell and settled and set off again. The strings joined in the background like a sweet celestial choir, as the beautiful creature flapped her way from blossom to blossom. Then in a gradual diminuendo, ever so quietly it left the scene, just like his mother had done all those years ago. The orchestra was left without its inspiration, and keened sweetly for what might have been, as one by one, the instruments ceased to sound and the room was left in silence.

"You drinking your tea? It'll go cold."

She noticed the single tear that had traced a path down Mr. Noble's cheek.

"Oh yes. Of course."

Mr. Noble picked up the Pluto mug from the tabletop next to him. The tea was now lukewarm.

"What was that piece called?" Charles Noble heard his own voice crack, and cleared his throat noisily. His nose was full of cotton wool.

Dolly O'Durr read from the old tape.

"'Snapdragons' Dunno who its by. It don't say on here."

"Oh. I've never heard it before"

Charles Noble blinked.

"Thank-you, Dolly."

# CHAPTER FOURTEEN
## October

## THE GURU

Mr. Noble was very excited, and couldn't concentrate on his work at all. Someone had asked for the profit figures for 2013, and he had given them the binding costs for 2012. Mr. Prood, the Managing Director, had been none too pleased and had actually phoned Mr. Noble on the old intercom system to tell him to "pull his trousers up". Mr. Noble realised that the old boy had meant "socks," but he was certainly not going to contradict him.

Fagg's Cafe was aptly named, and always seemed to be full of heavy smokers with racking coughs, but it was where Mr. Noble repaired on bad days. There was something comforting about the smell of cigarettes, greasy breakfasts, and breaking the punitive new anti-smoking laws. And Sid Pratt was a jolly soul.

Mr. Noble took a seat near the window to avoid breathing too much smoke, but a big man in vest and tattoos came over and slammed it shut. Mr. Noble took the magazine from his real leather briefcase just as he was joined at the table by an unshaven man in a leather jacket, with a cheroot clenched in his teeth. The man looked across the table at Mr. Noble, who was stirring his cup of decaffeinated instant coffee with a plastic spoon. He was never allowed sugar at home, and this was a special treat.

"All-right?" said the man, looking at the wall.

"All right?" replied Mr. Noble, looking down at the magazine.

"Karuna Lunar" had been named after a celebrated Californian lifestyle guru who had recently retired from public life after announcing that she was an alcoholic, but the magazine had now been taken over by Donna and Chip Courtenay whom Mr. Noble had met only very recently. It had been at a 'spiritual networking day' at the Old Town Hall, when Mr. Noble had been having a candle stuck in his ear by a fat lady wearing a Tibetan duvet cover that he had seen the willowy Donna wearing a white dress in the classic Greek style ministering graciously to an elderly gentleman under a notice proclaiming "Spiritual Healing Special Offer."

Mrs. Noble wasn't at all interested in his "alternative" activities, and was far away, so Mr. Noble had felt quite relaxed in going over as soon as the previous client had risen unsteadily from the couch, and offering himself for treatment. It had been wonderful. Donna's presence so close to him, and Donna's heady and liberally applied perfume had sent Mr. Noble to a place of peace which he didn't wish to leave. It had only been when Donna had shouted "Wake up! That's your lot!" into his recently candled ear that he returned to consciousness and allowed someone else from the worried looking and fast-diminishing queue to take his place.

Later that day, he had accompanied Donna and Chip to the Naff Tikka Restaurant and Takeaway in the Precinct, and had somehow agreed, in his professional capacity, to look over their books for them, and to host a day at his home in Hillside Close for the globetrotting guru, Dwane Atlantis. This was the cause of his excitement. Dwane was, by all accounts, a quite extraordinary man with unique psychic powers, and a special mission to help humanity climb up out of the mess it had made of the world through its selfishness and greed. Although Mr. Atlantis normally charged £250 for his one-day "You Can Have It All" workshop, Mr. Noble, as official host, would pay a special price of £150 only, a cost that would decrease by £10 for each participant he could sign up. He was, understandably, very keen to sign up a minimum of fifteen participants.

Mr. Noble opened the magazine. And there it was. Mr. Atlantis was certainly no shrinking violet. The top half of page three was an "art" photo of a naked man, well no, not quite naked. Mr. Noble adjusted his reading glasses, and, peering more closely at Mr. Atlantis's genital area, he realised that the subject was wearing a golden thong. The man in the leather jacket cleared his throat ostentatiously and moved to another table, mumbling under his breath. Mr. Noble didn't notice. He was looking at the god-like male figure playing a flute and sitting on a rock at the edge of the ocean. Golden rays from the setting sun illuminated the man, reflecting in the limpid blue eyes that matched precisely the shade of the docile sea. His thick, curly yellow hair, too, was lit up by the sun's rays and stood out from his head like a halo. Underneath the photograph was the title of the article: "The Pied Piper of Detroit."

Dwane Atlantis had apparently been born in Detroit in the thirties, the son of an unemployed car worker and a Norwegian mother he'd never known. The thirties?! Mr. Noble took another look at the flautist in the picture. No! That was surely the body of a much younger man. Mr. Noble returned to the article. At a very young age, Dwane Atlantis, then called Randy Limbowski, had seen a spaceship passing his window, and heard a voice.

"You came from this spaceship, Randy, and you are to give my message to the world. You remember Atlantis, Randy, so I want you to call yourself Dwane Atlantis, and keep listening out for my messages."

The boy had not told anyone, even his father, until, after a series of out-of-body experiences, the voice had returned to tell him he had special healing powers and he must use them to heal the planet and its occupants. He was told to leave his father, who had a very dark consciousness, change his name immediately to Dwane Atlantis, and start to give healing workshops at $50 a time.

Mr. Noble looked again at the inspirational picture. Mr. Atlantis really did look very youthful, and very man-shaped. He leaned forward and, pushing his reading glasses up to the top of his nose, examined the guru's physique more closely. A shaven-headed, younger man, with a ring in his ear had sat down opposite Mr. Noble, and now looked intently across at the illustration. Mr. Noble looked up, and the young man gave him a smile. Mr. Noble smiled back, and said "Good morning."

The young man lifted the mug of tea to his lips, and continued to smile at Mr. Noble with his warm brown eyes, which dropped to the photograph, and then, raised once more, looked quizzically into Mr. Noble's.

"Very nice," he said, still smiling. "Friend of yours?"

The young man licked his lips slowly and luxuriously and smiled once more. Suddenly, Mr. Noble felt a pressing desire to be somewhere else. Anywhere else. He shot up off his seat, completely forgetting his cold poached egg on toast, and his half-drunk mug of coffee, stuffed the magazine into his briefcase, and, avoiding his companion's enveloping gaze, strode on long legs to the door and stretched into the street.

Charles Noble timed his exit perfectly, as it turned out. Seconds after he left the café, it was raided by armed police from the newly-formed Anti-Smoking Action Squad.

Donna and Chip Courtenay came around for supper the next night, when Mrs. Noble had gone with her sister to see "St. Wilfred's - The Musical." Mr. Noble wasn't much of a cook, but he had prepared a vegetarian spaghetti Bolognese, and heated some Painsbury's garlic bread in the oven for his guests. An end-of-bin bottle of Painsbury's own label Bardolino proved difficult to open when Mr. Noble should have been stirring the Bolognese, but eventually the hard plastic plug detached itself from the neck of the bottle as Mr. Noble's arm felt as if it had detached itself from his shoulder. Grimacing in pain, he took the open bottle and three small glasses through to the dining room and put them on the table.

By the time the door chimes sounded in the hall, Mr. Noble was trying to give himself a deep, healing right shoulder massage with his left hand, whilst striving to scrape the bolognese sauce off the bottom of the saucepan with a wooden spoon in his right. With no steadying downward pressure on the pan, the inevitable happened, and the saucepan shot across the top of the stove on to the floor, where it landed Bolognese-side down.

Donna and Chip were a little taken aback by the wild-eyed appearance of the figure who opened the front door, wearing amongst other things, a floral apron and a green bow tie.

"Oh, hello" it said, moving immediately away from them down the hallway.

"Come in. Make yourself comfortable in there."

The tall jerky figure that was disappearing into the kitchen indicated the dining room, and was gone.

A slightly strangled voice issued from the kitchen.

"Help yourselves to some wine"."

The Abba tape that had been playing stopped abruptly, and the machine switched off. The Courtenays helped themselves to some wine.

"Just a temporary hiccup," said the voice. Donna and Chip looked at each other, but didn't speak. They sat obediently on the high-backed chairs, and helped themselves to some more wine.

"Nice curtains" said Donna.

"Yes; they are" her partner replied.

"Are we early?"

"No", said Chip. Chip raised his voice.

"How are you, Charles?"

"Oh, fine. Fine. I won't be a minute. Everything under control" came the voice.

"Are you sure you're all right?" Donna called.

"Yes, never been better" came the reply. "Help yourselves to some wine."

Mr. Noble couldn't find the parmesan, and had some difficulty in serving the very long spaghetti strands out of the saucepan, where some had stuck, limpet-like, to the base, and others showed all too much alacrity in emerging on to the plates, in the company of scores of their peers, slithering down in a squirming stream to the kitchen floor. But by the time he'd finished, the platefuls of food looked faintly impressionistic, with their overhanging strands of pasta and trailing pools of lumpy red sauce.

"Mmmmm" went Chip Courtenay, now divested of his overcoat, and cheered by the savoury dish before him.

"Delicious!"

"Better try it first" said Mr. Noble, moving forward to accept the other man's belated hug, but then holding back awkwardly in the clinch. The smell of after-shave was overpowering.

Donna, whose coat had joined that of her partner in the hall, was wearing a white dress again, and stepped around the table to greet her host. Mr. Noble hugged her with a warmer, more natural feeling as the liberally perfumed Donna slipped trustingly into his arms, and received a big manly squeeze and a squashed dollop of Bolognese sauce from the front of Mr. Noble's apron on her spotless bosom.

"That was nice, Charles."

Mr. Noble felt embarrassed, and moving to his chair at the end of the table, sat down and gestured for his guests to follow suit.

"I'm sorry we didn't bring any wine. But we didn't know if you drank alcohol."

"Oh, that's quite all right" replied Mr. Noble, smiling and reaching for the bottle of Bardolino.

"I don't drink much, you know. Like to keep myself fit. Just a small glass for me."

But Mr. Noble didn't even get a small glass. The bottle was quite empty.

Donna and Chip ate their Bolognese slowly. Some of the long pieces of spaghetti were stuck together, hard and tough, and the Bolognese sauce had an oddly disinfected nuance of flavour, reminiscent of Painsbury's All-Purpose Cleaner. ("Three for the price of two until the end of the month"). Donna and Chip kept picking up the empty bottle of Bardolino out of sheer force of habit but the glasses remained empty. Mr. Noble did not maintain a wine cellar. In fact Mr. Noble never normally kept wine on the premises. Or any alcohol, come to that.

There had been an exception to this rule, however, the previous week, when Mr. Noble had asked Jennifer if she would help him host the Dwane Atlantis day. He had bought her half a bottle of Cherry Brandy before popping the question, and it had done the trick.

It was only the second time in their ten years of partnership that her husband had offered her this old favourite. The first had been on their wedding night in Worthing, and it had sent her straight off to sleep. But this was nevertheless a romantic gesture, and knowing how important his place in the local spiritual hierarchy was to Mr. Noble, she had agreed to entertain up to twenty people, including Mr. Atlantis and his co-focaliser, Ms. Flow, on the following Saturday. Jennifer wouldn't take part in the proceedings, of course, but would hover helpfully in the kitchen, serving herb teas, and a healthy lunchtime salad to participants at the appropriate times.

Chip moved some congealed spaghetti pieces to the corner of his plate.

"And how does Mrs. Noble feel about the day?"

Mr. Noble looked down at the little pile of food.

"Oh. She's looking forward to it. Very much."

Donna was examining a small black object on a tine of her fork.

"Shame we couldn't meet her beforehand" she observed, putting down her spoon and fork on the heap of spaghetti on her plate with a sense of finality. She felt she could do with a drink.

"We brought the DVD."

"The DVD?" Mr. Noble didn't remember anything about a DVD.

"Yes, Charles. Can I help you set up the machine?" Donna moved round the back of Mr. Noble's chair, and he inhaled deeply of the floral perfume that followed her.

"Oh-er. Yes, of course. I'll just rinse these dishes."

Donna was feeling irritable. It was a long time since she had eaten such an awful meal.

"No. That can wait, Charles. We want you to see Dwane right now."

But Mr. Noble was already in the kitchen. He couldn't bear washing-up hanging around. And Donna wasn't as charming as her perfume. Donna removed a DVD of "My Fair Lady" from the machine, and held it up for Chip to see. His nostrils quivered and his mouth turned down hard at the corners. Mr. Noble was cleaning the plates fastidiously in the kitchen. He held them up this way and that in the light. He added a little more washing-up liquid to the bowl. He was happy for the first time that evening. He started to sing "Seventy-six

Trombones" in a high reedy voice.

Charles Noble turned off the standard lamp in the corner as a picture of Dwane Atlantis appeared on the screen. He was speaking into a golden mobile phone and looking the viewer in the eye.
"Hello; Pied Piper calling."
Mr. Noble became aware of Donna and Chip breathing very deeply and in unison as the camera panned back to show that Dwane was in the wilderness, high up on a rocky plateau, and was wearing a white robe. Mr. Atlantis put away the mobile into a fold at the waist of his robe. An extraordinarily deep voice-over voice, which sounded somehow familiar, asked:
"Is this man human? Or (Pause) something else?"
This last phrase was uttered with such penetrating pregnancy that Mr. Noble suddenly felt very uncomfortable. He looked across at the Courtenays, but they were clearly elsewhere, their eyes shining and their pupils wide. Mr. Noble didn't like the way things were going, and tried to think of something really prosaic to break the spell that was being woven in his dining room. His new dentures came swiftly to mind.
The deep voice continued to transfix Donna and Chip, whilst Mr. Noble tried to remember exactly what Mr. Prood had said to him on Thursday in the lift. Whatever it was, it had left him with a feeling of unease, and he now found himself looking down at an earwig crossing the carpet, and the combination of these unorgasmic visions succeeded in closing him down to the magnetic voices and images issuing from his 20" Kikabuchi. Donna Courtenay looked across at Mr. Noble for a moment, and noting his wandering attention, gave a brutal hiss to bring him back. Mr. Noble looked across at her.
"Watch!" she breathed, as the white-robed figure started to make unfamiliar gestures and signs in the direction of the sun, and then removed his white robe, and hung it on a nearby cactus.

The photography was accomplished. As the camera moved around the golden muscled figure in the golden thong, and the golden rays of the sun reflected mellowly from the shining body, Mr. Noble realised that Dwane Atlantis was wearing a thick coating of oil. Suddenly Dwane raised his arms in the air and started to chant. There were no recognisable words, indeed no consonants in the strange deep sounds that filled the room. One strident vowel sound followed another. It reminded Mr. Noble of Mr.Mac.Tavish, the French master at Pinchley Grammar, who had forced his class to mouth French vowel sounds into a mirror. "Aaaaaaah!" "Ayeeeeeee!" "Eeeeeeeee!" "O-o-o-o-o-o-o!" "Yeeeeeeeeew!" Only Mr. Mac.Tavish had been fully clothed at the time, and had not been gesturing wildly at the sky. Suddenly a bird appeared from nowhere, and perched on Dwane Atlantis's shoulder, and Dwane, smiling, reached up and tenderly brought the creature down. The voice-over asked "Could this man be a re-incarnation of our beloved St. Francis of Assisi?"

Then a well-groomed goat appeared suddenly on screen. Mr. Noble thought it appeared so suddenly, indeed, that it could have been pushed. Dwane smiled again and fondled the goat's head. The bird jumped up on top of Dwane's head and started frenziedly pecking at something in his halo of curly golden hair. Mr. Noble thought for a moment that the halo seemed to move. The scene changed abruptly.

It was much, much later that evening that Donna and Chip Courtenay took their leave of an exhausted Mr. Noble, who sat down heavily in the Parker Knoll wing chair that had belonged to his mother, and started biting his nails. It was all arranged. Dwane Atlantis and Gaia Flow would be arriving at 8am on Saturday from the Pinchley Biltong for an "intimate focalisers' meditation" which would include Donna and Chip, and Charles. And Jennifer. Mr. Noble had promised his wife that she wouldn't have to participate in the day's events, except on the catering front, but Donna had been very persuasive. Mr. Noble was trying to think of a way to broach the matter with his wife, when he heard her key in the door.

Jennifer Noble had enjoyed her evening out at "St. Wilfred's-The Musical," and was humming the catchy chorus, "We're All Going to St. Wilfred's" as she entered the room.

She was not completely surprised to find her husband fast asleep in the chair.  He had been finding work a bit of a challenge recently.  Mrs. Noble quietly fetched the brush and pan, and started to brush up the little pieces of fingernail that littered her carpet.  Then, wrinkling her nostrils, she went to the oven and removed the garlic bread, blackened and untouched, and dropped it in the plastic wastebin, which seemed to be full of spaghetti.

Chip Courtenay stamped on the brakes.  But he still struck the creature a glancing blow as he brought his Ford Probe to a screeching halt.

"It's a thirty limit round here" said his partner.  Chip flung open his door, and went round to the front of the car, dreading what he might find. But it wasn't as bad as he had thought.  A shaggy dog was getting to its feet with a small whine, and shaking itself.

"Hey boy! I'm sorry. I didn't see you."

Filfy O'Durr was feeling confused, but the man's sympathetic tone was unmistakeable.  The man was holding out his hand in friendship, so putting on a good show of feeling much worse than he felt, Filfy staggered across to the man and allowed himself to be caressed.  He loved being stroked, even by someone who smelled so penetratingly of  "Macho Miasma" after-shave.  Donna shouted from the car.

"Come on, Chip!  He's all right!  It's just a dog, for God's sake!  We've got to get some sleep."

But Chip was enjoying his meeting, and took Filfy round to the passenger door to meet her.  It was unfortunate that as Filfy came alongside, he received his second heavy blow of the evening as an angry Donna threw open the door to round on her partner.  As Filfy was hurled backwards into a low brick wall, he caught the stench of the woman's perfume and the smell of anger.  Filfy's heckles rose as he regained his feet.  He wouldn't forget "Abandoned" in a hurry.  Filfy growled and showed his teeth.  Donna didn't jump out of the car as had been her intention, but quickly slammed the door, and wound down the window.

"Chip!  Get in here!" she screeched.  Chip got in, and drove silently at just thirty miles per hour  to the hotel.

Mr. Noble was not known in Hillside Close for his sociability, so it came as quite a surprise to Mrs. O'Durr, and Mr. Bultitude, and Jim Drane, and the Grinders, and a number of other local residents, to find themselves telephoned by their neighbour in a very hail-fellow-well-met manner, and agreeing to welcome him into their homes so he could introduce them to Dwane Atlantis and his works by means of a video called "The Pied Piper of Detroit".

Mr. Noble hadn't told his wife that he needed to fill at least fifteen places, and that, if he didn't, their holiday in Frinton could be at risk. Mavis Noble was impressed with the enthusiasm that took her husband out of the house on so many nights when they would normally have been sitting watching "St. Wilfred's", or "Celebrity Underpants", or "The End of the World" together.

She made him a hot drink as soon as he got home each night, full of enthusiasm and tales of new participants signing up, and she made a real effort to sound excited about the day she dreaded so.  The only night she felt she let her husband down in his new endeavour was when he arrived home delighted that Randy Breed and Jenda Steamwell had signed up, whilst Jennifer was watching a highly publicised episode of "St. Wilfred's".  She was hanging on to Jim Manley's every word as he confronted a serial-killer in the bell tower, and she showed all too plainly that this took precedence over news of the neighbours or Mr. Atlantis.   Had she seen the video or met Donna or Chip, she might have taken a different view.

Dr. Nipp had signed up for the day.  Now retired from his private practice in Charmers Green, he liked to keep abreast of healing in all its forms, and had been experiencing depressive moments since losing his wife the previous year. He had found solace in D.I.Y., and his detached bungalow in Bishops Mead was replete with decking, loft extension, and a half-finished library, whilst his garage had come to resemble a Council Maintenance Depot.  Benches overflowed with electric drills and sanders, paintbrushes, metal brackets, and hammers, mallets, and handtools of all kinds. Walls were plastered with garden forks and hoes, and wheelbarrows, and extension leads, and green plastic netting, and the space under the benches filled with tins of ship's varnish, rubbing compound, creosote, rust remover, paints in all the colours of the rainbow, and at least four gallons of Painsbury's "Everyday" white spirit. It was a treasure-house that Filfy O'Durr loved to explore. Sniffing gloss paint and white spirit took him right out of his brain to a place where all humans were kind and considerate, and dogs, even scruffy mongrels, were constantly loved to bits.

On the morning of the "You Can Have It All" workshop, of which of course, he was in total ignorance, Filfy trotted around to Doctor Nipp's house, and was soon nuzzling a half–empty tin of white gloss paint and sniffing ardently of the partially dried paint-spills down the side of the tin.
Mrs. O'Durr had been behaving very strangely the night before, wandering around the house in a white dress and singing gospel songs in a raucous contralto, causing Filfy and, indeed, Mr. O'Durr to become concerned that she might be breaking down altogether. So Filfy felt he needed his fix, as the paint tin rolled off the end of the shelf and crashed to the floor. The lid burst open and dollops of brilliant white paint landed on the floor, the stepladders, the lawnmower, and on Dr. Nipp's shiny black Wurstwagen Volleyball.
Swish! Swish! went Filfy's inspired tail as he left the garage at a silent trot. Dr. Nipp's car was left with a futuristic speed stripe down the nearside, much of it resembling the silhouette of the Andes around Machu Picchu. Filfy was left with a distinctive white tip to his tail.

Dr. Nipp liked Mr. Noble and had found himself wishing that more of his patients would look after their bodies as he did. Dr. Nipp's pension didn't look as generous as it had when he had hung up his stethoscope, so the title of the day's workshop, "You Can Have it All" was a real attraction. As for "The Pied Piper of Detroit," well, he would be judged on his merits measured against the absolutes of both British orthodox medicine and the clear canons of the Church of England. He had mentioned the day to Cyril Downmouth to test his reaction, really, and it had been as the doctor suspected. The Reverend Downmouth's lips went very thin when he heard about the claims of Dwane Atlantis, and disappeared altogether when he heard the price of admission.

Jim Drane (65), who was very constipated, knew Mr. Noble from the occasional "All right?" they exchanged on the Pinchley Priory Bowling Green, and having just resigned from the Pinchley Ramblers after a falling out with the rambling focaliser, Cynthia Mee-Boss, was at a loose end on Saturday. In fact, he had been at a loose end most Saturdays since his wife had left him for a rodeo rider from Hard Bend, Arkansas. And, whilst Randy Breed and Jenda Steamwell certainly seemed to relate well to the "Pied Piper" video, their motivation in accepting Mr. Noble's invitation was entirely selfish. Their neighbours were all potential members of the Randy Breed Fan Club. It was definitely worth a few bucks to attend such a familiar sort of occasion although Jenda was to turn up late in the hope that she wouldn't be asked the full price by Mr. Noble. In the event, and in the clearest of terms, she was.

The Bultitudes arrived in designer clothing, and parked their Jaguar 'Z' Type at the front of the house. They had travelled from number 17, and they were both wearing white shoes. Mr. and Mrs. Bultitude were true networkers. They belonged to the Pinchley Historical Society, the Pinchley Light Operatic Society, the Pinchley Lawn Tennis Club, the Pinchley Dining Club, the Pinchley Wine Appreciation Society, and were founder members of the Pinchley Operagoers and the Pinchley Adult Video Club. But they were never too busy to extend their interests into new areas. Mr. Noble was especially pleased at the Bultitudes' acceptance, and his smile had been positively radiant when Mr. Bultitude had produced a silver clip of banknotes from his lightweight cream suit and paid in cash.

Both Major Margulies and Miss. Potts had been disappointed in love. The former had enjoyed a long but not very illustrious military career, during which he had for a while been aide-de-camp to the heroic General Fox-Phypps. That was before the general had blown himself up on the parade ground at Aldershot whilst demonstrating grenade-throwing techniques to some of his juniors after a very heavy session in the Officers' Mess. It had only been after this tragedy that the major had learned that the late general had been demonstrating some more successful and explosive techniques on Mrs. Margulies, whom he had promptly divorced.

Miss. Potts should have been Mrs. Armitage-Shanks since April, when Kevin Armitage-Shanks had arrived at the Church of the Dead Martyrs to announce "I do not love this woman." In a scene very reminiscent of a recent episode of "St. Wilfred's," he had thrown the ring to the floor, and marched, distraught, out of the west door. The black and white and grey and apricot congregation had been left dumbfounded. Miss Potts, pale as a lily, was left clutching a lucky sweep and a blood-red posy, and the Reverend Downmouth had been left wringing his bony hands.

So Mr. Noble put on his most compassionate voice when the young woman opened the door.
"Hello, Miss Potts," he said, stuttering slightly in his anxiety to sound appropriate, and actually enunciating "Miss. Spots."
"Oh, hello, Mr. Doughball." Miss. Potts sounded as if she had been crying. She beckoned her visitor through the bead curtain into the front room. Before long, Mr. Noble found himself perched on a beanbag, and sipping verbena and chamomile tea from a brass bowl. Miss. Potts seemed to have lit a campfire on top of the sideboard, and Mr. Noble found the smoke from the cedarwood and myrrh incense irritated his lungs. He coughed in great spasms as Miss. Potts told him how deeply hurt she was, and how she hoped Mr. Atlantis could help someone whose heart had been so cruelly broken.
Two spare looking Siamese cats had by this time colonised Mr. Noble's bony lap. Mr. Noble tried to move them, but they clung on to his green corduroys. And they had very sharp claws.

The golden figure of Dwane Atlantis filled the screen.  Mr. Noble started to breathe deeply, and suffered another coughing fit.  As his thin body shook, Karuna and Siddartha clung on for dear life, and he spilled verbena and chamomile on the coconut matting.  He looked guiltily across at Miss. Potts. But Miss. Potts was elsewhere.  Her pupils were dilated and she was breathing very deeply.  Her eyes did not leave the screen as Mr. Atlantis started waving his arms in the air.  The Pied Piper of Detroit clearly had a new convert.

Whilst Mr. Noble was choking in Miss. Potts's front room, Dwane Atlantis and Gaia Flow were themselves preparing for the weekend.  In his role as the "resurrected" St. Francis of Assisi, it was important that Dwane Atlantis should have the right animals to help him demonstrate the special rapport he had with all dumb creatures, and so it was entirely natural that he should today be visiting the premises of Brighter Beasts ("Fully Trained Animals for Stage and Screen") in West Wilton.  After interviewing a number of highly trained animals, Dwane decided first upon a donkey called Delvin, who responded promptly to at least six whispered commands and who seemed to take a great liking to the visitors.  As a back-up, Wayne chose a big, black, friendly mongrel with shining eyes and, it was claimed, an IQ of one hundred and sixty.  Murphy had an unusual white tip to his electric tail.

The thin electronic tones of "All Things Bright and Beautiful" made the dog jump, as Dwane Atlantis answered his mobile.
"Pied Piper speaking.  How are you today, brother?"
Gaia Flow dug him painfully in the ribs, and pointed archly at her dainty heart-shaped watch.  After a moment, Dwane's voice changed to that of an answering machine.
"Mr. Atlantis is away on a healing mission.  Please call back next week.  Bless you."
He addressed himself once more to the dog.
"Well, boy; it's good to know you.  Now, before we go, let's try a trick or two, shall we?"

187

Dwane Atlantis, Gaia Flow, and Charles and Jennifer Noble joined hands in the middle of the front room. Dwane was wearing a simple white robe and looking very tanned. Gaia was wearing a simple classic white dress that emphasised the rich golden brown of her skin. Mr. Noble was wearing a pair of grey flannels from Burton's, with a beige Aertex shirt which made his skin look even paler than usual, and Mrs. Noble was wearing brown slacks, a green top from Big and Classy, and a very worried expression. Jennifer Noble had joined the circle next to her husband, but Gaia had insisted that they should not stand together, because it would "disrupt the energies", so Jennifer was now standing between the two visitors. Charles looked encouragingly across the circle at his wife, who dropped her eyes to his feet and wondered why he had worn those awful sandals when he had a nice new pair of loafers. "All Things Bright and Beautiful" filled the room. Dwane Atlantis produced his mobile from under his robe, and said "Pied Piper" in a honeyed tone. Gaia Flow made a gesture of exasperation. Dwane caught it, and immediately added "Mr. Atlantis is abroad. Please call back on Monday. Bless you".

Suddenly, Gaia Flow was speaking.

"Oh, Great One, who has called us here today, we greet you."

"We greet you."

Dwane Atlantis echoed the welcome. "And we greet in joy our friends Charles and er..."

"Jennifer" said Mr. Noble.

"Jennifer" repeated Gaia Flow.

"Dear Jennifer" said Dwane Atlantis.

"Now we ask that your energy and your power may be with Dwane today."

Dwane Atlantis said "Amen."

"And in this regard we ask you to help Charles and er ..."

"Jennifer" said Mr. Noble.

"Jennifer" said Gaia Flow.

"Dear Jennifer" breathed Dwane.

"And to energise Dwane so that he may be a true channel of our beloved St. Francis of Assisi today. Or any other holy brother who may care to speak through him."

Dwane Atlantis said "Amen."

Charles Noble mouthed "Amen", but no sound came.  His wife remained silent.


Gaia Flow grasped Mavis Noble's hand so tightly she wanted to cry out, and Mr. Noble was certainly taken aback by the power of the grip.  He was also taken aback by the strange sound that started to arise from Gaia's throat.  As the deep, primal, sexy sound rose to a crescendo, he felt his hands being raised by his neighbours.  He stole a glance at his wife opposite, and registered her tight-shut eyes and pinched mouth, as her arms, too, were raised aloft.  There was a tearing sound from under the arm of the Big and Classy top.  Gaia Flow didn't seem to notice.

"Aaaaaaaarghhhh!"  "Aaaaaaaaaaaarghhh!"

Dwane joined in with his mellow baritone. "Maaaaaaaaaaaaaaaaaaaarghh!"  "Baaaaaaaaaaaaaaaaaaaaaaaargh!"

Mr. Noble felt a squeeze of his hand, and realised that he too was supposed to be sounding.

"Aaaaaarghhh!"

The note was uncertain and constrained.

"Aaaaaarghhhh!  Ahem!"

Mr. Noble started coughing.  The door chimes sounded in the hall.

"That can wait" said Gaia Flow, with finality.

"Aaaaaaaaaaaaaarghhh!"

It was some five minutes later that Donna and Chip Courtenay were admitted by an apologetic Mr. Noble.  Donna was wearing the same white dress as Gaia Flow and that familiar perfume, and for a moment Mr. Noble felt a strange giddiness as he embraced her.  He gave a much meaner, much narrower hug to Chip, who was looking very stressed, after running over a fox in Bishops Mead.  And a cat in Hillside Way.  Chip Courtenay seemed quite relieved to have missed the opening invocation, but his wife was not.  In fact she was quite upset.

"You should have let me drive. All that time nursing dead vermin!"

Donna was a good ten years younger than Gaia Flow, but on seeing the similarity of their attire and their long blond hair,

Jennifer Noble put her hands to her face.

"Oh! You look just like twins!"

In the event, Gaia Flow didn't look any more flattered than did Donna. In fact the comment seemed to be totally ignored.

Filfy was concerned. Mrs. O'Durr had risen before eight, for one thing. And had a shower. Filfy had stood nonplussed outside the bathroom door and listened to the water and to his mistress singing "When the Saints Go Marching In."

Instead of attacking his generous bowl of Brahmaputra Vindaloo Doggie Chunks before Mrs. O'Durr had even put it down, Filfy stood and looked quizzically at his mistress. The torn "Olympic Champion" top and the old trainer pants had been supplanted by a billowy, spotless white dress. Was that "Madame Sexy" he could smell? And what on earth had she done to her hair? Filfy slowly began to eat his breakfast, but with one eye firmly fixed on the transformed Mrs. O'Durr.

The latter, who had already taken an amazed Mr. O'Durr a cup of tea, opened the kitchen door. It was a lovely morning. She breathed in the sweet air.

"You're meeting someone very special today, Filf" she said.

Filfy O'Durr continued to lick his plate across the floor, without taking his eyes off his mistress. Mrs. O'Durr suddenly stopped humming "Amazing Grace."

"What's that bleeding donkey doing next door?!"

The ring-tone sounded on Mrs. O'Durr's mobile, and, as usual, she couldn't find it. She thought the sound was coming from the sitting room, where she seemed to recall making a confused phone-in on "Are You a Genius?" the previous night. But as she lifted cushions from chairs, and threw the inflatable settee across the room, the notes of "I Can't Get no Satisfaction" continued to goad her to a frenzy. Filfy heard exactly where the sound was coming from, and brought the phone from the kitchen wastebin, dropped it before his mistress, and smiled uncertainly. Mrs. O'Durr grabbed the phone and gave Filfy a muscular stroking.

"Oh, what a clever boy! What a genius. Good boy, Filf!"

Filfy glowed in the approbation. He loved to please his mistress more than anything else in the world. This was going to be a good day!

In the front room, the muster was all but complete. When Mr. Noble had told his pet-owning neighbours about Dwane Atlantis's special rapport with animals, Miss. Potts, Major Margulies, and Mrs. O'Durr had all asked to bring their pets, and Mr. Noble had agreed, much to the consternation of Mr. Atlantis and Ms. Flow. But income from the day would be reduced if these animals were barred, and "Brighter Beasts" had not come cheap. So it was agreed in the end that they should attend, subject to good behaviour. Major Margulies sat to attention on his cane-backed chair with Arabella bolt-upright underneath, whilst Jennifer Potts hung on to her chair with one hand and stroked the two  apprehensive looking Siamese cats that clung painfully to her lap. Dr. Nipp, wearing a dark suit and a long expression sat on the piano stool, looking straight ahead, next to a silent Mr. Bultitude who was wearing a Pinchley Bowling Club blazer and sipping green tea from a mug saying "Head Gardener."

In the corner by the tray of cheap biscuits stood the suntanned Randy Breed in a white suit which co-ordinated perfectly with the shade of Jenda Steamwell's low-cut dress. Dave and Sue Grinder, who were both wearing Sparks and Mincer's  slacks with sky-blue matching tops, and who had their hands in eachother's pockets, stood listening to Donna Courtenay as she described a recent adventure  at London Zoo, during which Dwane had saved her from a zealous armadillo. Sue looked across the room at the devout looking man in the simple white robe who was sitting in the lotus position, eyes downcast, meditating on a candle's flame, and trying to work out how much he would be making from the day. The chimes sounded once more, and Mavis Noble answered the door to her next door neighbour, whom she didn't recognise at all on account of the white dress and the alien coiffure. But, of course, she recognised Filfy O'Durr at once.

"Oh, Filfy. And er Mrs. O'Durr" she added, without warmth. Mrs. O'Durr was pulled into the front door by a powerful yank on the lead.

"Hello" she said, not looking at her neighbour. "In here, is it?" Mrs. Noble was feeling a little distracted, and was hoping that filthy dog from next door wouldn't make a mess on her white shagpile. Mrs. O'Durr and her dog went through into the living room, where Dwane Atlantis had completed his meditation, and where Dr. Nipp found his attention wandering. Tomorrow, weather permitting, he would paint the new library shelves with some thinned-down eucalyptus gloss.

"Oh, Great White Spirit," Dwane Atlantis intoned.

"Hear! Hear!" said Doctor Nipp.


Later in the day, when all present had enjoyed a healthy vegetarian lunch, carefully prepared and cleared by Mrs. Noble, who had then rapidly retreated into the kitchen and locked the door, Dwane Atlantis and Gaia Flow moved to the second stage of the day's proceedings with a question and answer session.

"If you would care to search your consciousness for a question", said Gaia Flow, "then I'm sure that Dwane, or St. Francis of Assisi, or perhaps some other risen one will be delighted to answer it."

There was a long silence. Miss. Potts made a small noise.

"Yes, my dear?" Dwane sounded very compassionate.

"What exactly do you mean when you say you can have it all, Dwane?"

Dwane Atlantis closed his eyes, and breathed deeply. Then with great gentleness, and only a hint of the harsh accent of Detroit, he replied.

"I mean exactly what I say, sister of mine.. It's all there for you, Miss. Chambers."

"Miss. Potts."

"Huh? Oh, yeah. Sure. You can have it all. You just have to learn how to receive. The universe is limitless. How could your gifts be limited? Are you so special that you receive less than anyone else?" Miss. Potts leaned forward.

"Well, yes. I think I do, actually. I was engaged to be

married..."

Filfy O'Durr stirred under the reproduction Victorian dining chair, and growled distantly. He was dreaming about his youth. Karuna and Siddartha arched their backs on Miss. Potts's lap. Miss. Potts grimaced before continuing.

"Kevin promised he'd marry me.." Her voice broke.

"You say I can have it all. But I can't have Kevin."

There was a long silence before the traumatised Chip Courtenay spoke for the first time.

"What would St. Francis say if you killed an animal? Accidentally. Well, two animals, actually."


Mrs. O'Durr looked at her large orange watch as Filfy emerged expectantly from beneath her chair.

"So what does 'you can have it all' mean, then?"

Dave Grinder was massaging his wife's neck, and wondering why he had come. Gaia Flow spoke.

"Dave; please cease the massage."

Dave Grinder ceased the massage, and said "Well?"

"It's all about self-worth, Dave" said Dwane Atlantis, throwing off his white robe with a flourish. The robe landed on Filfy O'Durr's head, and Filfy sneezed it off together with the accompanying smell of aftershave and sweet almond oil. Everyone else in the room looked at the almost naked guru, who was raising his arms above his head and making strange gestures as if he were drawing something down on himself. He broke out into a smile.

"I am not separate from you, Dave. I am so, so lovable. Look at me, Dave."

Dave Grinder caressed his wife's bottom and looked in some consternation at Dwane Atlantis. The golden thong had a strange, angular bulge in it. The man seemed to be deformed, but very well-endowed. Miss. Potts was looking at the same spot. So was Mr. Noble. And Dr. Nipp, and Sue Grinder, and Jim Drane and Mrs. O'Durr. The Bultitudes were looking out of the window where their new car was sparkling in the sun.

"Are you lovable, Dave?"

Sue Grinder put her hand up under her husband's blue Sparks

and Mincers' teeshirt and tickled him.
"Oh, he is, Dwane; he is."

Gaia Flow had left the room, and Mr. Noble's eyes played over the unclothed figure under the open window. If you screwed up your eyes, Dwane Atlantis's body looked quite youthful, but if you opened your eyes wide, the lack of tone in the skin was apparent. Mr. Noble opened his eyes wide as a donkey's head appeared at the window and pushed its way through his wife's lace curtains. Dwane Atlantis turned in gentle surprise.
"Well, looky here" he said. "Here's someone who needs no lessons in self-esteem. They seek me out. The animals."
"It's just like having St. Francis in the room" said Donna Courtenay, fixing her eyes, too, on the thong.
"Come on, old boy. Let's have a hug."
Had Dwane consulted those who knew Delvin better than he, it would have been made clear that if there was one thing Delvin didn't like, it was hugging. As the guru bent down and took the swarthy donkey's neck in his arms, Delvin made a noise like a Harley Davidson, and tried to bite Dwane's head off. He only succeeded in removing the curly blond wig. Suddenly the donkey's head was withdrawn from the aperture, and a bald Dwane Atlantis turned to face his flock.
The flock now included two spitting Siamese cats, a yapping Shih Tzu, and a big black mongrel trying to have his way with a standard lamp.
"Here y'are, boy."
Dwane Atlantis couldn't give up now, even though he could see his golden halo being tossed carelessly in the air in next door's garden by a playful Delvin. He would have to make a greater success of the St. Francis routine with the dog who seemed to have taken to him at their last meeting. The guru produced a bone from a "Fallmart" plastic carrier bag, and the dog, losing interest in the standard lamp that was by now in the horizontal plane, grabbed the offering, and bounded out of the door. Everyone looked at Mrs O'Durr.
"He's going to bury it" she said.
"Oh. Nice."

Dwane Atlantis was getting a sinking feeling. He put his hand up to his shining head and smoothed out the non-existent hair. Then he remembered the bird. He turned to Donna.

"Let free the dove of peace."

Donna reached down and opened the covered cage by her feet. Dr. Nipp looked at her purple toenails, wondering whether they were painted or if Donna was suffering from a serious fungal infection, and then at the snow-white dove that flew out into the room. Everyone took up defensive positions. Major Margulies spoke for the first time since his arrival.

"No need to panic. It's got its own radar."

The highly trained dove settled on Dwane Atlantis's shoulder, and allowed him to stroke her tenderly.

"This dove is a sign of peace" Dwane intoned.

Gaia Flow spoke in a very reverent voice. "Our beloved St. Francis of Assissi. See how the dove of peace responds to him."

The dove of peace responded by doing a copious poop on Dwane Atlantis's shoulder, just as Filfy O'Durr came in with a big smile on his face, and a tail that had lost control of itself. He had buried the bone in a spot that only he could find, and seen off the mongrel from Brighter Beasts who had been awaiting his call in the garden. He was feeling pretty darned pleased with himself. This was a good day! And look! There was a white bird given him to play with! Filfy jumped up and tried to grab the white dove of peace. Sadly, the dove of peace was so shocked by Filfy's innocent assault that it had a seizure, and fell off Duane Atlantis's shoulder to the floor, stone dead.

Dr. Nipp started to polish his spectacles.

"And what's your next trick, Mr. Atlantis?"

Chip Courtenay whispered "It wasn't me, Dwane."

Dwane Atlantis dropped to his knees, took the dead bird into his cupped hands, and appeared to breathe a prayer over it. He then passed the corpse summarily back to Donna, who dropped it back in the cage, and slammed the door.

Randy Breed said "Rest in peace."

Filfy O'Durr, who didn't really know the difference

between life and death bounded towards the cage, sniffing violently, and as he came abreast of Donna Courtenay, he stopped suddenly. The smell of "Abandoned" and fear and anger was overpowering, and very familiar. He turned to the woman and gave his most frightening growl.

"Grrrrrrrrrrrrr!"

Donna paled beneath the tan and rose to move away. Filfy lowered his head, and followed her. Everyone sat transfixed, except Dwane, who, in an amazingly deep and friendly tone called

"Whoa there, boy!" The asshole dog certainly hadn't behaved like this when they'd chosen it.

Filfy continued to advance, and Donna stepped back on the guru's ingrowing toenail.

"Ouch! You silly bitch!"

"Call him off , will you!" cried Donna. "He's a mad dog!"

"My dog's not mad!" Dolly O'Durr rose and pushed her face into Donna's.

"Who do you think you are, you cow?"

Mrs. O'Durr was starting to experience serious alcohol and nicotine withdrawal symptoms, and her white dress was quite crumpled. Filfy looked over his shoulder at his mistress. He liked her like that. All this soulful stuff didn't suit her at all. Oh! How he loved her! Truly he would do anything for her.

Mr. Noble looked despairingly around the room at his neighbours, and at his persuaders. The day had not gone to plan. His reputation would have taken a serious knock. He looked at his watch. Perhaps he should be subtly bringing matters to a close. He should never have invited that O'Durr woman. And he had definitely seen enough of Dwane Atlantis. Then a phone sounded..

The reedy electronic tones of "All Things Bright and Beautiful" alerted the room to  another incoming call for the "Pied Piper of Detroit."  But Dwane Atlantis was busy massaging his inflamed toe and was slow to answer. Filfy O'Durr saw yet another opportunity to delight his mistress. He leapt forward and his jaws closed on the phone through the golden garment.  He pulled hard and produced the device, still ringing, together with its sheltering thong.   Filfy's tail lost control of itself again as he dropped the still warm mobile into his mistress's lap.    Distractedly, Mrs. O'Durr removed the thong and lifted the phone to her ear.

"Hello.  No.  Mr. Atlantis is indisposed.  I mean exposed.  Call back later.  Bless you."

# CHAPTER FIFTEEN
## November

## GUY FAWKES NIGHT

The O'Durrs' radio was permanently tuned to "Radio Pinchley" these days, because Channelle's new boyfriend, Hassan, had landed a job on the station as a D.J.

Filfy O'Durr liked Hassan, who had recently brought him a "Radio Pinchley" mascot in the form of a floppy-eared rabbit. The rabbit had been torn to shreds and eaten within hours, but the friendship survived. Filfy, who was alone in the kitchen, pricked his ears and barked as Hassan's deep voice filled the room:

"And now, RP fans, just hold on to your hats. And please don't forget to keep your pets in tonight. We have a special bonfire night request for my friend, Filfy O'Durr. Are you listening, Filfy? Filfy?"

Filfy was indeed listening. His head was held on one side, and his ears were pricked like stilettos.

"Walkies, Filfy! Walkies!"

Filfy O'Durr pranced around the table to the cupboard where his lead was kept. He looked back, puzzled, in the direction of the voice, and barked once.

"No, Filfy. Not this time, old friend. But we've got a tune for you. This one's specially for you. 'How Much is that Doggie in the Window?'"

Filfy recognised the words and stood up, his tail swishing electrically. It was the song Mrs. O'Durr had sung to him for years after she had brought him back from the animal shelter on the happiest day of his life. A great smile overspread his features, and his heart moved to the music.

Next door, Mr. Noble was also listening to the radio, as he went through the fireworks assembled for his grandson's visit later in the day. He had spent far more than he had intended. The little box didn't seem to have much in it considering what he'd laid out. He hadn't planned on entertaining his son nor his grandson, Armalite, but he was fond of the little boy, and saw him so rarely that he had to take any opportunity that arose to spend time with him.

"I suppose it'll be worth it," he said under his breath, as he picked up a small Silver Fountain and carefully read the instructions.

"Cup of tea, dear?" Jennifer Noble's voice floated sweetly up the stairs.

"Lapsang Souchong, please dear."

Mr. Noble returned guiltily to the bathroom where he had been fixing tiles over the handbasin. He pressed hard, as a voice in his earpiece warned listeners to keep their pets indoors tonight and to avoid the deadly "Atomic Landmines" being imported from Korea. For a delightful moment Mr. Noble saw himself lighting the blue touchpaper on an "Atomic Landmine" that was taped to Filfy O'Durr's chest.

Mrs. Noble appeared at the door with a bone china cup and saucer and a dusty biscuit from the bottom of the tin. Her husband didn't hear her because he was concentrating hard on fixing a tile on an awkward corner above the sink. The tip of his tongue protruded from chapped lips as he listened apprehensively to a news item about a suspected terrorist cell in Bendon. Mrs. Noble bent down and raised her voice.

"Charles!!"

Charles Noble went rigid, and the tile fell with a crash into the basin. He took a deep breath, and with a supreme effort of will kept his voice more or less even. But there was still the suggestion of a hiss as he spoke.

"Please don't do that again dear."

Down at Pinchley Park, Councillor Bert Cheeseman was feeling satisfied with his morning's work. The bonfire was complete, and the guy was now sitting on top. It was an eerily accurate representation of Javed Johnson, the Primident.

"All right, lads. That'll do for now. Back to base."

The gang of helpers from the Council Offices, clearly identified by their bright yellow jackets with "Council" on the back, broke up into small groups and disappeared in the direction of the park gates. Councillor Conn, who had entered into the proceedings with gusto, was so warmed up by the unaccustomed activity that he left his discarded yellow jacket around the back of the bonfire.

Councillor Cheeseman looked warmly after his departing staff, and, taking the key from his pocket he let himself into the green-painted pavilion.

It was an impressive collection of fireworks, and all items had been sorted into order. In the bay marked "8p.m." was parked a large trolley packed with "Starfinder" rockets.

These would make a spectacular start to the display. He could hear the mighty "swish" of the launching rockets already; he could see them exploding in a dozen different colours high above Pinchley. And he could see the wonder on the upturned children's faces as they reflected green one moment and red the next, and then disappeared altogether in the darkness of the November night. He could hear the thunderous "Airbombs" explode, and the "oooh's" and the "aaah's" of the spectators. And then he could see them all listening to his welcoming speech from the steps of the pavilion. The pavilion built by his own great-grandfather. He saw it all. But he didn't see the shaggy head of Filfy O'Durr at the window.

Councillor Cheeseman whizzed a giant "Catherine Wheel" freely around on its axis. It was still spinning as he picked up a "Godzilla Thunderburst" and admired its radiant livery. It was very impressive. But it paled in comparison with the magnificently arrayed artefacts next to it. Councillor Cheeseman picked one up. It was heavy, rounded like a cannon-ball and had an inordinately long fuse. He felt the power of the thing, and took a very deep breath. Then, putting the firework down carefully, he put on his glasses to read the label. After several warnings, ("This firework am dangerous", "This more bomb than a firework" and "Save life and read instructions good") he came to the conclusion that the "Atomic Landmine" needed an experienced manager. He himself would handle it tonight.

Channelle O'Durr sat on the blowup settee at number 27, Hillside Close, eating the chocolates that Hassan had bought her. She rifled through the empty brown papers at the bottom of the box and realised she'd finished them. As she threw the empty box into the corner, a little trail of brown papers floated to the floor, marking its trajectory. She stood up and brushed down her tank-top and noticed that some of the chocolate crumbs had melted on to her tightly stretched black jeans. The credits for the latest episode of "St. Wilfred's" were rolling fast, when she called into the kitchen.
"What you doing?"
Hassan was cleaning the worktop with Filfy O'Durr in attendance. Filfy remembered that last time he had cleaned the worktop, he had given him a Doggie Treat, so why not today? Hassan bent down and patted the shaggy upraised head, which was retracted so that the mouth would be in the correct alignment to receive a delicious morsel. The mouth opened expectantly.
"Not today, mate. Come on through."

"Listen to this." Channelle indicated the television, on which a serious looking Pinchley Television reporter was standing outside a lock-up garage in Bendon.
"The stash of bomb-making equipment was found in this garage. Inspector Pete Balmer says this is the biggest such find in the south of England since the recent intensive searches began."
This was followed by the picture of a uniformed police inspector standing in front of a picture of The Queen and saying "This is the biggest such find in the South of England since the recent intensive searches began." Looking past the camera, he asked "Was that all right?"
Then suddenly the new Primident appeared, sitting in front of an impressive looking bookcase, with a picture of his large family next to him. His teeth were very white, his beard was

luxuriant, and there was excitement in the large dark eyes.
"Tonight is Guy Fawkes Night" he began.
"It is part of our British heritage, and marks the time when religious fundamentalists tried by dint of explosives to do away with the mother of parliaments, and democracy itself."
Hassan grabbed the remote and turned the television off. He couldn't stand Javed Johnson.
"You've eaten all the confounded chocolates," he said, retrieving the empty box and papers and dropping them in the wastepaper basket.

Dr. Nipp had been president of the Pinchley Bonfire Society since his retirement. He took his duties seriously. As an Anglican and a member of the Church of the Dead Martyrs, he had to be open-handed in regard to the Catholics in the community who also wanted to celebrate on November 5th. His own group, known as 'The Martyrs' was older than 'The Virgins' and took pride of place each year in the torchlight procession that wound around the narrow streets of the Old Town before the Grand Assembly in Pinchley Park.
But this year was different. A third group had applied for membership, and for the right to join the procession. Although they were more recent arrivals in the Pinchley community, the Muslims had become a respected yet vociferous minority. Their High School had become a bye-word for quality education, and their children were held up as a model for the rowdier and more drunken Christians. Some Pinchley mothers had indeed been so impressed that they had converted to Islam and started smacking their children again. In fact Penny Armitage-Shanks whose face was normally wreathed in smiles looked quite frightening as she now drove up to the school gates at the wheel of her shiny black Erebus people carrier wearing a burqa. The first morning she'd worn it, Mrs. Peeble, the lollypop lady, had looked up at the driver, and collapsed in a faint on the crossing.

"It's a question of tradition, you know, Dr. Siddique" said Dr. Nipp.
"Yes, Dr. Nipp. You are speaking to the right man about

tradition, sir."

Dr. Siddique had been chair of the Pinchley Multicultural Committee for seven years now.

"We too have traditions, sir, and our people indubitably have respect for your own. That is why we want to march in the procession."

Ralph Nipp massaged the worry stone in his right hand.

"But, Doctor; if you had only given us more notice. You know, this event has been going on for some hundreds of years. It's not an instant procession. It's taken centuries for the Anglicans and the Catholics to come together you know. And this, this is a celebration of that, that conciliation. It would not be right to admit a third party without long consultation on the matter, you know."

Dr. Siddique looked startled.

"Is that yours, sir?" he asked, indicating the large dishevelled mongrel that was peering in through the French windows. Ralph Nipp, irritated to have been cut off in mid flow, strutted to the window and gave Filfy O'Durr a dismissive gesture.

"Away! Off!" he called, optimistically. The dog was on his hind legs and was almost as tall as the doctor. Filfy O'Durr yawned and arched his back. His claws rasped on the dried up paint as the grandfather clock in the corner of the room chimed twelve. Dr. Nipp pulled a cord and a curtain swished across the window. The dog disappeared.

The visitor had stopped before a photograph of a large class of medical students.

"If only you could dismiss me as easily as you just dismissed that dog, sir! So you're a St. Thomas's man? I was at Tommy's."

Ralph Nipp looked the visitor in the eye for the first time that day.

"You were?"

"Class of '63, sir."

"Well, well" replied the host.

"Well, well, well." A light came into Ralph Nipp's one good eye.

"You must have been under Padgett?"

"Oh yes. And Prendergast."

"Prendergast! Ha! Old Prendergast.."

"You a rugger man?"

"Number eight."

"You look like a number eight. I was fly half. They called me 'Nippy'. My friends, that is."

Dr. Siddique smiled.

"Of course. And what, sir, do your friends call you now?"

Ralph Nipp looked past the visitor in the direction of the walnut drinks cabinet.

"Can I offer you something?"

He found himself wavering slightly. Did his visitor drink alcohol?

"Er…a fruit juice perhaps. Or a .."

Dr. Siddique looked over his shoulder as his host opened the cabinet door.

"Do you have a nice dry Sherry? A Palo Cortado, perhaps?"

The "Martyrs" and the "Virgins" and the "Saracens" marched down Pinchley High Street shoulder to shoulder that night, and the crowd greeted them ecstatically as they raised their fiery torches to the heavens. Doctors Nipp and Siddique, together with Father O'Grady and Cyril Downmouth led the procession to the park in Dr. Nipp's vintage Hillman Straight Six, huge headlights pointing the way. The night was mild and dry, so they travelled with the roof down, and waved at the onlookers with smiles of transparent good cheer.

George O'Durr, who had nothing to do with the council, was wearing Councillor Conn's yellow council jacket with which Filfy had presented him earlier that day, and trying not to let the dog pull him off his feet as he approached Pinchley Park. He had forgotten all about the display; in fact he had forgotten it was November 5th until fireworks started to blossom in the sky after sunset. But Filfy O'Durr hadn't forgotten. He wasn't exactly frightened of the noise like most pets were, but it did have a strange effect on the old dog. He had discovered over the years that if he didn't stop moving when fireworks were about, his reaction to the sudden noises was becalmed somewhat, and the whole experience became less traumatic.

George O'Durr did his best to humour Filfy by throwing a large solid rubber ball as far as he could for the dog to chase. The ball had a long strap attached to it to give the thrower extra power for long distances, and Filfy happily burned off some of his surplus energy by streaking after it like a greyhound across the park. He had a little difficulty with the 'retrieve' because the ball was so big that he could scarcely get his jaws around it. He normally liked to tease the unathletic Mr. O'Durr by dropping the ball a few yards from him, and then grab it again as his master moved to pick it up. But tonight, he hadn't been fed before the walk, so he was behaving perfectly and bringing back the ball to Mr. O'Durr's feet each time. And each time, Mr. O'Durr, who really liked his new yellow jacket, rewarded Filfy with a Vindaloo Chew.

It was as Filfy was happily bounding across Pinchley Park in the direction of the pavilion that he heard the growl. It was a low threatening sound, and Filfy recognised it immediately, and stopped, allowing the ball to bounce into the bushes from which the sound came. There was only one growl like that in Pinchley. It was the fighting dog, Gripper Butt. And yes, there was the unmistakeable odour of his master. Beefburger, onions, and stale smalls. Yes; and there was the trademark Union Jack waistcoat. The canine one.

Filfy flinched as Gripper Butt, on hind legs, and with a slavering maw, put all his considerable weight on the heavy chain that held him in the shadow of a municipal rhododendron. But Darren Butt yanked on the chain viciously and the dog's bloodcurdling growl of pure murderous hatred was cut off in mid-sentence and the dog pawed the air with an agonised whimper as he was pulled back mercilessly into the bushes. Filfy's ball was not forthcoming. The only thing that issued forth from the bushes was a four-letter word from the black-shirted and blacked-up Darren Butt, as Gripper fell backwards into his master's recently-dug trench, knocked over the stack of Monster Thunderclaps, and broke the shaft on one of the giant rockets. The rockets were lined up on a launching rack. And they all pointed in the direction of the pavilion.

By the time Filfy had returned via some fascinating scents to the spot where he had left his master, he had forgotten all about the ball. His brain simply wasn't wired to hold on to bad things. Mr. O'Durr had disappeared, and the procession, headed by the three local dignitaries in their beautiful car had entered the park. They were closely followed by a stumbling group of buxom majorettes, a float carrying a group of half-naked women and the flashing sign 'Pinchley Women's Institute,' the Pinchley Combined Cadets Drum Corps, the Bendon Silver Band, and torch bearers brightly arrayed as Martyrs, Virgins, and Saracens. The Saracens, with their brilliantly coloured Ali Baba trousers and waistcoats, and flashing scimitars drew the biggest cheer from the crowd of excited spectators.

Just as Dr. Nipp stepped down from the Hillman at the pavilion steps to be welcomed by a beaming Councillor Cheeseman, the first rocket hit the side of the wooden building in a shower of sparks. Councillor Cheeseman staggered backwards as a second rocket exploded against the wall, and shot great shining gobbets of red and green fire in the direction of the crowd. Some people applauded, whereas others looked apprehensively in the direction from which the attack had come.

As the councillor opened the door of the building with a spectacular flourish of the key, and entered the pavilion with Doctor Nipp, the third rocket struck. It crashed through the window and the interior was suddenly illuminated with greens and golds and reds before the doctor had even had time to turn on the light. The place was a tinder box, a magazine. Realising his life was now imperilled, Councillor Cheeseman looked desperately around him for help. Dr. Nipp was frozen to the spot, and the councillor was about to run for it when he saw a yellow-jacketed council employee at the front of the crowd that ringed the pavilion.

"You!" he shouted . "Here! Quick!"

There was no doubting the authority in the voice. George O'Durr never understood why he responded so readily, but before he knew it, he was at the top of the pavilion steps, whilst behind him, a panic-stricken retreat was taking place as more rockets hit their target and revellers realised the imminent danger from the sparkling pavilion. Children, cadets, drummers, mothers, Saracens, Virgins, and Martyrs fled the scene, accompanied by the Reverend Downmouth. Father O'Grady kept crossing himself, intoning "Holy Mother of God!" and jerkily up-ending a hip flask in the direction of his mouth.

"Come back! Come back!" shouted Dr. Siddique in bitter disappointment.

"It's all right. Everything's under control! The council has everything under control!" Councillor Cheeseman ducked as a Supersonic Targetfinder rocket nearly took off his head.

Inside the pavilion, George O'Durr was fighting for his life. The invading rockets had ignited the touch paper on a Royal Cascade and a Giant Catherine Wheel. The Catherine Wheel had already started spinning merrily and distributing potentially lethal sparks around the room, and so George O'Durr jumped up and down on the Royal Cascade touchpaper, sweating profusely and shouting "Die, you bugger! Die!"

Councillor Cheeseman put his head around the door.

"Everything under control here?" he asked as another rocket hit the wall where his head had just been.

"Fuck off!" George O'Durr had no time for pleasantries as he saw that the long fuse on one of the deadlier looking fireworks had caught. It was an Atomic Landmine, but Mr. O'Durr wasn't interested in what it was. He was only interested in getting it as far away from himself as possible. The fuse itself was sparkling as if it were a firework of its own, so he didn't stand on ceremony.

Grabbing the globe by its heavy snake-like fuse, he barged past Councillor Cheeseman to the door and hurled the Atomic Landmine with all his strength into the darkness, where it bounced with awful precision in the direction of Darren Butt's hiding place in the municipal rhododendrons.

Filfy O'Durr, who had been investigating a dead mole, saw the ball bounce across his rather blurred field of vision, and unable to stop himself, bounded after it. The still sparking fuse made it impossible to miss. But when it rolled into the bank of rhododendrons, Filfy stopped short. Although he generally had a short memory, he remembered Gripper Butt.

Suddenly the ball was thrown from the bushes. Oh! Joy! Someone else wanted to play with him. Filfy didn't really care if it was Darren Butt or Mr. O'Durr. Anyone would do. And he was hungry for a Vindaloo Doggie Treat. Ed's Burger van had disappeared with the crowd before Filfy had had time to make himself known. Off after the bouncing Atomic Landmine he went, oblivious of the dangerously shortening fuse, and back to the rhododendrons he pranced with the ball in his jaws. As he dropped it and it rolled into the trench that Darren Butt had dug for himself, Filfy saw no Doggie Treat. So he turned and started to run towards the pavilion in anticipation of another throw. But the ball was inadvertently retained. As Darren Butt scrabbled around desperately at one end of the trench, and Gripper foamed at the mouth at the other, the sparks stopped as the end of the fuse was consumed.

The fusillade of rockets had ceased, and George O'Durr suddenly realised he had saved the day. Councillor Cheeseman's head appeared round the pavilion door.

"All clear?"

George O'Durr took a deep breath, and assumed a modest expression.

"You could say that, squire."

The councillor, whose notes for his welcoming speech were by now blowing across Pinchley Park in the gathering westerly wind, stepped forward and draped his arm around the trembling George O'Durr's shoulders.

"Good job. Good job. Well done! Well done! It's..er.. George, isn't it? I really didn't realise you were on our staff. Shows just how out of touch I am!"

George O'Durr assumed a sphynx-like expression.

"Perhaps we'll have to think about promotion. Was that the National Front, would you say?"

Before George O'Durr could answer, and as the wailing of a police siren came closer, an immense fireball accompanied by a series of deafening explosions arose from a rhododendron patch in the middle distance.

"Dunno.  Well, if it was, it ain't now, guv'nor."

Suddenly George O'Durr was feeling cold.

"Come on Filf.  We're for home."

## CHAPTER SIXTEEN
### December

## CHRISTMAS CAROL.

It was Christmas Day. Hillside Close lay silent under a powdering of snow, and a dark crystal sky. Everyone except Mr. and Mrs. O'Durr had done their shopping. Indeed, the shelves at Painsbury's Executive Supamacromarket at Bugsden Corner looked as if they had been stripped by a swarm of giant locusts straight out of Bisney's new animation, "The Locust King."

The O'Durrs had indeed visited the new Fesco Hyperturbostore at the Blodgett Centre. They had been forced to go by taxi, because Mr. O'Durr had failed to put antifreeze in his car before the coldest December day for two decades. Everyone else had bought turkeys, mince pies, and crystallised fruits, Christmas Puddings, huge tins of chocolates and fancy biscuits, and strangely shaped bottles containing exotic foreign liqueurs like 'Rumba!Rumba!' They had purchased electronic devices costing hundreds of pounds that their children had seen on the telly, multi-coloured plastic water guns of immense power, boxes of crackers containing useful objects like miniature screwdrivers, and plastic signet rings, and the year's favourite children's gift, a full-size "Squeeze Me Suzie" Mandarin swearing doll.

But George and Dolly O'Durr had totally forgotten to buy anything at all for their daughter or, indeed, for their dog. (Channelle had asked for a weekend at a health spa or a house coat like her mum's from "Big and Classy", whilst Filfy had asked for nothing).
No, the O'Durrs had spent almost all their money on their addictions. Mr. O'Durr had purchased ten five-pint cans of

Buster's Lager, five hundred Caskett's Killer Number Ones, and had also bought a five-pint can of Buster's for his wife, who didn't drink lager. Not to be outdone, Mrs. O'Durr had bought six bottles of Birnoff, and received one free on a special offer, and stolen one from the shelf when Ernst Kesselring and Jeremiah Mbogu, the recently recruited security men, were trying on their new uniforms. She had also purchased five hundred Undertakers High Tar Cheerio Tipped, and pilfered another two hundred whilst Sharon Bust had been busy on the phone to her drug-crazed boyfriend in the cubby hole at the back of the counter. It had been Sharon's first day in the job, and, coincidentally, her last. Mrs. O'Durr had also spent £20 out of the housekeeping on the Lottery, because she felt this was definitely her lucky week, and she needed some new tights.

Of course, the O'Durrs had to buy some food. Mr. O'Durr had insisted on getting twenty tins of "Mercury" sardines on a special twenty for the price of fifteen offer, and lots of unhealthy snacks like Blotchers Pork Bottom Scratchings, and Dripping Krunchos, and Fabbs Full Fat Luxury Executive Fries. He had refused to stop chatting up the young demonstrator with green hair and a pierced nose, who was dispensing free samples of Ballybunnion Cream to bewildered pensioners, so Mrs. O'Durr left him to stagger round the great store under her own steam, with Filfy O'Durr sitting in a state of joy atop the purchases in the trolley.

Naturally, Filfy wasn't left out when it came to food shopping. In fact, in terms of priority his eats were right up there with the tobacco and the alcohol. As soon as Filfy came abeam of the huge mountain of Brahmaputra Vindaloo Doggie Chunks on an "Unrepeatable Offer," he leapt like a spring lamb out of the trolley and charged the edifice, knocking down tins to left and right, and pooing next to the deli counter in sheer delight.

By the time the store manager, Mr. Mac.Swear had been called, and the area had been freshened with Shapp's Summer Morning Deodorant Spray, which wasn't much of an improvement, Mrs. O'Durr had moved swiftly to aisle number sixty-three, which was full of giant nodding Father Christmases going "Ho! Ho! Ho!"

Mrs. O'Durr stood smoking and chatting with Filfy as Mr. Wellborne, of Polite Taxis, packed the boot of his new Skoda with her shopping, and told her "That dog will have to go on your lap," whilst hoping he wouldn't be forced to ask her to extinguish her cigarette. As the car left the forecourt with smoke curling from its rear window, Mrs. O'Durr's husband was coming to realise that the white liquid that the bemused demonstrator had been pouring out for him was not good for his digestion. She had failed to inform Mr. O'Durr that in Ballybunnion Cream, she was not demonstrating a new Irish liqueur, but an expensive foot preparation from Franco-Swiss Laboratories S.A. of Geneva.

Next door at number twenty-six, the Nobles were well-prepared to entertain over the holiday. Mr. Noble had a week off from Prood's Educational Books. And, although he felt a little uneasy about seeing his son, Lightworker, after such a long break, he was certainly looking forward to seeing his only grandson, who was now six years old. His daughter-in-law would sadly not be present, as she had left the country following the only Christmas she had spent at Hillside Close, and that was three years ago now. As for Lightworker, he had almost forgiven his father for the name he had been given, and was actually looking at the possibility of changing it by deed poll. He felt it would help him in his career in the Parachute Regiment.
In a funny sort of way, he was quite looking forward to seeing his unusual father once more, together with his motherly wife. But he was a little on edge about the visit. He knew the old man would preach peace and forgiveness, when Lightworker was much more interested in a few beers and some good nosh, and telling his tales of the dangerous and exciting life he enjoyed as a para in the Home Counties. No; Armalite was to grow up a man. In a world where there were no free lunches, peace and forgiveness were not qualities he wished to

encourage in his son.

Mr. Noble was not one to follow the crowd, and refused to have a Christmas tree in the house on the grounds that such an indulgence would speed up global warming. Instead, he had found a tasteful man-made lotus blossom with creamy, pink-tipped petals, together with a little carved Chinese (or was it Japanese?) god in Sparks and Mincers new multifaith department, and he had put them together in the centre of the reproduction marble fireplace in the front room. Unfortunately, Mrs. Noble's enthusiastic feather-dusting on Christmas Eve had done for the little god, and he was now laying in shards in the new transparent Kitchen-Chic wastebin, uncomfortably close to a decomposing kipper.

Other aspects of the Nobles' Christmas were orthodox; well, more or less. Not too many of the men of Hillside Close, for example, took all their clothes off and chanted at the moon from the middle of their front lawn at five o'clock on Boxing morning. But Mrs. Noble had her own ideas about the festival, and didn't let her husband depart too far from the traditional joys of an English family Christmas.

She insisted, for example, that everyone sit and listen to the Primident's inspirational and heartwarming speech from Kensington Palace about the year's disasters. This year Javed Johnson was to amuse some by dressing up as Father Christmas and talking about lassa fever and his mother-in-law. Mrs. Noble had made a special effort in the kitchen, cooking her own organic mince pies which incorporated cement-like pastry and very little mince, most of which found its way on to the pie's exterior in the form of a bitter and burnt-tasting glue. Her rich dark fruitcake was marred by the tooth-crackingly hard, brilliant white icing.

The previous year, Mr. Noble recalled, his dentures had imploded as he had tried to breach his wife's impregnable confection. This time, he ostentatiously left all his icing on the side of his plate, and complimented his wife with a thin smile.

"Excellent cake, dear," he said, with the very faintest of emphasis on the 'cake.'

"Now, dear. You watch your favourite programme, and I'll do the washing up."

Mr. Noble couldn't bear to watch "St. Wilfred's", and he also felt he needed some time to himself. He felt liverish, the two glasses of cheap Beaujolais from Kostbusters had gone to his head, and he had had quite enough of his son's stories of life in the Paras.

The latter asked "Do you want a hand, Charlie? I got some cracking jokes – men only if you know what I mean."

Mr. Noble rose from the table with a dyspeptic look and started to pile the tea plates.

"No thanks, Lightworker. You look after your mother. And I'd rather you called me Dad, if you don't mind."

Charles Noble took a deep breath and smiled as he surveyed the acres of dirty washing up that awaited him in the little kitchen. Then he closed the door, shutting out the hated sound of the "St. Wilfred's" signature tune, and opened the door leading to the garden for some fresh December air. He ran the hot water, and switched on the radio. "Good evening, ladies and gentlemen," announced an unctuous male voice.

"We bring you tidings of great joy. Welcome to our third multifaith Christmas celebration from St Paul's Cathedral."

Mr. Noble guiltily stripped a piece of white meat from the turkey, popped it in his mouth, and put the remaining bird out of the way on the top of the fridge. Then he snapped the radio off as two dark eyes out in the garden registered his every move.

It was little later in the afternoon that Jennifer Noble sat back luxuriously in the cushions of the settee and said "This is what I call a Christmas."

She popped another Painsbury's "Belle Luxe" Belgian Chocolate into her mouth, took a sip of Vintage Character Port and then a bite of Kendal Mint Cake. The mint cake, which was very strong, went down the wrong way, and Jennifer Noble started to choke, much to Lightworker's annoyance.

"Shut up, Jen, will you? I can't hear what he's saying."

The Reverend Jim Manley was indeed saying something, but it

was drowned out by the terrible coughing and agonising gasps coming from the Parker Knoll settee.

"Grandma!" Little Armalite was alarmed, and copying a move he had seen one of his Dad's training videos for prospective Paras, he jumped up on the settee and slapped his grandma's face with ferocious force. Mrs. Noble screamed.

The boy's father said "Well done boy! Now; shut up, will you? I'm trying to listen to this."

Mrs. Noble started choking again. She was going very red in the face.

"Merry Christmas, Mrs. Salahuddin," said Jim Manley, as he handed a very beautiful parishioner a red rose.

Mr. Noble had heard the scream, but he finished making a perfect job of cleaning the encrusted roasting tray, and meditated for a moment before washing his hands carefully with Painsbury's Male Nourishment Honeysuckle Executive Handwash, and then drying them on some Painsbury's Double Quilted Aloe Vera and Juniper Kitchen Roll. Then he strode through into the living room.

"Did I hear you scream, dear?"

His timing was not good. Lightworker was just giving Mrs. Noble a hearty slap, and she screamed again, and collapsed on the floor in a shower of Belgian chocolates. Mr. Noble took one step forward, and hit his son with a ramrod straight left. Lightworker fell back on to the settee.

Little Armalite shouted excitedly "Come on Gramps!" as his father groaned and raised a grimy handkerchief to his bleeding nose. Mr. Noble bent down to his wife, who was breathing more easily now.

"Are you all right, dear? I think I've broken my fingers. Can I get you one of your pills?"

"No, Charles. A glass of Port. And give me a hug, will you?"

Mr. Noble sat down and gave his wife a hug. It proved to be a long hug which he found he enjoyed. It actually lasted, on and off, to the end of the programme, long after Lightworker had stormed out of the house with his son in his arms.

"What's he doing there?"

Filfy O'Durr was standing in the doorway from the kitchen.

"Oh, no!"

Mr. Noble leapt up and lunged for the dog, but Filfy was much too quick, and was out in the garden before Mr. Noble entered the kitchen, where he stopped and slowly took in the scene of devastation. The big plate from the top of the fridge was smashed into a hundred pieces on the floor, and all that remained of the turkey was bones. They were spread over the kitchen floor like branches in Potteridge Woods after a storm.

The receptionist at Pinchley General Hospital A. & E. was not helpful.
"You'll have to wait. It could be hours."
Phat Pong stared dispassionately at the screen.
"Sit down in that corridor. If you can find a seat."
He suddenly laughed loudly.
"Dr. Wellington- Lumumba is very busy today."
"And what do you want, squire?" he asked of a man with his head swathed in bloody bandages.
Mr. Noble walked down corridor "H" and sat down in the one empty chair between a very thin glassy eyed white woman who was talking to herself, and a  black man who was weeping.
Mr. Noble picked up a copy of "Perfect Gardening" and tried to concentrate on an article entitled "How to get Brown Patches out of Your Lawn." But it was beyond him. His right hand was very painful, and he found himself reliving the instant when he had punched his son on the nose.
He had never punched anyone before. He felt sickened by the memory of the moment, and yet somehow buoyed up by it. What would he tell Dr. Wellington-Lumumba when he asked him how he had come by the injury? Would he tell him it had been in protection of his wife against a trained assailant? Or would he pass it off lightly with something like "Well, you know how these family Christmases can be. Ha! Ha!?"
In the event, Dr. Wellington-Lumumba was not at all interested in how Mr. Noble had come by his injuries. She just handed him a card and said "Take that down to X Ray."

Mr. Noble arrived home at midnight, feeling very sorry for himself. By the time he climbed the stairs he had already decided that next morning's car-wash would have to wait.

"Is that you, dear?"

He opened the door of his wife's bedroom.

"Hello, dear. Is that you?"

"Yes. It's me."

"What time is it?"

"It's twelve. Past midnight."

"Oh. Shouldn't you be cleaning the car?"

"It's Christmas Day. Or, rather it was. I'm not doing it today. I'm only just back from the hospital."

Jennifer Noble sat up in bed. She was wearing mauve and she had a mark on her cheek.

"Oh! Happy Christmas, Charles!

Charles Noble sat down on the bed they had until so recently shared, and his eyes were irrevocably drawn to the magnificent white marble valley between her breasts.

"Happy Christmas. I'm tired, dear."

"Yes, of course you are. Get your clothes off, and come to Jennifer. She'll make you feel better."

"Yes, dear. My hand's hurting."

"Then we'll kiss it better, won't we. It's Christmas. Get your clothes off."

Despite some difficulty undoing buttons with his injured hand, Charles Noble was down to his Sparks and Mincers puce Y-Fronts in no time. His knees seemed to be trembling.

"I'm not feeling too well. And I'm up at five, remember."


At five-thirty a.m., Mrs. O'Durr was enduring a nightmare in which she was being pursued around Fesco's by Mr. Mac. Swear and a rabid Filfy O'Durr who had been retrained as a ruthless security dog. The store manager was shouting something quite unintelligibly Glaswegian, and yelling to his staff in a strange, penetrating voice.

"Call the cops!" "Call the cops!"

Exhausted from pushing a huge Fesco super- leviathan trolley with faulty electronic navigation, full of pilfered Birnoff, and cornered by a scarily aggressive Filfy O'Durr, Mrs. O'Durr had to slow down, and as she did so, Mr. Mac. Swear's enunciations slowed.... and slowed. Gasping for breath, Mrs. O'Durr looked over her shoulder to see what Filfy was up to, and collided with a vast Rudolph the Red Nosed Reindeer (£50 To Clear) singing "Jingle Bells." Mr. Mac.Swear was still calling, but the words sounded slow and distant. What was that?

"On! On!"

Was he encouraging her to flee? Mrs. O'Durr decided to leave the store without delay. She tried to change direction towards the end checkout, but the great trolley had other ideas. Like a crazed juggernaut, it detached itself violently from its driver's short fingers, and drove straight through the wall, immediately adjacent to the vacant Life Insurance counter. Mrs. O'Durr lost her footing, and on the seat of her jogging bottoms, she slid across the highly polished floor in the direction of a set of double rubber doors marked "Giant Shredder This Way." Mr. Mac. Swear was still not giving up. "On! On!"

Mrs. O'Durr collided with a male mannequin in a light grey suit marked "Savile Row Tailored" and awoke.

But that sound was still there. Mrs. O'Durr opened her eyes, fearfully, and looked around her, the covers pulled up to her ears.

"Ommmm! Ommmm!"

The tone was unmistakeable. Mr. Mac. Swear was somewhere down below. The reedy, penetrating voice called to her from outside the covers, outside the room. Indeed, as she took a grip on herself, she realised it was floating up to her from somewhere at the front of the house.

"Ommmmm!" "Ommmmm!"

Mrs. O'Durr struggled out of the musty sheets, and, disengaging herself from her dormant husband's unappealing armpit, she lurched to the window in billowing Winceyette.

"Ommmmm!" "Ommmmm!"

Mrs. O'Durr tried to wipe the icy condensation off the inside of the window, and failed. She fetched a hairy comb from the dressing table and scraped away at the window pane, clearing a tiny patch of glass. But then the comb broke.

"Bugger!"

She peered through the little porthole of clear glass.

"Ommmmm!" "Ommmm!"

With an inrush of freezing breath, she recognised the pale and solitary figure below. "Ommmmm!" "Ommmmm!"

Mrs. O'Durr yanked open the window.

"OMMMMM!" "OMMMMM!" "OMMMMM!"

Yes, it was that muppet next door!

"Oy! You! Oy! Yes, you! Oy, Noble!"

"OMMMMM!" "OMMMMM!"

"Cut out that 'ommin' at five o'clock in the bleeding morning!".

"OMMMMM!" "OMMMM!"

"You hear me, eh?! Charlie Noble!!"

"OMMMMM!" "OMMMMM!"

"Right, you little git, you've asked for it!"

Mrs. O'Durr slammed the window shut, bustled, shivering, past her snoring husband, donned a faded rayon housecoat from behind the door, and shouted. "FILFY!"

The bedclothes moved, but it wasn't Mr. O'Durr. Filfy pushed out a mud-caked paw, then a dreamy dark eye appeared under shaggy brows. Then the whole sleepy, despoiled animal struggled out of bed, and followed the scent of his beloved mistress downstairs to the front door. Mrs. O'Durr opened it, and Filfy looked out. If he had been blessed with hands, he would have rubbed his eyes in disbelief.

"OMMMMMM!" "OMMMMMM!"

It was his next-door-neighbour, completely unclothed except for a bandage on his right hand. Pointing at the unmistakeably slender, pale, and shivering figure in the next garden, Mrs. O'Durr screeched "Get him, Filf!" and trembled both with excitement and bitter cold in her covering of Winceyette, rayon, and dried perspiration.

Suddenly, Filfy O'Durr was awake. The morning chill, the anticipation of the chase, to say nothing of the intensity of his desire to please his mistress; all conspired to galvanise him as he leapt out of the front door, like a dog half his age, in sheer, helpless abandon. He loved attacking Charles Noble.

"OMMMMM!" "OMMMMM!"

With a primeval growl drawn from deep within, Filfy O'Durr

launched himself in the direction of the reverent figure sitting unprotected in the lotus position in the middle of next door's lawn.

"OMMMMMM!" "OMMMMMM!"

On previous occasions, Mr. Noble had taken to his heels at Filfy's first approach, but this time he paid the dog no heed whatsoever. And what was that white thing on his hand? And the strange odour that accompanied it? Filfy O'Durr halted in mid-stride. His old instincts suddenly seemed to drain from him.

"OMMMMM!" "OMMMMM!"

Somewhere in Mr. Noble's plaintive, penetrating chant, Filfy heard something he'd never heard before. Something was definitely different. Filfy stopped next to a notice saying "Please Keep Off The Grass". He shook his head from side to side. Something about the sound, something about the sheer defencelessness, the fearlessness of the slim, erect figure on the perfect winter lawn touched his canine soul.

"OMMMMMM!" "OMMMMMM!"

Something in the strange chant entered him, and caressed him and, stilling his more basic instincts, made him suddenly aware of the oneness of all life.

Filfy O'Durr stood stock still, and opened his mouth hesitantly. His steaming breath took life in the still air.

"GRRR-ORRR! GRRR-ORRR!"

This was not easy. But Filfy just had to do it.

"GRRR-ORRRR! GRRR-ORRRRR!"

"GRRR-OMMM!" GRRROMMM!"

"GRRR-OMMMMMMM!                    GRRRRRRRRR-OMMMMMMMMMM!"

Filfy, with a totally new sense of the most profound humility, sat down quietly next to his valiant neighbour. Mr. Noble was far, far away, and blissfully unaware of his new companion. Filfy O'Durr adopted a sort of studied canine lotus position, and raised his eyes to the great star that shone overhead.. As Mr. Noble continued to chant in his other-worldly reverie, he became gradually aware of a second, deeper voice that joined him from somewhere in eternity. He was not alone!

"Ommmmmmmm!  Ommmmmmmmm!"

"GRRRRR-OMMMMMMM!  GRRRRR-OMMMMMM!
GRRRRR-OMMMMM!"

      And thus it was that a man and a dog, together and as one under the stars, welcomed the Holy Child at Christmas.
"OMMMMM!" "OMMMMM!"
"GRRR-OMMMMM!" "GRRR-OMMMMM!"

      As the great star shone down on Hillside Close, Lightworker and Armalite Noble and Mrs. Noble and Mr. O'Durr were still in lands of dreams, and quite unaware of the brightly illuminated scene below.  Mrs. O'Durr still stood alone on her doorstep with her mouth open, pinching herself in an attempt to wake up from yet another nightmare.  She felt left out somehow.
"OMMMMMM!"  "OMMMMMM!"
"GRRR-OMMMMMMMM!"  "GRRR-OMMMMMMMMM!"

But Mr. Noble and Filfy O'Durr, imperfect man and scruffy old hound, were joined irrevocably this new morning, somewhere in Heaven.

# FILFY O'DURR ON THE WEB

Log in to **filfyodurr.co.uk**

For **FILFY'S BLOG,**

and for

**FILFY O'DURR,
THE WORLD'S FIRST CANINE
AGONY AUNT!**

**WOOF!  WOOF!**

Lightning Source UK Ltd.
Milton Keynes UK
09 October 2010

160998UK00002B/63/P